DUST TO SMOKE

THE LAST TRITAN, BOOK III

MYRA DANVERS

FOREWORD

Make sure you sign up for Myra's Newsletter so you never miss sexy NSFW art, free things, exclusive deals, and loads of other cool shit you do not want to miss...

Sign up for Myra's Newsletter today!

To Alina Lane.
You fit me into your busy schedule to help me get this book over the finish line, and I cannot thank you enough. You're a gem, your questions and opinions filled my burnt-out soggy bacon with the good kind of fire, and my whole family is tired of listening to me gush about how grateful I am to you.
If hugs were for me, I'd owe you a really good squish.
As it is, I'm prolly gonna do something weird and chaotic to show my gratitude. Like delivering a larder of dead birds and rodents to your door step at 4:13 am. Or... I dunno... delivering chapters of Atom and Evil unto your inbox as they come together...
You know.
Normal shit.

1

She was dying.

I could feel it on the wind.

Hear it in the quiet hiss and pop of heated crackling coming from within her depleted husk.

Could see it in the quiet glow still flickering in her veins, where dying embers glowed a soft, gentle blue in muscles with nothing left to give. Her body intact, and yet... badly compromised.

Death.

It was there in the pull behind my ribs, where she'd touched me with her gifts. Where she'd built protection I had thought to be a trap. Blinded by my helpless fury and never-ending quest for vengeance.

My impotent, boundless rage... and helpless, unforgivable ignorance.

And now it was too late. My apologies would land on ears that only looked perfect. Their inner workings intact, the structure sound enough, but... connected to nothing.

The Head Priestess couldn't be saved from the bone chilling void.

I knew it.

Deeply.

Still, I reached for her. Crushed beneath the protective weight of a possessive male, I extended one trembling hand and took her ankle in hand. Wrapped it in fingers grimy with soot—stained by the ashen remains of the elites she'd sent to escort her into the void—and threw everything I had into the abyss.

To bring her back.

Fueling her dying body with what little remained of my corrupted gifts.

"*Mila.*"

It was a warning in a voice I didn't quite hate.

One I ignored as I wilted beneath his weight, faltering with the effort needed to sustain her broken shell when I had so little left to give. Desperate to hold her here, on this side of the veil.

Where I *needed* her.

Where I could apologize for the hurt I'd caused.

Chaos reigned all around me. The screams of the dying and ruined were a haunting symphony, wailing in tribute to the power of Tritan's last true priestess. A master of the art, whose death meant the loss of wisdom I couldn't begin to fathom.

Flickering with a poisonous green, flames consumed the podium that was meant to be our final stand. Sluggish, but hot enough to crisp the cheeks of any daring or foolish enough to get too close.

I felt nothing.

Nothing but the dusting of frost, burned by the bone-chilling cold of the quiet place she'd gone… where I meant to follow…

"*Mila, stop.*"

But I couldn't!

Not now, not as I watched her lips turn blue. Her chest so still. And her skin… it was… crumbling. Flaking, to be carried off on a sinister wind. Damage *he* could fix, surely. The same way I'd seen him do before, using stolen priestess magic to heal himself. All I had to do was stop the flames from seeping through the cracks…

A warm, calloused palm caressed my cheek a moment before lips moved against my ear. "You have to let her go."

It was cruel to ask for such a thing when I hadn't given everything I could in the attempt to save her.

"There's nothing more you can do."

At this, a wordless sound of pain and denial crackled over my lips. Aggravating the blisters lining my throat, where I'd inhaled the searing heat of her final moments. The dust and smoke of her doomed escort.

Long fingers carded through my hair, soothing, despite the catch of callouses that pulled at my scalp. "Let her go before she takes you with her, little warrior. Before she takes us both."

My grip tightened around that slender ankle.

Nails biting into flesh growing cold and spongy, dimpled in a way that seemed unable to bounce back. Still, I held on, despite the way the cold spread. "I... I don't care..."

Lips pressed to the corner of my jaw, the rasp of his beard prickling against my ear. "Your fight isn't over," he murmured and caught my chin. Turning my eyes away from the woman I'd failed, he ensnared me with an unblinking stare. Trapped me in twin pools of swirling, inky depths that seemed so much more than bottomless. Brimming with so much that would have to go unnamed.

A primal call to arms, he dared me to fight. Issued a challenge in a language I couldn't speak but could no longer ignore.

Anguish splintered through my chest, and I sobbed, torn right down the middle. Brushing up against her spirit, just once more, before he reeled me in with a leash I'd handed him. Allowed a single, silent farewell before he pulled me back from the edge with the reins I no longer held, he smiled as he fit me with a muzzle built by the very best of my kind.

And it was a kindness, in a way. To ease that terrible burden from shoulders too slumped to carry it for another moment.

Sasha slipped away, fading into nothingness so quickly and irrevocably, that for a moment I wasn't sure if she'd ever really existed at all.

"She's gone."

It was spoken in a voice thick with pain. One I didn't recognize as mine or his.

It simply was.

He brushed a lock of tangled hair back from my face, careful where it stuck to tear-stained cheeks tacky with grime. Patient, he was content to wait, ignoring the flames and the chaos. The screams of his people and mine.

And to my horror, a flood of tears washed over my lashes—I saw it in the reflection of eyes gone dark as pitch. "She... she *killed* herself," I rasped, eyes wide. Reeling, my hairline growing damp and itchy. "Killed them all."

"I know," he whispered, and traced the delicate angles made wet with shock, brushing at the deluge of tears that tracked down my cheeks and cleansed me of the soot of the dead.

"It was a trap. The"—I whined—"the instant he touched th-that cannon, h-he—" Traumatized, gut wrenching sobs broke through my illusion of inner strength. Thawed the frost and left nothing but anguish in the hollow. Cinders that began to smoke with the threat of new heat.

Hushing me, he sat back and pulled me into his lap, cradling my cheek tight against his chest, where my tears were hidden from the hordes of frantic Caledonians trying to escape. Where they might dry against his skin and couldn't be burned away by the heat of Sasha's final stand or the puddle of noxious plasma that had swallowed a general whole. "She knew what she was doing."

The offer of comfort bought only another flood of pitiful anguish, and I clung to him.

My enemy.

A man I'd hated.

The only one who knew *exactly* what it was that twisted and lashed behind my ribs. Clawing for freedom until my throat was wet and raw, singed by the caustic burn of gifts I'd been cursed with.

He knew because he was already inside.

Fingers winding tight into the sodden fabric of his formal wear—gritty with a dusting of unspeakable grime—my lips moved of their own volition. "She died an empath," I murmured, quiet enough that I wasn't sure he heard my confession. "And I gave her the idea. It was my fault," I whispered, and it echoed all around us with the ring of truth. "I killed the Head Priestess."

2

Dust.

It clogged my lungs. Acidic and choking, it was all that remained of the six elites Sasha had sent to their doom. And what very little that remained was still hot enough that they continued smoldering with the threat of combustion. Ashes on the wind.

But it was nothing, *nothing*, to the tiny fleck of horror held in a brittle cage.

A beast named empath.

It was an entity I no longer controlled—and it was starving.

I was starving.

As if he were reacting to the mere thought, I felt the leash tighten about my throat. Throttling the empath before it could lash out. A possessive squeeze from the man who owned it, for it was no longer my crutch.

I'd traded it on a whim, reduced the power of

Tritan's greatest secret to nothing more than a weapon. Placed it in empire hands. Cocked. Loaded. Primed and begging for the fight. A commodity traded. Assigned value.

If he wanted the empath, he could have it.

All of it.

A cage of hard muscle flexed around me, and without a word, he pressed my cheek to his chest. Cupping the opposite side of my jaw, he filled my lungs with a breath that wasn't poisoned with the smoking husk of a woman who might have been a friend, before she was nothing.

It was... peace.

Stability in the crush.

An anchor in hands that squeezed hard enough to leave marks of ownership... that held all the pieces together and refused to let them crumble, despite the cracks gaping wider with every passing, soggy breath.

But it was only a moment.

Brittle, as delicate things most often were.

And he couldn't hold me forever. He was too tired. Too drained from all that had come before.

Foreign, cruel hands found my nape. The touch bit deep, and I felt it all the way through the muscle and into bone an instant before ragged fingernails scored me from collarbone to shoulder blade. Before I was torn from Asher's embrace in a rush of invasive violence.

A glimpse of burly shoulders. Dark, frenzied eyes rimmed in blood-flecked white. And hands. Hands caked to the elbow in silver soot. Eyes glassy with murder. A face I didn't know, energy I couldn't bring myself to taste, despite the hollow spot where the empath starved.

Because I knew.

Knew what was there, lurking in that sharp, narrow glare, for I'd seen it before.

It was vengeance.

And it *always* tasted like *more*.

"*You*," he spat, this soldier I didn't know. A man whose every errant molecule trembled with fury. Whose spittle misted my face, thick with malice and bitter, sick hatred. All of it directed at me. "Vile *whore*."

I blinked. Taken off guard by the aggression that shattered the hush, and saw an elite who reeked of feral madness. Whose every crinkle was caked with a thin film of fine grey ash—who looked at me and knew without asking who was to blame for the carnage smoking all around us. I could see it in the veins pulsing around dark eyes, tiny lines blackened by the death of an empath.

Infected by what Sasha had done.

As if the ashes of his fallen comrades had soaked through his skin and left him tainted.

"Reese," he snarled, and shoved me back, posturing when I landed with a thump on the raised dias. Palms crammed full of splinters, I skidded to a halt. "Aiden. Khal. Eidic. *You* killed them—"

Uttering a wordless snarl, the captain surged between us. His shoulders bunched. High and tight. His feet braced shoulder width apart.

But it was a bluff.

There was precious little left between us. No whisper of the true potential the captain now wielded with the empath at his disposal, nor a hint of the living embodiment of both sides of the spectrum.

We were drained.

Utterly ravenous for more energy than what was strictly required to keep our hearts beating.

Unless...

The thought was fleeting. Hardly more than a second.

But I felt the sentiment pass from me to him. The urge to indulge. To take a sip of the vibrant, seething pot of rage threatening to boil over and taste what this mad elite might offer. Drink deep of his energy, and replenish what I'd burned in trying to save her...

To *survive* so that Sasha's sacrifice would not be wasted.

A moment was all it took. An instant of that desperate grasping, and the empath took every scrap of freedom not offered. Reaching, clawing toward the vibrant life force laid out before us. A feast of boundless energy too tempting for morals or virtue or pithy fucking *reason*.

"She killed them, Rawlings," the other elite spat, oblivious to the danger coiled in the captain's shadow. The whites of his eyes gleaming in a face coated in grime. The dust was all that remained of the men he'd named. "She and Sasha both. Fuckin' witches. She's got elite blood on her hands—your fucking golden girl—and you know it. Our *brothers*." He drew his weapon. Muzzle aimed at his feet, where flickering green flames dribbled from the muzzle, shaken free by a grip that trembled with every wild thrashing beat of his heart. "You're not leaving with her. I won't let you."

At this, something in the captain... shifted. A smile that went unseen, one that was not meant for me, but keenly felt all the same. I felt him swell, as if he'd outgrown his skin. Felt it when something... *else* surged up from deep inside.

It was a thing that saw the empath for all her savage, chaotic needs, and meant to see them fulfilled.

Pure, raw energy pushed at the cracks, and where he'd been deplete, he now felt...

... Dangerous.

Stretched too thin, stuffed too full, he was running on vapor and fumes, all at once. Unstable energy built and lashed, snarling where I could only watch, entranced.

It was familiar as it was foreign. Alien, despite the scent of something that matched.

There was so much potential left untapped...

"Step aside, Rawlings," the other elite barked, his weapon inching up. Held tight in a fist that trembled not with fear, but fury. "Little witch has to pay for what she's done."

"She's mine."

It was a voice that promised to ignite the wind. Deeper than any ocean, it rippled through the soft tissue behind my eyes. Jiggled the fat and jelly until my brain threatened to slip down the back of my nape in a liquid, greasy smear.

But the other elite seemed not to hear the warning.

Ignorant to the hint of power that blinded me to all else.

"I saw the way Sasha spoke to her. Spillin' secrets and whispers before she did what she done. *She knows something,*" the other spat, but when his gaze fell on me, it was with eyes rolling white. Spittle strung between top and bottom lip, a gummy tether that quivered without breaking as he spoke. "Or worse, your little bitch had something to do with what happened here, Rawlings, an' you fuckin' know it." Lip curled around a sneer, disgust etched in his every grimy line, he looked me up and down, then said, "You'd choose her, then? Over us?"

But to this, the captain's answer was a wordless snarl. A possessive guttural thing that sent shivers through my blood and bade me still. Utterly frozen, commanded to watch him work, I was immobile. From breath to bone, from untrained priestess to empath, I stilled. Enthralled by what only I could see.

The captain swelled, fists and jaw clenched, his every muscle locked into place as unstable energy shoved at the seams. Drawing on the dregs of an empty barrel, on the very stuff that kept his heart and lungs moving, it was power that lashed and promised to deal the sort of damage meant to leave pure devastation in its wake.

Saving nothing, it was a thing that would spend every last drop in defense of what was *his.*

Every. Last. Drop.

There was a moment that promised clarity. An instant of knowing without comprehending *exactly* what I was seeing. A truth that lay just out of sight, hidden beyond a thin veil separated between two split seconds of time.

And it was beautiful.

"Get back!"

My breath caught as the moment was shattered by a voice I recognized. One that sliced through the pandemonium of a crowd driven to blind panic, and bade the flexing power swirling around the captain to stall on the cusp of freedom. Turning one unblinking corona toward the voice snarling at the crowd to, "Get back, you animals! I said *back!*"

Marco.

Weapon raised, he swung elbows at the crowd of terrorized citizens and carved a path through the bodies, and snarled, "HEY! *RAWLINGS!* Get your shit together, old man! Look at me! *ME!* "

But the other elite before us was undeterred, his attention unbroken by the interruption, he was instead driven to take a menacing step toward me. Toward *us.* "Your girl needs to be questioned, Rawlings. Punished."

"CAPTAIN ASHER RAWLINGS!" Marco grunted, and shoved an old lady aside before he leapt onto the podium in a swirl of dust and smoke. "Contain your shit before I'm forced to contain *you.*"

And then I saw what the other elite did not. That Marco's weapon was held in a grip that did not tremble—*and was fixed directly to the captain's heart.*

I blinked, and missed the moment it took the captain to wrestle that unstable thing back. Forcing it down deep, where not even I might catch a glimpse. "Sorry, Dez," Asher drawled, but that cultured purr was ragged and thin. His brow pale and damp. Waxy beneath his tan. "Not your call to make."

Exhaling a breath that tasted of deep relief, Marco's chin dipped in a tiny, almost imperceptible nod. And then, without another instant of aggressive hesitation, he swung in a perfect half circle and trained his aim at Dez. "*Move.*"

"Come along, pet," Asher murmured, and wrapped a clammy palm around my elbow. "Time to go."

As if in a dream, I did not fight him. Couldn't. Not with legs made of watery clouds, and a neck too loose and rubbery to support my head.

"Fuck," Asher hissed, and lifted me in arms scarcely more reliable than my own boneless meat-sacks. I could feel it in the way he trembled, straining to bear my weight. Feeble, his muscles deplete.

"Move your rickety old man ass *right fucking now!*" Marco snarled, backing us off the podium and into the seething masses. Finger not quite on the trigger as a wave of civilians swept onto the stage to avoid the pools of liquid plasma still glowing with enough heat to leave what remained of General Tilcot bubbling with the reek of roasting pork.

My head lolled, only to be caught in the crook of Asher's arm. Bleary eyed, my attention was snared by the shimmer of turbulent emotions hovering above the crowd. As if it were a cloud, a tantalizing miasma of panic and fear. Of primal *feeling* so thick in the air my mouth watered at a sight no one else could see.

"It's... chaos..." I whispered, hypnotized by it. And then, lifting one trembling hand, I reached. Fingers outstretched, so I might catch a passing sleeve. Brush against an exposed forearm. Touch what I desperately needed to taste so I might stop the burning, aching cold where an inferno no longer burned.

All I needed was a single instant of contact...

"Don't," the captain barked, and trapped my fingers in his palm. Squeezing too hard. Enough that my joints groaned, my lips drawing back in a hiss of pain and protest. "Focus *here*," he whispered, lips dragging across the edge of my jaw. Inky gaze wild as his eyes darted back and forth in my periphery.

"It's so..." I shook my head, refusing him. "*Beautiful.*"

Strong white teeth flashed, a warning forced between his lips. "Mila. *Don't*. Don't you fucking dare."

But his promise of retribution came too late. Falling on ears deaf to everything but the oppressive hum of bone-crushing grief.

"Yes..." I whispered, and reached into the seething dark. Soaking myself in it, I rolled my neck as it washed over me. The pain... the anguish and the heartbreak.

It was mine to endure.

A punishment earned. Exactly what I deserved, for in return for my blind, stubborn ignorance, I was to suffer agony before I followed Sasha into the welcoming dark.

I exhaled, and let my mind go blank. Seeing everything around me through the eyes of a conduit. A void that needed to be filled with the teeming waves of chaos swelling all around me.

From the distance, the captain cursed. Deep, vicious, it was a sentiment that reverberated through his very bone. "Marco," he hissed, "get us out of here. *Now*."

"And how exactly would you like me to proceed?" the soldier retorted, his every line tight. "The only way out is *through*."

The captain's fingers tightened. My face pressed almost into his armpit when he hiked me up. "She's got no control," he said, scraped raw and left open. Vulnerable. Barely holding on. "I-I can't stop her. Can't hold her back for much longer. And then... if she takes me with her..."

Something... unspoken passed between them. Utterly beyond my comprehension, though I felt the morbid weight of it and knew without understanding that it was a deadly something they spoke of. It was there, in the way Marco's knuckles went white around the grip of his weapon, the dry click of his throat working to choke down a swallow.

And it was there in the fumes of grim determination shimmering across the captain's skin.

I pulled a breath between the points of my teeth and groaned as a hint of what I needed burst behind my eyes.

Murder.

The duty and conviction of a career soldier.

I shivered and burrowed deeper into Asher's arms as energy pulsed through my system. Amplified by the swarming legion, I groaned and felt it when that energy lashed out.

A fight broke out somewhere behind us.

I could feel the dull thud of connecting fists vibrating in the air, could feel the impact of each strike as if it were my own flesh rippling with the force.

Breath hitching around a ragged inhale, my spine arched and bowed.

"Fuck," Asher snarled, and pressed me closer still. My face buried against his throat, his fingers bunched and tangled at the back of my skull. All but smothered against his chest.

Heartbreak, confusion, excitement, terror, bloodlust... it was all right there. The entire emotional spectrum swirling around us. So thick in the air I didn't need to touch to feast on what was so readily available.

I was a conduit.

And I would take.

Eyes rolling back, I let it wash over me. "*Yessss...*"

Voice hoarse, the captain's shout was the only thing that could penetrate the fog. "Mila, *stop!*"

But I couldn't.

This was the only path. The answer I needed, that Sasha had died to protect.

I was just a weapon in the hands of an enemy.

Energy pulsed through me, through Asher, and straight into the gathered Caledonian civilians.

A subsonic boom that flattened grass, people, and anything inside my immediate radius of influence.

For the space of a single breath, there was nothing.

And then...

Pandemonium.

People crawling over each other. Desperate and trying to flee without a whisper of regard for those caught beneath their feet. Well-dressed officials, elegant ladies, terrified slaves—all of them were consumed by animal instinct. A single, seething mass of the collective. With eyes rolling white, lips frothed with foaming spittle. Reduced, one and all, to a writhing mass of consciousness hell-bent on consuming itself.

I watched, entranced, as two waves of people collided in the centre of the clearing, their panicked screams blending to create a symphony of horror. Faces lit by the eerie green glow left over from the general's final, deadly act.

I watched as hapless individuals were thrown from the herd, stumbling and tripping in all directions. Watched as ankles twisted and snapped, observed the dull lowing of chattel until, without so much as a backward glance, several bodies landed in the pool of plasma.

Upon contact, clothing burst into flames. Skin crackled and split, shriveling as it gave up any whisper of moisture that might have been. Not so much burning, as melting. I watched a shelf of meat char and slip free of the bone, until all that was left behind was a greasy smear and the wretched, garbled screams that spattered before they died.

Some part of me knew to wince. Understood that their deaths would not be easy, for I was with them until the very end. Knew that I'd all but taken their hands and walked them into the arms of doom.

But everything else?

I indulged in the now-familiar electric tingle of life giving over to death. A tingle that sizzled high at the back of my throat, where I'd been singed by flames hotter than even those that made instant amputees of those too weak to fight. It was a tingle that soothed, even as it destroyed.

Starving for more, I was a glutton for their suffering.

Paralyzed by it.

Consumed, just as they were. My eyes blank and unseeing as the depth of feeling washed away everything else.

I could do nothing but feel. Aching where my silken dress touched my skin, ears assaulted by the commotion of the riot, nauseated by the scent of death and panic—I was drowning beneath the onslaught as it washed through me. Smothered by the rise of the empath who feasted on the gluttonous excess, who took every spare millimeter of freedom, and ran.

It was chaos. Untethered, wild chaos.

The beauty of destruction—of venting my repressed rage on the citizens who'd grown fat and opulent on Tritan's suffering—was equalled only by the pain of being pulled in every conceivable direction all at once. Too much, too thin, too *hungry.*

Energy, hot and pure, burned through my mind. Wrapped about my shoulders, winding around my hips in a band of searing heat, it was an embrace as much as it was a tether. An answer to my directionless flailing.

Asher.

In an instant, I knew.

He was hiding a secret as deadly as my own.

I knew it as effortlessly as I knew to draw my next breath and then exhale.

It was a thing I recognized in my blood. In the electric tingle at the back of my throat.

Nature's answer to the empath.

Balance between unseeable forces, and so, *so much potential left untapped...*

3

A searing heat flashed past my dangling arm. Singing the fine hairs and leaving the scent of ozone burning thick in the air.

I blinked.

Foggy and not quite lucid.

All around us, bodies. Some still uttering garbled, soggy screams. Some were quiet and still, reduced to little more than obstacles that forced Asher and Marco to step on things that squelched and crunched. Each unsteady footfall jostled me where I hung limp from his arms.

They were running. Fast as they could, despite the obstacles and the carnage and the chaos.

Another flash of vibrant, noxious green energy sailed over our heads. Illuminating the riot in a single frozen blink that refused to fade, even when I squeezed my eyes shut and tried not to see what I could feel with such clarity.

It was Marco who voiced the truth of the horror.

"They're firing on civilians," he whispered, aghast. His eyes rimmed in white as he looked back. Back toward the only branch of the military that seemed unaffected by the swirling eddies of poisonous energy rippling through the weakest minds.

The elites.

"We don't have time," the captain rasped. "Keep pushing. Keep moving. Get us out of here, before I lose what little control I've got left."

"But—"

"I don't care if you have to mow down a line of women and children," the captain spat, making no effort to disguise the desperate edge to harsh words. "It'll be less horrific than what'll happen if I can't stop her—"

"Please! Please help me..."

It was a woman.

Shuddering around wretched, ugly sobs as she staggered back and forth in the middle of an obliterated street. One of her legs bore the bulk of her weight, while the other... the other was... *wrong.*

Crooked at the knee.

She'd been trampled. Burned.

For a moment, the captain stilled. Faced with the reality of a dying woman, his breathing grew ragged, his arms trembled as he strained to hold my dead weight. Fought not to keep pushing forward as a nagging sense of duty flushed through his system. His throat clicked around a dry swallow as something twisted in his chest before it was promptly squashed.

Neatly tucked away, deep inside, where I couldn't reach it.

And then, "Can you walk?" he said. Not unkind, despite the obvious flaw in asking her to do such an impossible thing.

She couldn't.

We could all see it.

But she nodded anyway, reaching for Marco with both hands as she shored up what little strength remained and readied herself to fight through it.

I knew, because I was with her too. Felt the hopeless courage when she pulled it tight about her narrow shoulders, as if it were a cloak that might shield her from what would come next.

A sob bubbled through my lips. "It *hurts…*" I mewled, twisting away from the intense agony wafting off that ruined woman. A pain so visceral, I was driven to lift my head and look. Scowling through the burn of salty anguish as she took another step and wailed anew.

"Come're," Marco murmured, tucking his weapon into its holster before reaching out to her. "Take ol' Marco's hands. Easy, love. That's right—"

It happened in blinding flashes.

Tableaus burned into my memory as an errant blast from an elite weapon finally landed true.

A blast that incinerated her before she could utter another helpless screech—her death was brilliant and blinding. So bright that I could see straight through her flesh to what lay beneath. The image of her contorted skeleton was seared into my memory against a backdrop of green.

Green flames.

Green bones.

Green death.

Flung aside by the booming heat that followed, I sailed through the night. Weightless, until I crashed in a tangled heap of limbs that were mine and his, my head struck the uneven cobbles hard enough that, for a moment, I saw nothing at all. *Felt* nothing.

Not the impact. Not the emotions of a horde, nor the oppressive force of Asher's unshakable will.

Blessed nothingness.

Dazed but still conscious, I couldn't bring myself to react beyond a blink at the electric shock of life yielding to death as the woman was simply... obliterated in the flames. A shuddering gasp whispered over my lips as the last of her sour dregs vanished into the void, leaving me to untangle myself from her energy. Disoriented. Bleeding freely into the dirt, where I lay limp beneath Asher's dead weight.

His bulk pressed me into the cobbles, with no awareness that he was crushing me beneath him.

Shallow breath ruffling the fine hairs on my nape was the only indication that he was merely unconscious. Not dead.

I was... *free.*

Just for a moment. Just long enough to be reminded what it felt like, before he woke and reeled me back in.

There wasn't time to luxuriate in it. Not enough of

anything to enjoy my moment, for I was too drained. Too deplete and worn through. I hadn't even the strength to heft him off me and take a full, luxurious breath.

Boots crunched somewhere off to my left.

Boots attached to the vibrant signature of an unbound Caledonian elite.

And I knew, without bothering to twist my head, just who it was who'd fired that deadly shot. Who'd killed an unarmed, injured woman when he'd meant to kill *me*.

Dez.

He'd followed us from the podium, infected with a poisonous rage not quite his own.

I looked. Chest rising and falling in an uneven shudder as my head fell to the side, trapped beneath Asher's dead weight.

Pinned...

... but not quite helpless.

Watching through a blur as something hot tracked through the grime on my cheeks. Blood or tears or sweat, I couldn't begin to offer a guess, because a conduit couldn't care about such insignificant details.

"I told you she'd pay, Rawlings," Dez said, a horrible smirk crinkling one corner of his lips as he crunched over hideous things. "She's got to answer for what she done. What she knows."

Violence erupted from the centre of my very being. A wordless denial, it was the very definition of survival. Pure and primal, I ensnared Marco with a barbed lash, for it was my turn to brandish a monster on a leash.

As if he were an ill-fitting cloak, I made space for myself inside Marco's heart. Shoved aside anything that wasn't pure, cold vengeance, and was with him when he staggered to his feet with a guttural roar. Felt every intimate facet of his temper as it was uncorked. Full of adrenaline and rage, the soldier scrambled up. Tripping only once, before he fell on Dez from behind.

A maelstrom of heavy fists fell. Ribs, kidneys, jaw, and cheeks—Marco was everywhere all at once. His weapon forgotten where it had been holstered at his hip.

I felt the male satisfaction and the hurt. The victory and the lancing crunch of bones buckling under the assault.

Everything.

Joy.

Rage.

Fear. Pain.

Bloodlust.Arousalexcitement*terrorlust*—

It blended and swirled.

I couldn't escape. Couldn't so much as blink, not even when Dez's heart sputtered and his lungs seized as something jagged sliced through dense muscle and unleashed a flood that smothered his next breath with the weight of a choking, crimson ocean.

Victim and assailant, I felt it all.

Every second that leached into the next, and when Dez's heart began to flounder and sputter beneath the onslaught, I was overcome by a seductive lure. One intent on dragging us all into the dark. It was a soothing blanket of frigid nothing that banked the flames consuming me from the inside out—a numbing wash I embraced with a ragged breath.

A muffled groan puffed against my nape, and with a stuttering gasp the captain began to shift above me. "Ssstop," he slurred. Driven to fight the seeping cold, even as I tried to welcome it. "Marco," he rasped, and lifted his head as if it didn't weigh thousands upon thousands of pounds. As if the weight of it didn't strain his neck all the way down to his lower back. "Enough. Marco, that—that's enough..."

I shivered when the noose tightened about my throat once more. Bones rattled inside my skull when the captain forced me back, my teeth clacking together when my skull bumped the cobbles and he crammed the empath back inside her cage of flesh. Canceling my murderous intentions so he could release the soldier from my grip with an effort that left me cold. Freezing solid in the heart of an inferno.

Marco coughed. Just once before he staggered back. Landing hard, he sat, braced against the cobbles as he stared between his knees. Horror etched into every grime-caked line as he stared at the wreckage of what he'd done. "A-Asher—"

"He's dead." The captain's grip tightened at the top of my thigh, and I felt his jaw bulge when his teeth chattered. And then in a hard voice that showed nothing of the turmoil I could feel swirling inside his chest, he said again, "He's dead. We have to go. Now, before anyone else gets too close. Before she—"

"Right." Marco pulled a haggard breath between clenched teeth. Gagging at the sight of the dead elite before his eyes went to his knuckles. Inspecting where the skin had torn and peeled back, leaving a hint of yellow and white that didn't bother to bleed. "And the woman—is she—did I—"

"She died in the blast," the captain said. Firm. Easing the other man's heart. "It was… she didn't feel it. Didn't even know what happened."

With a tight nod, Marco swallowed.

He swallowed again, and again, before his breath burst over his lips and he forced himself to stand. Swaying before he gathered himself and turned to pull the captain up with unsteady hands anchored beneath his armpits.

And then, as they towered above me, Marco said, "Dez wasn't wrong," in a careful tone. "If she can't be controlled, should she be put down—"

"Not now," the captain snapped, and slipped greedy hands beneath the backs of my knees. Cradling my head and neck with a grip that trembled.

"Look around, mate," Marco returned, dark eyes intent on mine. Cheeks sallow and waxy beneath his tan, his voice tinny and far away as his face began to blur. Doubling as my eyelids grew too heavy to lift.

"It was Sasha," Asher hissed. The imprint of his fingers the only thing I could feel as everything grew numb with a dusting of frost.

"Sasha's dead. She didn't do"—Marco gestured wildly around us—"*this.*"

To that, Asher had nothing to say. No rebuttal that would spare me from the truth as he had Marco. No possessive squeeze that wrapped me in a confusing cloud of hated comfort. And no flicker of soothing energy to supplement what I'd lost and ease the burn of frigid cold.

His jaw flexed as he pulled a whistling breath through nostrils pinched white and bloodless. And then, with eyes gone dark as pitch, he caught my gaze in one that was carefully controlled. His every flickering emotion shuttered and locked down tight where I couldn't begin to wonder what it all meant.

Ignoring the dull throb pounding away at the base of his skull, he pulled the rest of my strength from my soul in a single, merciless gulp and did not blink.

Letting me fall into swirling, inky nothingness of pupils blown wide as they might go.

I fell...

My last thought a question not quite asked.

Because I wasn't sure if I'd ever open my eyes again.

4

I woke to the murmur of far off voices.

Listening to the sound of conversation ebbing and flowing above me, I was pulled up from the bottom of a deep, dark ocean.

Lost somewhere in the fog obscuring what was left of my mind.

Somewhere I'd been *put*.

Where I'd been meant to stay.

I reached without thinking, testing the limits of my new bonds. Trying for the surface... where I might breach through to find a lungful of crisp, light air that wasn't bogged down by the stench of failure. Of guilt.

In an instant, I was surrounded in light. Scalding attention from a single, burning corona that did not blink but managed to scowl as I began to burn even while I drowned.

The attention of a leviathan—it engulfed me.

Completely.

And with a sneer, I was flung back into the depths with a contemptuous flick—a casual lash of power I was forbidden to taste, even though it had once been mine. Found wanting by a better monster, I was banished into a bottomless pit that held a gravity all its own.

Made to watch the chasm between us grow, for the deeper I fell, the higher he soared. Floating, until all I could see was shimmering, gleaming white that grew more brilliant with each dragging moment I wallowed in darkness.

A wall.

But this one wasn't protection against elite attackers.

No, it was a prison.

Protection for *them*.

Against *me*.

Crafted by an expert, it was fed by my own life force. Impenetrable, affording him full, easy access to my power, without the risk of infection from all that I was. A wall meant to blind me to the work he was doing beyond it. Tinkering with power I didn't understand, no matter that it had been mine.

Still, I tried.

Tried to claw my way up, toward freedom.

All I managed was a twitch. A dull lurch of limbs hidden beneath sheets that reeked of *him*.

My lids were gummy.

Heavy and crusted closed.

And though I tried to scream as my wings were

clipped back to the root, a hoarse groan was all that escaped my lips.

"Sleep."

It was the only word I knew. The only one I understood, for it wasn't an offer.

It was a command that shook my bones. Dragging at my will with a nagging, silent reminder of what I'd promised to give in exchange for this ocean of numb.

Some part of me refused. Knew to hate this all-consuming cold for the lie it really was.

The part that ached for the hurt and couldn't be caged—not entirely.

Not by a wall with no ceiling.

And then something cool landed across my brow. A cold compress paired with a gentle touch and soothing hands. The touch of a healer. Hushed words and whispered sentiment that held no meaning and brought no comfort...

... because that touch was absent any spark of delicate priestess energy.

Because Sasha was dead.

An anguished sob clawed through my vocal cords, tearing blisters that left me choking on blood as I gathered a scream that might be capable of describing my fury. My pain and sorrow.

The bone crushing guilt.

She was dead.

And it was my fault.

But even that was robbed from me.

"*Sleep.*"

Those hands began to tremble with the burden of

their lie, quaking at the effort to uphold the illusion, even as a feminine voice tried to promise and appease.

A laugh raced up from the bottom of my lungs. Some dying morsel of rebellion desperate to be vented, before that too, was snuffed out. Choked, horrible madness seeking an outlet before I cracked and gore spilled through the gaps.

I *wanted* to laugh.

Needed to scream and claw and fight and rage until there was nothing left but a blessed wash of nothing that I'd tasted in a mass of seething, panicked Caledonians. My truest nature unleashed.

Again, my fingers twitched, but that was all.

Except the light of the wall, growing ever stronger as it feasted on everything I might have been, before I was *nothing*.

It matched me beat for beat. Spinning a gossamer web of lies around every part of me, he wove commands through my sinew. Installed failsafes that were so much worse than the leash I'd handed over myself, for these were commands that were etched into bone.

He countered my every attempt to escape before I couldn't tell the difference between my thoughts and his—and he did it with a breathtaking ease I knew to fear even then. Even as I was herded back, *down*. Into the dark, where I was freed of the burden of my empathy.

Where I could be numb.

Just as I'd wanted.

The last thing I heard before the screaming dark washed over me was the sound of his voice. Murmuring words I couldn't understand. Low and deep. A rumble that engulfed me with a blanket of oblivion.

5

Liquid heat pulsed through my blood.

Hot. Savage. *Desperate.*

It was a lure.

One I couldn't help but take, for it pulled me up from the muck and the mire. A gentle tug, the shifting of sediment slipping off heavy, useless limbs, and I was able to take a breath. Lids fluttering open to find that I was not alone in the gloom.

He was watching me with a dark intensity amid a swirling backdrop of mist and fog. Face a careful, indifferent mask that couldn't hide what was lurking just beneath the surface. In the unforgiving gleam shimmering in that inky, walled off glare. It was there in the quick, shallow breaths, and the electric tingle singing through my blood.

Want.

Frustrated, furious, futile need.

It was a poison. Rot, spreading through my veins. Leaving aching fever in its wake.

Cheeks hot, my back grew tight. Muscles twisting until I arched with a raspy, guttural groan. Clenching, my head tilted back to expose the length of my throat in a display I made with unconscious ease.

His grin was predatory.

Unblinking, alien, and utterly fixated on my helpless posturing, for I couldn't hide what he could plainly see. What he could sense down in the dark, lurking in flushed skin growing slick and swollen.

Need.

It echoed in each and every flutter of my heart. Answering his call, my body wept for attention. For touch that would stretch and burn and remake even as it eased the ache of neglect. Forgiving the years of lonely solitude so I might learn this new way to burn.

Punishment, for all that I was. All I'd done.

He moved.

Like silk.

A swirl of twitching shadow through the fog, and in a blink, he was before me. Looming in close enough that I saw it when his mask slipped, and a smile curled in the corner of his lips.

It was not a relief.

Beneath the steely exterior, lust. Bubbling at a furious boil. Scarcely contained, despite the way his hand slipped behind my head. That his fingers were sure, even as they twisted in the fine hairs at my nape.

Because it was a trap. My compliance a sure thing that didn't beg for fevered intensity when he could command it at a whim.

He pressed that cruel smirk to my lips and I

groaned.

He swallowed it. Greedy when he pressed deeper, his tongue flicking in to taste, beard rasping against my cheeks and lips. He pressed me back, crushing me down as everything that he was began to swell. Growing, surging to fill every space where I wasn't, until he moved to claim that too.

I was consumed.

From every direction.

Every conceivable angle, inside and out—*Asher*.

The press of naked flesh burned and prickled, and I shivered at his touch. Unashamed by my nudity, because there was no space for such a thought. Not here, where there was nothing but need.

And I did...

Need.

I needed it hard. Fast. Needed him to boil over and fill the place where I ached most. I needed him to mark the spot that only he had ever touched, to burn away everything I'd ever been so I could do nothing but feel.

He only grew cooler. Angry, painful contempt barbed through my nerves. A thing that sat next to hatred in the way that it burned me.

His touch was measured, calculated, even as it drove me to madness. All but writhing, yet unable to so much as lift a hand to sate the pain he'd unleashed in my blood.

It was to be my punishment, this denial. Withholding what had become vital to the next painful beat of my heart.

Cruel, gentle fingers spread me, then. Teasing as they made a slow sweep of my entrance. Testing all that was molten and slick for him.

I sobbed.

Hips tilting back, trying to entice, I whined and couldn't stop. Robbed of all sense of pride or shame. Unable to speak or beg or pray. Frozen as he tormented me with the force of my own vicious, wretched desire.

That grin grew wicked and with a swirl of inky mist, he withdrew. Back behind a wall of gleaming white. Concealed by a fortress where I could not sense him, his fingers were replaced with a thick, blunt length that only promised to pierce into my depths and went no further.

He stilled.

Poised on the cusp of relief, he hovered out of sight. Out of reach. Waiting.

"*Please!*" It burst over lips cracked and bleeding. Born from desperation and madness, it was a thing I'd never meant to do, but hadn't a hope of avoiding. Not now, not in this place, where he was everything and everywhere. Where he saw and felt every lie. Every desperate half-truth that I'd never meant to voice used against me.

I begged.

I felt him smile, then. My enemy. Pleased when the pain became me and I turned to him for relief.

In a single, possessive thrust, he surged forward and—

6

I gasped.

Eyes snapping open, unseeing, I trembled all alone in dark sheets. In a dark room.

Soaked.

Drenched in anxious sweat, and... perhaps something more.

Cheeks flushed hot, my pulse thrashed in my blood. Felt in the hollow at the base of my throat. In my eyes and...

... between my legs.

Dreaming.

I'd been having a nightmare.

It wasn't real. I hadn't sobbed, hadn't begged to be fucked raw by my enemy as he—

"Mila?"

I jumped, a ragged screech spattering over my lips as I lurched away from that voice. Fingers clumsy, I scrambled to pull damp sheets up to my chin as if they might save me from a predator greater than any I'd ever known.

Asher.

He was there. *Right there.* Sitting on the edge of the bed. Looming in the dark. A shadow that blended with the night, and for a moment, as I was ensnared in that inky glare, I couldn't so much as draw a single breath.

He was so much more than the cruel, alien shade in the fog. Intense in a way that defied my senses, that pained my eyes to see after so long in the dark.

Vivid in a way that couldn't be real.

Dead.

I'd died with Sasha, and this was to be my punishment. To be tormented for my part in her end... eternally bound to *him.*

A breath hissed between the points of my teeth, and I squinted. Peeling truth from the ether.

Something was wrong.

My senses were... off. Skewed, just a little. Enough that I could sense a lie, but couldn't quite catch the thread that needed pulled.

I scrubbed at my eyes with the heels of my palms. Trying to peel away whatever magics were obscuring my sight enough to make everything blurry.

When I looked again, it was to find him perched on the edge of the mattress.

Surrounded by a slight shimmer I'd never noticed before. He was coiled as he watched me. *Ready.* Eyes glittering in the dark, but... they were sunken.

Rimmed in strain. Glassy, as if *he'd* been woken from a nightmare to find his enemy looming over him in sleep. And his hair—it was messy. Standing on end, it poked out at odd angles as if mussed by sleep or...

Twisting, desperate fingers driving him faster, begging with touch and nails and breathless sighs...

I swallowed the lump of something caught in my throat, and let my eyes wander. My gaze catching on hard edges and twisting shadows that were there one moment and gone in the next.

Couldn't help myself.

Couldn't help but notice that he was stark naked, and... painfully hard. Shining and taut, his pulse thrumming in a pearly drop that beaded at his tip the longer I looked. Growing with each passing, lurid second of eye contact with this weapon that had already dealt me a mortal blow.

"Mila?" he said again, but it was distorted. Tinny, as if from a long way off. The tone all kinds of wrong, for those two syllables on his lips had been laced with something that reeked of concern.

Relief flooded through me, because *that* was impossible. "Hallucinating," I slurred, and rolled over. Burrowing deeper into the pillows, I turned my back on the phantom from my darkest musings. And then, matter-of-fact, "'M dying, aren't I? Only way I'd beg for *that*. 'Sides. You can't be in two places at once..."

Sleep washed over me in a blanket of frigid numb.

The waves heavy with the dregs of a wry chuckle.

Any sinister hint of something not quite right was swallowed up by the welcoming dark.

7

I slept.

One hour bleeding into the next, unmarked. Hours that became days without much ceremony. One after the other. Pressing forward in a relentless march that seemed not to mind if I got up and rejoined the daily grind, or rotted right there in dark sheets.

A feast for a better monster. Threads of thin, elite silk binding me tighter and tighter with each breath. Until my every inhale saw those threads cut through my flesh, sinking in deep, until they'd become a part of me.

Until *he* was a part of me.

Raw, painful memories were glossed over by a subtle dusting of calm. Seething hatred flipped, until there was a confusing, pleasant blur of feeling that had rewritten who I'd been.

Sterilized.

Cool.

Efficient.

Fed a steady drip of elite energy, I turned my lagging, dizzy attention to the brightest flame and found it warm when I was so, *so* cold...

Still, part of me seethed. Cringing back from the wall I couldn't scale, even as it fed on my marrow. Hiding deep in the dark, alone, where he hadn't yet managed to touch me.

But my refuge grew tighter and smaller by the hour.

The temptation to indulge and be pampered was more enticing with each honeyed drop of dew that trickled over his wall with the command to drink what he offered.

Without ever once bothering to open my eyes, I could feel the coming and goings of several elites and their various entourages. Powerful men, made all the more vicious by the women bound and indentured to follow in their wake. Perfect little slaves, complacent and obedient.

The priestesses. Not a one equal to Sasha's pure might, but they haunted the halls of the captain's stolen brownstone just the same.

Their priestess magic was a taunting lure I was forbidden to taste.

And their grief... it oozed through the walls in a toxic sludge. Sticky. Dripping from the rafters in a constant acid rain that reached for me no matter how deeply I was buried, nor how impenetrable that wall. Each droplet burned. Each burn a throbbing reminder of what I'd done.

That Sasha was dead.

That it was my fault.

And the Caledonians agreed with me. *Heartily.*

For many countless days, I'd listened as they argued about what to do with me.

Publicly euthanize me as a token reparation to the families of those who'd died in the wake of the riot—but Asher was an asset trained by the Empire, and they couldn't risk killing him with the same blade. Not knowing if he'd survive my death.

Lobectomy to maintain access to the so-named *golden priestess* and the rarity that was the empath, without any of the risk of my continued sentience. But they had no idea if the empath was tied to me, Asher, or some unfortunate combination of the two.

Bind me with a second set of chains, as the late General Tilcot had intended. Both to help the captain carry the burden of being tied to one such as me, and to distribute my abundant power between more than one elite. But there was no one left who knew the history of the Tritan people. No one who they might ask to see if any of their many options might lead to consequences with an astronomical price.

They cycled through a thousand iterations of the same plans. Each one more horrible and creative than the last—none of them hinting that they had any idea of the truth of what had really happened.

It *wasn't* Sasha who'd killed dozens, upon dozens of unarmed Caledonian civilians.

It wasn't her grief and anger that had lashed out and sparked a deadly riot.

Marco had been right, for she'd already been dead.

And not even she could do something so vile from beyond the veil.

"Any idea how she did it?" Colonel Viridian asked for the twelfth time. "I just can't wrap my head around it. Priestesses don't have offensive capabilities—"

"Apparently they do," the captain returned, his tone biting. The exhaustion pounding through him the sort I could feel even across the room, for he'd been at this longer than any of the others. Forcing himself to stay awake. Vigilant as he fought to redirect suspicion away from us. To heap it back on Sasha's ghost, so we might escape the consequences of my actions.

His suffering was acute enough to draw me up from my comfortable stupor, and I looked. Found him dressed in the black and gold of his nation. Buttoned from wrists to throat. A thatch of messy black hair the only thing out of place. That, and deep shadows beneath, sunken, inky eyes.

Wretched, and running on fumes, he was sustained by what he took from me after he'd finished feeding his wall. Drinking down whatever was left of the empath's excess in great, heaving gulps.

"This isn't a joke," the colonel snapped, and scrubbed a hand down the white stubble speckling his cheeks. "A priestess as a weapon"—he coughed up an incredulous laugh—"how could we have missed that? How did *Harper* miss that? Sasha was *his* priestess. All this time, harboring a secret like that?" An indelicate snort. "It's unfathomable."

A few tense moments passed, and the hush was nearly enough to let me slip back into my stupor until a new voice broke the silence.

"The important question, gentlemen, isn't *how* we missed it," this new man said, and my bleary gaze flicked to a new face, unseeing. My eyes too heavy to focus and listen at the same time. "But how many of the other priestesses know about it. Was Sasha able to pass along some tender little scrap of knowledge before her death?"

This was a man smart enough to ask the *right* questions.

The first to guess at the secret knowledge I carried.

Every priestess who's ever been has the potential... to become an empath... a weapon...

I squinted from beneath my lashes, peering through a nest of blankets to take the measure of the man. Middle aged. Dark hair laced with wisps of silver that reached back from his temples, he was a handsome, statuesque man of bold Caledonian lineage. But it was his eyes that caught my attention. Stormy grey, his gaze was cutting. Eyes that could penetrate deep enough to see exactly what was meant to be hidden.

I felt the captain's glare before I saw it. The burning attention of my very own personal leviathan, he engulfed me with a net of unstable, frantic power. Commanding me to be still where I was entombed in his bedsheets, molten gold rushed through my veins in an instant. Trapping my breath in my lungs, my every muscle seized in searing bands looped about wrists and throat. Bands of gold that brooked no argument—and burned all the same.

Oblivious, Viridian scratched at his cheeks, absentminded, his fingernails rasping at silver stubble as he hummed and continued the thought. "Are we facing an uprising of suicidal priestesses with power enough to damage the Northern front from within? And if so, why now? Why wait five years? Why not strike when patriotic tempers were still hot?" At this, the colonel sighed, and said, "So many questions we've no answers to."

The third man didn't miss a beat, his stormy gaze fixed to Asher's profile. "What about *her*?" he asked. "I understand your girl and Harper's were spending a great deal of time together. It would be foolish to assume Sasha didn't attempt to pass her something before she died. An object, perhaps? Information, at the very least."

Nervous anger danced through him into me, poison that leached through a barb lodged deep inside my heart. "I carried her out of that riot myself, Lieutenant General Hastings," the captain snapped. Jaw bunching at the corner, his knuckles going white where they were clenched beneath the table, unseen. And there, on his brow, the evidence of the effort he expended—a sheen of anxious sweat. "We've been under 'round the clock surveillance since the demonstration, and thanks to Dez' wild accusations about an untrained fledgling priestess somehow causing that riot"—he sneered—"we haven't so much as left this room in eight fucking days." At this, he laughed, and it was a brittle, wild thing. Reeking of desperation hardly concealed. "She's barely opened her eyes since, and if"—a curse, and the captain cracked his neck, scrubbing at the small hairs at his nape—"*if* Sasha had managed to pass something to her, I can assure you, I'd have already found it."

"This isn't an attack on your character, son," Viridian soothed. "We've got hundreds of elites to think of, here."

The other man didn't so much as blink.

For a moment, there was silence. Tense quiet broken by the familiar sound of a bottle being uncorked. Glass clinking, liquid sloshing. And then, "She was spattered with gore during the riot," the captain murmured, calmer now. "She was standing right beside Sasha when Reese and the rest caught fire. The grease..."

I felt him shudder and knew the white rimming glassy eyes wasn't a show.

Those men had been his comrades. Friends.

Men whose deaths had been ugly. Whose dust had coated our skin, caked in the fine lines. Men whose grime had lined our noses and throats, their taste left to linger long after that horror had been scraped and scoured away. An essence I wouldn't soon forget.

"I couldn't get it off. Not at first. Stripped her down and cleaned her up best I could without visiting the baths." The captain paused, tipped his head back, and swallowed half a glass of amber liquor in a single gulp, then refilled his drink without bothering to conceal the way his hand trembled. "She had nothing but the dress I put her in myself."

"Yes," Lieutenant General Hastings replied. Droll, despite the grim weight of the subject. "How very distressing that must have been. But I'd like to hear you say it, Captain Rawlings. Without the flowery imagery. There can be no question of your innocence in this."

Another tense silence dominated the room as the captain struggled with the edges of a frayed temper. And then, "Lieutenant General Hastings, sir, I've found nothing the late Head Priestess could have given Mila that might teach her how to kill an elite. She had nothing but her dress, and precious few places to hide something where I couldn't find it."

"Yes," the Lieutenant General hummed, unmoved, "but that's not quite what I asked, now was it?"

Ice washed through Asher's blood, and his hold on me began to slip. But even without the leash, I couldn't bring myself to move. To draw attention to myself in the presence of this man.

Lieutenant General Hastings.

Just another head of the snake to replace the one who'd come before it.

"By your own admission," the Lieutenant General said in a low, cultured hum, "the girl stood close enough to hear Sasha's final words, did she not?"

To this, the captain had nothing to say. No clever maneuvering or subtle diversions.

He'd been trapped.

And I watched as his chin dipped in a single, terse nod.

"Given that we cannot interrogate what's left of Sasha's corpse," the Lieutenant General said, and did not blink, "I presume you don't need to imagine how important those words may be to the empire's interests?"

I heard the *click* of the captain's throat working around a dry swallow. Felt it stick. "No, sir. I understand."

"Good. *Good.*" The Lieutenant General clapped his hands, then stood. Turning his stormy gaze toward me at last. "Now wake her up."

8

Clearing his throat, the captain rushed to step between the Lieutenant General and where I lay ensconced in his bed. "Sir, with all due respect—"

"Denied."

The captain blinked, his lips gaping around a mouthful of shocked nothing. "Sir," he said after a moment, "she isn't ready for an interrogation."

Raising one dark brow, the Lieutenant General hummed, and said merely, "Oh?"

Fists clenched at his sides, cheeks sallow with a sheen of sickly green, Asher swallowed and tried again. "She was—Mila was... *damaged* during the riot. Her mind—"

"Shall be all the easier to pry open if it's already cracked," the Lieutenant General said. Flippant. Unbuttoning his cufflinks as he stood, rolling his sleeves back, one careful fold at a time.

Pale, sweating, the captain tried again. "Sir, please, you don't understand. Mila is—she's—"

"That's quite enough, Captain Rawlings," the Lieutenant General snapped. "Simply put, I do not care if this girl is depressed." He laughed. "I don't care if she's been shitting uncontrollably or if her mind is a bowl of fetid, curdled stew. I've got a national security crisis, a rancid puddle that used to be one of our most decorated generals, and the remains of his slave who was, until last week, the absolute picture of obedience and a trophy of Caledonian triumph— until this one irrelevant slip of a girl appeared as if conjured from the ether. I'm getting answers directly from the mouth of the last one to speak to said invaluable slave," he said, and lifted his forefinger to point directly at me, "and you will not interfere another second longer. Understood?"

This time, the captain didn't hesitate. "Yes, sir. Understood."

Without a word, Colonel Viridian pulled out a seat, his face set in a grim, tight mask as the captain sat with a heavy thump. Shoulders slumped in defeat.

I didn't watch Asher's long fingers slide through his hair. Didn't watch them clench in dark, unruly tresses as his jaw worked and his head dipped to hang between his fists and his attention drifted *in*.

Didn't need to see the terror etched deep into the lines on his face to know that he was expecting doom.

And I didn't need the captain to seize my every muscle in a burning, golden fist to know the exact flavor of mortal terror my personal leviathan was trying to choke down.

That despite all his workings to unmake me in his image—as a mockery of the ideal, Caledonian slave —it was all for naught.

Instead, I was made to feel it. His every flicking emotion a drug I couldn't resist. Beseeching, he fed me a desperate tendril and tugged on the cocoon he'd spun around me. A single thread of fire, it was a reminder that he alone sustained me, even if it was poisoned with every breath.

And through the wall, he let a single, desperate sentiment echo down into the depths.

A plea.

Desperate, vulnerable. On the edge of shameless, wordless begging.

Pass this test.

I shuddered.

Buried beneath a heap of blankets, frozen by pulsing bands of molten gold, I let my eyes drift closed as the Lieutenant General approached. Measuring each breath by the soft falls of his feet, I worked to affect the air of someone in a deep, dream-less sleep.

Becoming the lie.

Pulling back the blankets, the Lieutenant General was gentle when he might have been cruel. Exposing me to the chill outside of my nest, he peeled the sheet away from where I'd buried my face, and said, "Release her, captain," in a low, commanding murmur when he saw the gold lacing every inch of my skin.

For a moment, I thought Asher might outright disobey him and damn the consequences. He let the silence drag on long enough that the tension in the room grew brittle.

And then, simply, "I can't."

It was a quiet, tight-lipped admission.

I felt the Lieutenant General frown. "You... can't?" he asked. "Or won't?"

"Won't," the captain admitted, forcing the words through clenched teeth. "Mila"—the captain cleared his throat and tried again. "Her power is... unique. Impressive and incredible, yes. Absolutely. But she wasn't trained in the temple, and as a result, this so-called empath, it's... unstable. To the point of being all-but unusable." He laughed, low and bitter. "It's taken everything I have to hold her in check since Sasha died."

The Lieutenant General turned and straightened in one fluid motion, and with him, the energy in the room shifted. "Eight days?" he said after a moment, incredulous. "You've held her in thrall for eight days?"

The captain lifted one shoulder. "More or less."

Another weighted pause stained the room before the Lieutenant General said, "Why? What do you think might happen if you let her go?"

"I'm not... entirely certain," Asher hedged, but I knew it for the lie it really was.

Because despite the heavy fog, I remembered *exactly* what would happen if he let me go.

"Well, then. It's long past time we find out. Release her," the Lieutenant General said again. An order, and this time, I felt a cool touch on my forearm an instant before I felt everything else. "At the ready, Viridian."

His hands were cold, and through them, I felt what had the captain in such a lather.

Power.

Distinct. The unmistakable signature of an elite, though he lacked the pure clarity I'd grown so familiar with. The effortless, casual power Asher wielded with such crisp efficiency was absent in Lieutenant General Hastings. Or at least, he wasn't quite the equal of the man who held my leash, despite being his superior.

But the man reeked of power he had no right to possess.

For though it was tainted with the metallic stink of an elite, it was *priestess* magic.

The other side of the coin.

Another enigma, just the same as Asher, for it seemed those who could wield both sides of the spectrum weren't quite as rare as I'd been led to believe.

... This is a secret the empire can never possess... that they all have the potential... each and every one who's ever lived... so much untapped potential...

Before I could taste my next breath, I knew the sort of power I'd been born with was *not* the only kind to fear. That Asher was leery of this man he could kill with ease, cautious to the point of self-harm in his effort to out maneuver the other elite? It gave new perspective into the man who had everything it took to climb the political ranks in the Caledonian aristocracy, but who was seemingly content to play the soldier. Disguised as just another obedient cog in the machine, taking orders from lesser men when he had more than enough pure might to see his every whim obeyed.

"Mila," the Lieutenant General said, his voice a low, soothing hum. Demanding my attention. Drawing me toward him. And through his palm, I felt his power plod through my blood. Crude. Absent even the merest hint of elegance required to build a wall like the one Asher had built to imprison me, but it was enough that I knew the Lieutenant General could feel any attempt I might make to evade his questions.

And then I understood what the captain did not. That it was futile to resist, for the Lieutenant General would feel it, even if he hadn't the tools to understand the exact nature of the deception. I understood, in a brief moment of burning clarity, that it would be so much easier to simply give the man *exactly* what he wanted.

The truth.

Asher was trying to hide it in clever cracks between words, in some vain attempt to conjure a rescue from beyond the veil. A rescue that simply wouldn't come, because my one and only ally was already dead.

"Open your eyes," the Lieutenant General murmured. Lacing his words with a compulsion to obey.

My lashes fluttered open as I allowed myself to be swept away in the lure of his unique blend of energy. Watching from my lonely island in the dark. Not permitted to do more than taste the feast laid out before me, I turned my bleary gaze toward this new threat and did not blink. Obedient, but damaged. The very picture of what Asher had painted. Exactly the perfect little slave girl the Lieutenant General wanted to see.

No more. No less.

"My name is Lieutenant General Hastings," he said, and folded one over-large hand around my fingers. Enveloping my frigid digits in a warm pocket that was little more than a disguise for this insidious interrogation. "I need to ask you a few questions. About General Tilcot's death, and the events that came before and after."

I swallowed, and let the truth bleed through my cracks.

And then I told him *everything*.

"It was my fault," I said, and meant every syllable. "I killed General Tilcot."

In my peripheral, I saw the captain's eyebrows jump. Heard the bubble of hysterical laughter before he was able to contain it. And felt the lightheaded rush of adrenaline as Asher prepared to die. Doomed at last, by my words.

Head snapping back, the Lieutenant General frowned and said, "Is that so?"

"He meant for me to die," I rasped, voice a parched croak of unused tissue. "Meant for the captain to die at the demonstration, like we almost did on the field. Burned up from the inside out, until there was nothing left of either of us but a dried up husk." I let a tiny, unhinged smirk play at the corner of my lips, and leaned in to whisper, "But he fell into his own trap. His legs... they melted." I took a haggard breath. "Can you smell it? Taste what's left? I can." I swallowed again, and let my tongue peek out to wet dry lips. "There's nothing left but the grease and you can't scrape it off. I've tried." With my free hand, I scratched at my throat. Scratched and scratched, murmuring, "Tried and tried and tried and—"

The Lieutenant General was careful to keep the bubble of disgust tucked neatly away, but I felt it all the same. "Horrible business," he cooed, and his thumbs traced a pattern between the thumb and index finger of my captured hand. "Here. Let's have a sip of something stronger than water, to help wash away such a traumatic memory."

Without blinking, I let him feed me a generous gulp of amber liquid straight from his own glass.

"Swallow it down, now," he hummed, and offered a kind smile. "Every drop. That's it. Good girl. Now tell me about the general's slave. Sasha, was her name? What was her part in what happened? We haven't been able to sort that out."

Tears flooded my lashes, unbidden. "She *shone*," I breathed. "From the inside out."

"Yes," he drawled, "so I heard. But what did she say to you before—"

"I tried *so hard*," I hissed, forcing the words between the points of my teeth. And my fingers— they found an anchor around the thick digits encasing them, nails biting into the flesh of the Lieutenant General's wrist as I fed him every poisonous drop of truth in a titanic flood of information. "But I couldn't fix it. I tried to pull her back," I whispered. Frantic, letting him feel the instability still rocking behind my ribs. Where failure throbbed with each guilty, treacherous beat of my heart. "Blue fire in her veins. Priestess magic," I rasped, clawing at his wrist. "She never taught me how to stop it, because I'm not a priestess. Just another play thing for an elite. A whore, trained to serve with a smile." A hysterical sob chattered through my teeth, but I flashed him the closest thing to a smile I could muster—and it was horrible. "They're extinct, now. The priestesses. The very last of them burned up in blue flames, and I killed her. She's dead because of me."

The Lieutenant General shook his head, but couldn't tear his gaze away from mine. "Hold on a moment. Back up. How exactly did you kill them—"

"Born to be a healer," I mumbled, face wet with tears. Prickly and hot. "But everything I touch dies. And I can still taste it. The rot."

Pressing the fingers of his free hand between his

eyes, the Lieutenant General pulled a slow breath between his lips. "Mila—"

"I'm a poison," I snarled, and used the leverage I had on his wrist to haul myself upright. To force him to look and see what remained of the empath. Getting right in his face, unblinking, so he might feel the true depth of my guilt seeping through his ribs. "Death was her only escape *from me.*"

"Did she say anything to you before she died?" the Lieutenant General pressed, his brow glistening with a thin layer of sweat. Pupils tiny pricks of darkness, even in the half light of Asher's bedroom. "What were her last words? Be exact, now."

At this, a wash of wretched heartbreak flooded through my chest, and I gasped out the words that burned the deepest. *"You're not a priestess, girl. Powerless. Soiled. Nothing but dust, just another tool to be used and discarded by the Empire. And now,"* I rasped in a singsong voice, *"the priestesses are all gone."*

For a moment, the Lieutenant General could only blink as he tried to untangle himself from the gossamer threads of netting I'd spun around him. Pulling back, first where only I could feel it, and then with a trembling hand, he wrenched his trapped fingers from my grip. Crimson half-moons oozed around the white imprints of my fingerprints.

Nodding, as if to himself, he patted my forearm, then said, "Thank you, Mila," in a voice that trembled beneath that cultured surface. "You've been a tremendous help. Why don't you close your eyes and get some rest. This has been a trying experience for you."

He stood.

Nodding again, he took a breath, and turned to the captain and Colonel Viridian. "Well," he said. "That was... an... experience."

From the captain, there was only grim silence. A clenched jaw, and white knuckles as he awaited his sentence.

"Captain Rawlings"—the Lieutenant General laughed—"to say you've earned a break is an understatement of criminal proportions."

A tiny breath of air left the captain's lips. "Thank you, sir, but I don't need a break—"

The Lieutenant General put up his left hand. "Nonsense. Complete and utter nonsense, and after five minutes with that girl, now we both know it." Shaking his head, he dabbed at the moisture on his brow, then reached for his overcoat. "No, you're excused from all duties going forward. And I'll need some time, but let me see what I can do about getting you some relief from so defective a priestess as this one."

I went still where I'd wilted in my nest.

Tension pinched the captain's brows, and he said, "Relief?" through tight lips.

"They're strictly experimental for now," the Lieutenant General replied, "but the research teams have developed a suppressor cuff that acts as a deadener for any energy wielder who wears it. There are some... unpleasant side effects," he added with a grimace, "but given the state of her, being indefinitely comatose might just be a kindness."

Ice washed down my nape, and I jolted in place. Eyes darting to the captain. To see what his reaction might be to the words 'suppressor cuffs' and 'indefinitely comatose'.

The captain gave his head a slow shake. "I didn't even think to ask about such a thing." And then, after a moment's pause, "Thank you, sir. I appreciate it."

"Don't mistake my sympathy for forgiveness," the Lieutenant General retorted. "This is why new priestesses are meant to be tested vigorously before being assigned to the elite most compatible to her needs. It takes extensive training to be ready to manage a properly trained girl, let alone one of such a disastrous nature. General Tilcot's reports were not generous to your character, captain, and if I wasn't already impressed by your handling of the girl over the last eight days, I'd probably already have plans to have you two torn apart and damn the consequences. Just as he recommended. Punishment for binding yourself to an asset that should have been claimed in the name of the empire." Dark brows rose almost high enough to meet his hairline. "A decision that *should* have been a royal one, I might add. Oh, I understand why you did it, just as easily as I understood Tilcot's impulse to try and steal her from you. By our own folly, priestesses are a dying breed, and that girl's all but made of raw power. Never felt anything quite like it. And if that power can be harnessed without risking some catastrophic fallout?"

That stormy gaze flicked over his shoulder, and

without err, the Lieutenant General met my eyes. His stare penetrated straight through me, pinning me in place as a slow smirk tugged at the corner of his lips. "She'll be an incredible asset. To whichever program she ends up in."

Nausea splashed at the back of my throat, but I fought to keep my expression harmless. Worked to keep the horrified disgust contained, behind that sterile, white wall where it couldn't lash out and sign our death warrants.

The Lieutenant General shrugged, and in a slow, cultured drawl, added, "But now that I have assessed her for myself, seen just how deeply she's been affected by the death of her would-be mentor, I'm not entirely certain you haven't gotten a punishment and a trophy all in one."

At this, a shaky, breathless huff of laughter puffed over the captain's lips. "An apt description, sir."

"Right." The Lieutenant General beckoned to Colonel Viridian, and readied himself to depart. "A guilty conscious does not make a murderer. And once we get her fitted with suppressors, the issue of her instability will be moot. Oh," he added. "You'll have to put in a request for a full-time carer for her, and I suggest you start filing that paperwork now, unless you're keen to change soiled garments yourself."

Clearing his throat, the captain's brows furrowed as he said, "Thank you, sir. I'll do just that."

And then he stood, seeing his superiors to the door. Exchanging tepid pleasantries with the man who'd just promised me a living death.

"We'll see you at the funeral, Rawlings," the Lieutenant General said from the hall. "Deepest condolences for your loss."

As I sat there listening to the low buzzing hum of horror as my blood roared in my ears, I couldn't quite decide which loss the Lieutenant General was referring to—the death of General Tilcot, or...

... *Me.*

9

Asher closed the door with a measured, steady *snick*.

Forehead bumping against the oaken grain, I watched him simply breathe. Eyes closed. Shoulders hunched as he took several dozen steadying inhales, forearm braced against the dark wood as he retreated inside himself.

Alone in the privacy of his mind, where I could no longer sense his every flicking emotion.

And then he laughed.

It was a single bark of sound that did little to bring comfort.

Incredulous, teetering toward outright madness, he laughed without bothering to lift his head from the wood. Shaking with mirth and the release of pent up tension.

"Fuck," he breathed at length, and scrubbed at his eyes hard enough that I winced for him. "*Fuck.*"

I swallowed, brow damp with a sickly sheen as

disgust rolled through me. The Lieutenant General's words echoed inside my head, over and over and over until I had to swallow back the acid splashing at the back of my throat or be sick right there in my nest.

"I have to say," Asher drawled after another series of unhinged, breathless bouts of laughter, "that was fucking incredible, Mila. Brilliant, even."

It was my turn to shrug, but it did little to quell the horrified nausea still rippling through my system.

Setting his back to the door with a thump, he turned to watch me from beneath the fan of dark, inscrutable lashes. Arms folded behind his back, jaw bunching at the corner as if he'd started several sentences only to bite them in half. "What I'm trying to say," he said when the silence dragged on, "is that you've impressed me, Mila."

I sneered. "Enough that I might avoid the privileges of being rendered a living corpse?"

A tight, uneasy little grin played at the edge of his lips. "One day at a time, pet."

"I wonder," I rasped, and began to peel back my layers with arms that were far, *far* weaker than anything I'd ever known before. Getting tangled in the sheets as the edges of my temper began to fray at last. "Who gets the profound honor of playing nursemaid to my corpse? Will it be Alicia? I'm sure that green-eyed little traitor would take some sick satisfaction from that. She'll get to bask in my victimhood and weep big, messy, extravagant tears over the injustice of it all. Or perhaps Beau would enjoy seeing me in such a state. Or perhaps—"

"Mila." He pushed off the door, arms still loosely clasped behind his back as he approached with careful, measured steps.

"Perhaps you'll just leave me to rot in the cellar on a bed of spilled rice," I spat, too tangled up to scramble back. Heart in my throat as the emotions that had been uncorked began to boil over. "Nice and out of the way. It's cold enough down there that my corpse might last for quite some time without you having to so much as worry about any unseemly messes I can't help but—"

"*Mila*," he said again. Quieter this time, despite the added force he applied to the word.

"*Indefinitely comatose!*" I hissed, my voice splintering as I clawed at the sheets and only grew more tangled. Kicking and thrashing, I screeched at the fabric that clung worse than the sticky grease of dead elites. "You fucking parasites are sick, Asher, *sick*—"

He took my wrists in strong, rough hands and bade me to still without filling my veins with molten force.

I wanted to tell him I'd prefer death. Wanted to scream and wail and beg, tell him that he could ask for whatever I had left—ask for whatever lurked in his darkest, most depraved fantasies and I'd give it to avoid such a horrific fate as what the Lieutenant General Hastings envisioned for me.

Anything but that.

Instead, my lip trembled.

Energy seeped through my skin. Waves of soothing, relentless calm that stopped my panicked ranting and forced my bewildered gaze down, to where his fingers were wrapped around my wrists, only to see a gentle pulsing gold lapping at my veins. With a touch, he fed me... *euphoria.* A drugging, relentless current that bled through the network of energy he'd built inside me while I'd been lost in the dark.

"One day at a time," he murmured, and with deft fingers, let go of my wrists and pulled the sheets away from my thighs. Freeing me from the cloying, sticky wrappings that had been my tomb for eight days.

My every muscle trembling with an emotion I couldn't quite name, I was still as he unwrapped me. Unnaturally calm, and struck by the horror of what this level of influence might mean. That with a touch, he could rearrange my emotions to suit his needs.

Fighting the urge to hide my breasts when they were exposed to the chill outside of my cocoon, my fists balled up. Nails biting my palms as I fought to look anywhere but those penetrating onyx eyes and share in a moment of rare camaraderie with the man who'd made this most recent horror possible in the first place.

Because it wasn't real.

And the real horror was forgetting just *who* was my enemy.

Twin bands of gold caught my eye, offering welcome distraction. Glowing with a dim, warm light, I traced the left one with the tip of my forefinger. "Eight days?" I whispered.

He hummed as he worked, but that was all.

Tracing the glow that illuminated the manacles, it

was my turn to laugh, but it was breathless and thin. The gold no longer filled my veins, as if his influence was muted, despite obviously being active. As if, in his bid to leash the empath, he'd gone deeper than the surface. Where I'd eventually grow... numb to his constant vigilance.

"It hardly even feels like pain anymore," I mused, voice trailing off as I wondered how long it would be until I didn't notice his influence inside me at all.

And it was then, as I shivered beneath his scrutiny, that I turned away and was shocked by the state of his quarters. Stacks of plates and uneaten food teetered by the door. A pile of dirty laundry, three empty bottles of wine, an entire platter of untouched fruit. Papers and documents scattered across the surface of his desk without so much as a hint of organization

"Confinement doesn't suit you," I snipped in a voice barely recognizable as mine, for it was reedy with disuse. Shivering with each forced syllable.

Warm fingers landed on the corner of my jaw, and he turned my face back, so he might drown me in a gaze of the inkiest pitch. "Do you remember the demonstration?" he murmured, and to his credit, his gaze didn't dip to everything he'd exposed. And why bother? It was nothing he hadn't been staring at for eight days anyway. The shine of a new toy well and truly worn away.

My lip curled, and I didn't dignify the question with anything more than that.

"Harper's funeral is tomorrow morning," he said,

fingers tracing the edge of my jaw back toward my ear. He tucked a lock of tangled silver-blonde hair away from my face.

A funeral meant a crowd.

A crowd full of emotional Caledonians. Peppered with the elites and their enslaved priestesses, each of them with a different reason for tears and theatrics.

All that energy... ripe... *readily available...*

The blood drained from my face in a dizzying rush, and I turned away from his touch. "I don't understand what that has to do with anything."

"Don't you?"

I swallowed the hard lump clogging my throat, but couldn't stop the screams from echoing up from the back of my mind. And with them, the scent and flavor of their former owners. Their unique energies, each signature one I could remember with painful, blinding clarity, if I dug deep enough. Remembered just how... *incredible* it had been to be a conduit for that type of power. With the seething masses unleashed, the very air had been charged with exactly the sort of energy I now desperately wanted to taste again.

The electric tingle of life giving over to death...

I remembered.

Of course I did.

Tears gathered at the edge of my lashes, but I forced them back, and said, "You think I'm responsible for the riot."

He said nothing, and the weight of that silence threatened to crack each and every one of my ribs.

"Do you blame me for Sasha's death, too, then?" I asked, and mustered the courage to glance at him from the corner of my eye.

Taking a tiny, insignificant pause in his perusal of my face, he blinked. And then, "No. Sasha's choices were her own, at the end."

"But not the riot."

"No," he said, "not the riot. You may have won us a victory here today, for now," he went on, "but it doesn't change what happened. Won't stop Hastings from coming back to test his theories and his new tech on a priestess he sees as a liability before she's an asset. Impressive or not, you bought us one more day and a sentence that might just be worse than death."

"Great. I'm a menace," I said, and made to return to my nest. Hiding the salty, traitorous wet soaking my lashes in a handkerchief of dark sheets. "Leave me here to rot and take your intended lady wife to the funeral. I'm sure Carina'll appreciate *that* deeply romantic gesture."

His hand darted out to stop me from cocooning back into the sheets, long fingers wrapping around my wrist. Concealing warm gold in the heart of his palm. "You can't stay in bed forever."

"Just getting accustomed to the inevitable," I snapped, trying to wrench away from his poisonous grasp, succeeding only in tugging him closer.

"You gave the empath to me, remember?" he said, and, taking advantage, he slipped in behind me. Enveloping me in his scent, his heat—his oppressive, domineering will locked away where I couldn't taste or touch or take. The fabric of his uniform was rough wherever I was soft. Arms slipping around my shoulders, he pulled me in tight. Wrapped me in an embrace I was too weak to fight off. "You traded it in exchange for freeing you from Sasha's prison." He paused, then. Lifting my left wrist, it was his turn to trace the softly glowing band of gold with the edge of his thumb. Making me look. "I didn't realize exactly what her wall was holding back, though I suppose, above anyone else, *I* should have known what you might be capable of."

I went very still. Hung on the edge of ignorance and bliss, dangling over an abyss where painful things went to fester and rot.

"And now that it's gone"—a huff of breath mussed the fine hairs at my nape—"now that *she's* gone, the burden of holding the empath in check has fallen to me."

"Train me," I rasped, twisting against his heat. "Like you promised, before—"

"Forty-six people died in that riot, Mila. Thirteen elites, most of which were Sasha's doing, but the rest... they were unarmed civilians provoked into unnatural violence. Violence that's been attributed to Sasha's final act. *Officially*. But the rumors whisper of a different culprit."

Something in my chest collapsed. A tiny, fragile sound escaping my lips from the battered corner of my soul that wasn't a smoking wreckage. "Please don't do this. I—" My eyes drifted shut on a painful squeeze, and I turned my face, whispering a shameful truth into sheets that couldn't judge me for a moment of weakness. "I don't want to be a weapon for the empire."

He clicked his tongue. "And yet," he murmured, letting his fingers tangle in my hair as he tugged it away from the slope of my neck. "You gave the empath to *me*," he said again, lips moving against my ear. Ghosting down the length of my neck. "A payment for services rendered." His fingers grew tight with greedy excitement and I felt the edges of a trap cinching tight around my throat. "Mine to do with as I please."

"Until Lieutenant General Hastings has me lobotomized," I whispered, shuddering with terrorized disgust.

"This is Caledonia," he returned, voice going hard. Grim. "And I warned you, Mila. Told you what would happen if you drew the attention of powerful men, that *you* would pay the higher price and *my* plans for you would go ignored." He cupped my chin and let rough fingers skate over the edge of my jaw. Turning my face, so he could see my eyes when he said, "I warned you of horrible things you've never thought to be terrified of, but still, you pushed until you found the edge of their tolerance. And now we reap the consequences of your actions." His fingers grew tight with scarcely concealed anger—a depth of feeling that flirted with hatred, it was an accusation and condemnation all in one. "You left me no choice."

I swallowed and it was thick with dawning horror, with the nagging sensation that... *something* wasn't right. My magic robbed of me in a way I couldn't define. After all... eight days was an eternity to a man who wielded the sort of power Asher had inherited. And my voice was ragged and thin when I whispered, "What did you do?"

He shrugged, despite the way dark eyes gleamed with the smug sheen of pride. "Let me show you."

10

Heart hammering, my chin dipped in a single nod.

I wanted to see.

Needed him to shine a light on the slithering things that hid in the dark, and left me with the creeping sense of wrong.

It was a permission he didn't need but he smiled as if indulging a small child.

And with an effortless flick, he swirled through my blood. Twisting. Tasting. A ravenous burn that didn't pour from his touch—it was summoned from within.

Already inside. Laced throughout my entire body, laid down with meticulous care, it was a network of energy waiting to rise at his command. A power that answered only to him.

I dragged a stuttering breath through my lips. Eyes wide, shocked as I stared into obsidian depths and saw the pale reflection of a helpless, lost little girl caught in tar. Marooned on an island, completely surrounded by an ocean of power.

Alone.

High at the back of my throat, a fragile whine crackled through the despair as the veil of ignorance began to lift and horrible understanding rushed through the cracks.

A grin spread across his lips. And against my spine, a growl rumbled through his chest. Guttural and deep. Dripping with the toxic wrappings of obsession, he ground his hips against the curve of my bottom and let me feel just how much he appreciated my reaction to what he'd done inside me.

But the show had only begun.

The kiss of dark flames lapped at the soft spot beneath my jaw. Elite energy saturated my skin—bubbling up from inside me in such a way that made me swell on a gasp. Bewildered by the way my muscles went liquid, jerking against him *without* the cruel burn of gold.

Because he had no need of such crude methods. Not anymore.

"I was forced to make... *other* arrangements while you slept," he said, and traced the outside of my thigh with his palm. "Had to get creative to contain the empath after the riot. After you'd tasted true power."

"A wall," I said, my voice reedy and thin with a desperate edge, trying to deny what I couldn't bear to admit. "Another one." And then, to flatter him, I added, "A *better* one."

He tisked. "Come, now. I expected better than *that* from my warrior priestess."

My lip trembled. Breath caught.

Because I knew.

The truth was woven through the very fabric of my being.

Undeniable.

That from this, there would be no escape. No clever maneuvering. No covert plans born from the shadows, for he ruled the dark and everything in it. My body. My mind. *Everything.*

"Nooo," I whined, an admission in a single syllable leaked through a quivering pout. Seeking comfort from the very man who'd ruined me, I was helpless, leaning into his touch when his thumb skated over the edge of my jaw. When he cupped the back of my neck and cradled my skull, leaning over me without an ounce of shame or regret.

"It was the only way," he murmured, and moved to cover me with his muscular frame. Blocking out the light, consuming my vision until there was nothing but him. "You have to know that, Mila. That you couldn't be trusted. I had no choice."

I tried to pull a ragged breath through my teeth, and failed. It was stuck in the clog blocking my throat. In the choking, wretched heartbreak gushing through the rip in my chest that was stuffed full of him.

He hushed me, kissing the corner of my eye. "It's over now. You'll never want for anything," he soothed, and his black gaze flicked down. Watching as he fingered my lips, exposing the point of modified canines, not quite able to disguise the gleam of greedy, dark flames flickering in his eyes. "You'll never have to fight, or struggle, or suffer again— unless it's for me," he murmured, and tipped my neck back, pressing our foreheads together. "But I promise you'll beg for this brand of torment, pet. Over"—he rocked against me—"and over again."

Breath hitching, I let my eyes drift closed. Shutting him out, trying to find some tiny forgotten place that was quiet, untouched by his power. His all-consuming awareness.

It didn't exist.

One rough hand slid down, to knead my breast. Tweaking a nipple that beaded beneath his touch with an eagerness that betrayed me. An excitement he felt before I could so much as try to disguise the rush of taboo lust.

Giddy with excitement, he pressed his lips to my ear and I felt the smirk catch in my hair. "Come," he whispered. "Let me show you how easy this can be."

I blushed. Hot and prickly, shamed by all the many things I had no control over. "Take what you want," I whispered, because despite the way my pulse pounded at my temples—in my wrists and throat—it didn't matter. The fight was over. Lost while I had been sleeping.

He pulled me from the sheets. Shifting first one, and then the other leg over the edge of the mattress, his hands dipped to my lower back as he helped me to stand. Supporting me when I swayed on unsteady, atrophied legs and clutched at his shirtfront with fingers that were thinner than I remembered them being. More claw-like than ever before.

He didn't sweep me off my feet. Didn't scoop me up and simply carry me—he let me walk, despite the thin layer of sweat that bloomed on my brow. Ignoring the way my nails caught on his skin as I clung to his shirt. Supporting me when I began to wheeze, without a single snarky word to point out the obvious deterioration of my muscle.

Because he knew.

Because he was already under my skin and understood just how badly I needed to cling to the illusion that I could control *something*, even this one small thing.

By the time he closed the bathroom door behind us, the room was spinning. My face and lips tingling and bloodless as the tiles danced in an alarming pattern that beckoned me to rest my head on the unforgiving floor. At speed. Regardless of the force.

"Sit."

I obeyed, plopping down onto the frigid toilet seat with the splat of naked skin. My knees folded without a second to spare, and I took several deep, steadying breaths with my eyes squeezed shut. Sound ringing in my ears, and nowhere else.

"Ready?" he said after several minutes of watching me fight the welcoming dark where a leviathan waited in the gloom.

I peeled my lids apart, squinting at him through one watery eye.

Yards of naked, bronzed flesh. Forearms crossed over tight muscle, utterly absent even the merest hint of shame, he was watching me from an unblinking glare. Cloaked in steamy mist, backed by the dim lighting. Still, except for measured breaths as he witnessed my struggle to remain upright.

"You'll feel better after a shower," he said.

I glanced at the shower stall, remembering the particulars of our last shared showering experience. The flash of a clenched fist that directed rope after rope of salty come as he marked me with his seed, then pushed it inside. "You think so, huh?"

A tight grin played at the corner of his lips. Quick. Devious. There and gone between one blink and the next, but long enough that I saw what lurked beneath. Beneath the ill-fitting cloak of an ally, there was a predator coiled and ready to spring.

He was playing with his food.

I knew it, but I took his hand anyway, allowing him to lead me into the shower.

A groan of pure bliss slipped between my lips before I could stop it. My every muscle going lax when a spray of warm water washed over me.

"Hands on the wall," he murmured, placing my palms himself so I could brace beneath the shower head.

Anchored to slippery tiles, I focused on drawing one long breath in. Letting it leak through clenched teeth as it went out.

I heard the click of a bottle being uncapped seconds before I felt strong hands worm their way into my scalp. Massaging my hair at the root.

I *melted.*

Whimpering as he paid special attention to the base of my skull, my temples, and the back corner of my jaw, a helpless groan spilled over my lips. And without meaning to my spine twisted and bowed, arching until my shoulder blades jutted back, until the tips of my breasts kissed the tiles and I hissed with the shock of cold.

"Here," he murmured, guiding my head back. Clear of the water, back until I bumped against the dense muscle of his shoulder, and...

... everything else.

Yards of slippery, prickly naked male flesh lined up against my back. *Achingly hard male flesh.*

"A-Asher—"

A deep hum rumbled through my ribs as long fingers wound through my sodden tresses, working at my scalp in such a way that my eyes all but rolled back. Serenaded by the crinkling pop of suds bursting against my ears. "Relax," he whispered, and slipped one strong hand around my ribs. Pulling me back, until I notched into place against him and could feel each steady beat of his heart against my spine.

Throbbing where he was stiff and lodged between the cheeks of my ass.

I swallowed, staring at the tiled ceiling. Blinking

beneath a crown of suds, I focused on drawing another breath between my lips, and *not* the way his fingers were inching... down. Massaging my neck. Trailing over my shoulders as he worked little circles into the muscle.

Forearm flexing, his hips strained in a shallow thrust. Cock slipping through slick bubbles that invited him to play.

Instead, he turned me with a gentle twist. Setting my back against the tiles so he might watch me from that hooded glare. One palm braced beside my cheek, he towered above me and sent his other hand to trace the slender column of my throat. Fingers soapy, he painted my collarbones in bubbles—then cupped my breast. Catching the nipple between forefinger and thumb. "Touch yourself," he murmured.

My lips parted on a soundless denial.

"Show me," he whispered, and added a maddening pressure to his grip on my nipple. Twisting until I squeaked and spread my feet before I collapsed on rubbery knees.

"I"—a trembling gasp caught in my throat, making me swallow and cough, even as I strained toward that delicious pain—"I can't."

In the glow of the chains, lit by his ever-present vigilance, wickedness gleamed at me in the dark. "You already know I don't have to ask," he said, and the chains hummed to life in a brief flicker of warning before fading back once more. "But I want to see. I want to watch you come apart for me," he rasped, forehead dipping to bump against mine as he released my nipple, and his soapy fingers darted lower.

"Asher—"

He cupped my mound. Heel of his palm grinding against my clit, he spread my lips with a single deft stroke, front to back, and found me entirely too wet to blame on even the deepest ocean. Slippery in a way water just *wasn't*. "I can feel how hungry this little cunt is," he said, tracing my opening with a languid lack of hurry. "But go ahead and tell me how this"— he pressed inside me with a slow push of his index— "is all my fault. That I made this pussy gush. The lies are so much richer when you're coming with them on your lips."

Hands balling into fists, a long, low whine was pulled up from the bottom of my chest as even the girth of a single finger stretched all that was swollen and far, *far* too ripe.

He pulled back with a wet squelch, took my wrist, and guided my own fingers to trace my clit in a slow circle. "Show me," he said again, almost pleading as he let go. Gaze fixed between us, his breath hot on my cheeks. "Please."

I sobbed, just the once. Hardly half a breath, but it was enough that I wobbled with the force of my shaking head. "I *can't*," I hissed, inexplicable tears gathered on my lashes. "I've never—without Carina —*I don't know how!*"

For a moment, all he did was frown. Eyes flicking back and forth between mine as he weighed my words and found them lacking, then turned to drink the truth straight from my veins. And I knew he was remembering the last time he'd asked and I'd readily given him a show. Donning the skin of a cheap seductress as if it were my usual cloak.

And then, a gentle, pulse throbbed beneath my skin, where I was helplessly ensnared. "Explain."

I couldn't stop the words from spilling over my lips. "Before you, I'd never—no one has ever—*I stole her energy*," I said in a fragmented rush. "Carina, I mean. Because she knew and I don't"—another sob, and I shivered in place, frozen beneath the weight of that bottomless stare—"But now I'm empty—*nothing*—and, and I—*I don't know what you want me to do!*"

"You were a virgin," he whispered. Eyes wide, voice a ragged, choked thing I could scarcely hear above the pounding rush of the shower. A realization of the truth that came far, *far* too late. "All those years living alone, fighting the empire, evading capture. You'd never been touched—*until me.*"

Heat bloomed in my face as a fat tear spilled down my cheek.

And then another.

And another.

A surge of feral, possessive elite *want* flooded my veins.

Absent even the barest hint of remorse for all he'd taken as his own, Asher caught me by the throat in a hand that was somehow rigid and gentle all at once. Pinning me to the tiles, he forced my chin back with his thumb and ensnared me in his inky glare.

"All those years," he breathed, nostrils flaring white with poorly disguised excitement, "*untouched*. A priestess of rare and untapped power, unknown to even her own people. A perfect fucking match to all the things I can never freely admit." He laughed, and then, "This cunt is *mine*," he snarled, and nudged my ankles apart. Stepping into the space, he hooked my left leg over his hip, forcing me to balance on one unsteady foot as his fingers found where I was aching and slick once more. "*Mine,*" he said again, and filled me with two fingers, pushing until my swollen petals met his palm in a horrifying squelch. "Say it. Tell me who owns this pussy."

Head spinning, tears spilling unchecked down my cheeks, I was helpless before his lust. Drowning without Sasha's wall to levee the flood, I couldn't blink. Couldn't look away from the man who'd taken everything.

But I refused to speak the words that would damn me forever and brand me inside and out as *his.*

His thumb found my clit. And with flawless precision, he pressed that swollen bean in a long, slow stroke. Bottom to top. Languid, despite the way the tension was building below my navel. That I was trembling on a leg that could barely support my weight.

Spread.

Vulnerable and pinned. Utterly helpless but to feel exactly what he wanted me to feel.

Straining toward him, my every muscle winding

tight enough to burst, I hurtled toward the edge. "Oh, fuck—"

"Ah, ah, ah," he breathed, and the chains flared to life as he took my orgasm and caught it on the edge of a blade. Holding me suspended over the abyss. "You're not getting off that easy," he drawled through a gleaming white grin. A smirk he pressed against my throat, the corner of my jaw, giving me a playful squeeze that threatened to cut off my air, before his lips found the space between my throat and shoulder. "Tell me whose pussy this is," he said against my skin. Teeth grazing the very same spot he'd marked when he'd fucked me raw from the back that very first time.

I tried to tell him to fuck off. Tried to snarl and rage, but my teeth chattered, and all I could muster was a helpless little mewl as he let me edge closer, only to pull me right back.

Pressing his cock against my thigh, I felt his grin as wicked amusement flicked through my blood. "Say it," he said, groaning against my throat, fingers buried so deep inside it was as if I could feel them wiggle behind my bellybutton. "I want to hear my name on your lips, little virgin. I want to hear you admit exactly who's responsible for making this pussy drip." Teeth playing at the tendon singing with exquisite tension, he nipped at the space between my shoulder and throat. Kissing the sting, he said, "You can't outlast me, Mila. I can feel everything. I know how hot you are, how badly you ache for me to stretch you out and fill you up. *Only me.*"

My head thumped back, and I tried to take a breath that wasn't obliterated by a choked sob.

"Just say my name," he rasped, and sent his thumb over my clit in another slow sweep that forced blood to rush out of that sensitive button, only for it to come surging back in a flood of exquisite agony. "Admit what we both already know, and I'll give you exactly what you need. I'll fill this cunt to over flowing as you milk me dry of every last drop."

"*Fuuu—*"

"This pussy was made to take my come," he growled, flicking his thumb faster and faster. Tormenting me with the cruel lash of pleasure denied. "I'm going to fuck you so deep, so hard, you won't be able to walk without my come gushing down your legs with every step. But don't worry, I'll make sure to keep you stuffed full. Over and over. So deep, so much. Every day, as often as I can. You'll take every single drop, until you're fat with it. Until you can come just by thinking about the next time I breed this tight little cunt..."

My lips moved around a plea, but the only sounds I made were the little *pop* at the beginning of the word. A tiny, strangled hiss at the end.

"That's it," he growled, "ride my hand, Mila. Feels good, doesn't it? Feels *right*."

Lips trembling, I let my chin dip in a single, invisible nod. Hips lurching helplessly as I did what he said.

"You're going to come hard enough to break my

fingers," he cooed, and hooked those digits behind my pelvic bone. "Just say it—"

"You!" I spat, and clung to his forearm with both hands. Nails biting deep when I felt the muscle beneath my fingers ripple, when he squeezed my throat just hard enough to make my vision sparkle. "You did this to me, you insufferable pig! Please—"

He tucked a grin against my collarbone. "Clever word games at a time like this?" he asked, and clicked his tongue. "Perhaps I wasn't clear enough." Withdrawing, Asher pulled his fingers free and went to his knees before me. Leaving me teetering on one leg as he shifted my trapped thigh over his shoulder and bullied his way between spread knees.

I staggered. Scrambling for purchase, until my fingers found their place in his hair. "A-Asher, what—what are you doing—"

"Making myself perfectly clear," he drawled, and didn't bother to glance up. No, that obsidian glare was fixed directly between my legs. To the spot he spread with both thumbs. "Who, Mila? Who owns this greedy little pussy?"

Teeth flashing, panic bubbled up in my chest. Warring with the tsunami of Caledonian lust running thick and hot through my blood, the two opposing forces clashed and became a blind, petrified thing that wanted to flee only half as much as it wanted to be caught and submitted.

But I tried.

Tried to stop him from doing whatever wicked thing had made his eyes go bottomless with want, but he flicked aside my efforts without bothering to slow, or blink, or even glance away from what lay between my spread thighs.

"Wait, d-don't. Y-You can't—"

"Oh, I think you'll find I can," he retorted, and then—

His tongue darted out.

Warm.

Wet.

Everywhere all at once, he licked me. Two fingers surging back inside, he pumped even as he found my clit and pulled it into a vacuum between his lips. Sucking until my leg finally gave out and I slid down the wall, laid out before him. A helpless puddle of desperate need, my knees fell apart, hips tilting back to give him better access. Reduced to a creature of primal instinct, I chased what he refused to give me.

Release.

"I'm going to be the first to swallow your come," he said, forcing the lewd words into my very centre, hardly bothering to stop his assault of lips and tongue and fingers. "The only one to taste this sweet cream. Say it," he demanded, and hooked his fingers once more, sending a tiny prickle of energy into the spot just behind my pelvic bone.

A spot that robbed me of all sense and sent the back of my skull thumping into the tiles, even as I drew him in closer with two fistfuls of inky black Caledonian hair.

"No one else," he growled, and pulled my throbbing clit into his mouth once more. Laving it with his tongue, only to release me with a lewd, sucking *pop*, then said, "Only me. *Ever.*"

"Only you," I rasped, hips undulating as I rode his face.

Because it was too much.

Because I couldn't think.

Couldn't breathe.

Couldn't even see anymore as he held my every muscle on the edge. His tongue lapping at tormented flesh, while his fingers worked a cruel dark magic I might not survive.

"Yours," I gasped, unprompted, drowning in the heat dancing on the tip of his tongue. "Only yours."

A smile spread across my mound. "My name," he insisted, as his fingers moved in a noisy blur.

"Asher! Asher, *please*—"

He obliged me.

Every muscle seizing, I came with a strangled squeal. Stunned by the force, I was reduced to a twitching mass of something vaguely Mila-shaped. Torn from my body as wave after wave of electric pleasure pumped through my blood, my next breath was a sob. A hiccuping, messy sob of release and bone-deep fucking gratitude. That it was over—that such a feeling could exist at all.

"Fuuck," he groaned, feasting between my legs. Noisy, shameless. Inky black eyes shining gold in the glow of my chains as he infiltrated my blood and dragged it out. Fingertips leaving little jolts of pure pleasure spiking through my cunt, he lapped at my delicate folds and drank down every drop.

"That's it," he murmured. "Keep going. You're not done yet."

I shook my head, tears spilling over as the shower washed them away.

With one final, mortifying slurp, he shifted. Kneeling over me, he flung my legs over his hips, pausing only to strum my clit and force my orgasm to echo long after it should have ended. And then, looming over me, blunt tip poised on the edge of aching flesh, he said, "Say it again."

Unmade, my resistance shattered, I didn't hesitate. Didn't stutter. Didn't blink. "Asher," I whispered, and damned myself with a brand that would never scrub off. "Asher. Asher. Ash—"

With toe-curling ease, he split me open and found my end. Pumping once, twice, he buried his face at my throat on the third frantic thrust. Snarling, fingers kneading at my hips where he held me still and open, I felt the harsh, familiar pinch of teeth seconds before the first pulse of elite, Caledonian seed sprayed into my depths.

I felt every heated lash.

Every pulsing, desperate jet of spilled cream as he pumped me full, just as he'd promised. Felt first through his base where he'd stretched me wide open, his cock kicked hard enough that my pussy rippled with every throbbing jet. And then through my blood, where he'd wound himself deep in a way that I might never be scourged of him. Helpless but to endure when he let his pleasure spill over that gleaming, white wall, and I fell again.

Hammered drunk on elite fumes.

Enslaved to this man who knew my every unspoken lie and felt nothing but possessive rage at the chance to mark me inside and out. Absent so much as a hint of remorse for taking what I didn't give, Asher's jealous poison seeped into my blood through each rope of sticky come until it became a lazy, contented sort of joy as he sluiced through the mess and played with the last dregs of my orgasm.

I was ruined.

A twitching mess. Boneless with pleasure. Stained with come and teeth and bruises and pink, flushed cheeks. My ankles were hooked and locked at his lower back, and me, with absolutely no memory of how *that* might have happened.

"Thank you," he murmured, filling my vision with eyes utterly void even the slightest hint of color, except for the reflection of gold. Looming, broad shoulders shielding me from the pounding fall of water beginning to go cold.

All I could muster was a blink. The tiniest flutter of questioning confusion that I didn't bother to voice, for he was in my blood. He felt the tendrils of shame and self-loathing as I tried to put myself back together, even with his cock still twitching and buried to the hilt.

"For today," he whispered, and cupped my cheek as he elaborated. "For not intentionally getting us killed." Trembling fingers pushed a mat of tangled, sodden hair back from my face, and for a moment, just a split instant, there was a shred of something...

vulnerable allowed to slip through his legendary control. "It's going to be good between us, Mila," he said. "*Easy*. Like this, all the time—"

A tentative knock at the bathroom door made him jerk, hunching over me like a wild thing refusing to give up its kill.

There was someone in his room.

11

"Captain Rawlings, sir?" It was a female voice. Tentative, but bracketed by a firm knock. One I recognized, even in my delirium. Alicia. The traitor with green eyes and high, elegant cheekbones. "My apologies, sir, but—"

"Alicia," the captain drawled, and reached one hand up. Twisting without looking, he turned the faucet off and ended our shower somehow dirtier than we'd begun it. "Come in."

I squeaked. Vision still blurry at the edges, limbs a mess of twitching, uncoordinated flesh and bone. "What—she can't—"

Asher frowned at me, as if genuinely unaware why I might protest. That I might not want to be seen in my current state, soaking wet and dripping inside and out. Nailed to the floor of a shower stall by the thick cock of my enemy, my pussy stretched around him tight enough to force him still as I fluttered and clenched, still lost in the throes of an unnatural orgasm.

But it was Alicia who demurred. "It's Carina, sir," she called from behind the door. "It would seem the Lieutenant General Hastings mentioned that you've been cleared. She's... uh... in the parlor."

The captain cursed then pulled out in a rush of salty heat that gushed from swollen lips, before he scooped me up from where I was puddled on the shower floor. "Tell her I'm indisposed," he snarled, and dragged a towel into the stall. A towel that was already damp and musty, cold against my skin as he wrapped it tight about my shoulders—and let me drip until my thighs were tacky and wet.

"She's"—Alicia cleared her throat—"rather insistent, sir. Marco can only distract her for so long."

A line of strong white teeth flashed at me in the dim lighting, and Asher's impotent fury crackled through my blood an instant before he let go a held breath. "Fine," he snapped, and guided me to sit on the toilet seat, checking to ensure I was steady before he turned. Wrenching the en suite door open, stark naked, he murmured something I couldn't hear beneath his breath, then closed the door in Alicia's face once more. Doing his best to block her sight.

Like a gentleman.

I watched him from my perch. Leery of the jarring shift in reality. Hair dripping where it lay in tangled snarls over my shoulders, hanging down my back in cold, dead silver-blonde serpents. Trying to gauge his mood, to see how receptive he might be to grant a favor, I took a ragged breath. "Asher," I began, licking my lips.

Another knock, and this time, Alicia opened the door herself. Just a crack. Just enough to slip one slender arm through the gap and pass the captain a bundle of dark fabric rimmed in gold.

He took it without a word of thanks, and said, "We'll be out in a moment."

I swallowed, and tried again. Calves quaking where I was braced on tiptoe, perched atop his toilet seat, clutching the musty towel high at the base of my throat. "I... I need to shower."

One dark brow lifted, but that was all.

"I'm... You..."

Dark flames crackled in that inky gaze, wicked amusement that traced a long, slow smirk at the corner of his lips and chased off his foul mood. "Spit it out."

"I..." I shook my head, blushing from the roots of my hair, all the way down my throat and into the towel clutched at my breast. "You came in me," I whispered, mortified. Fragile and brittle.

He growled low in his chest. Menacing, a deep rumble that preceded a storm of unstable want that flooded through him into me. "Fuck, that's hot," he rasped. Stalking closer. "My little virgin with a pussy full of come."

Heat flashed through my cheeks. But electricity sang through my nerves. Through everything that was still tender and clenching, my voice stolen as my blood rushed in my ears.

"No," he drawled, and peeled a tiny scrap of fabric off the top of the bundle Alicia had given him. "I think I prefer you like this. Dripping in my come, cheeks stained pink as you can't help but think about every spilled drop... Hoping no one notices..." Openly grinning now, he knelt before me. Hand gentle on my knee as he traced the length of my calf to my ankle, then lifted my foot from the floor. "It suits you."

"No," I retorted, watching him slip my foot through a hole in silky black panties. "It suits *you*."

His gaze flicked up, meeting my eye with sinister mirth dancing in inky pitch. And he shrugged. "Semantics."

"The general is dead," I said, trying a different angle when he moved on to my opposite foot, appealing to reason where emotion had failed me, time and again. "Who else would be bold enough to flaunt your Caledonian laws of ownership? Who else might try to touch me? To take me from you?" I swallowed, throat dry enough that it clicked in the quiet hanging heavy between us. "No one else can match the power you wield. Not now. And I'm not likely to soon forget what happened today. I don't need the reminder, or to r-reek of sour, used p-pussy. Asher, please," I breathed, and wound my fingers tighter into the fabric of the towel.

He slid the panties up my legs, then helped me to stand. Tugging the towel from my hooked fingers, he adjusted the silly scrap of fabric to his liking, then tipped my chin back with the backs of his knuckles.

Dark eyes flicking between mine, he ignored my plea. A question written on his brow. Seeking answers in my blood, where I couldn't hide them.

Where shame had crashed into lust and had become something new. My definition of sex forever tied to him. Defined in the swirl of an inky black glare, and rough fingers that took without asking.

And he knew it.

A crackle of devious, elite energy zipped through my skin. Reeking of victory and lewd, piqued interest. "You can go about convincing me after I've dealt with Carina, if you must. Until then," he murmured, and his thumb caught and pulled at my lower lip. "Knowing your panties are soaked through with my come *and* yours?" He tisked, tongue clicking as that wayward digit bumped over the points of my modified teeth. He loosed a ragged breath as a fresh wave of arousal began to build between us once more. "Knowing that my little virgin is soiled, inside and out?"

Trembling, I tried to step back. Couldn't, for I was already caught in that sticky trap.

"I can feel how you ache," he said again, voice a deep, quiet purr. "Even now, so soon after strangling my dick with a truly spectacular orgasm." Fingers bumping down, over bones that had never poked through my skin before, he cupped my mound over the panties. Tracing my clit with flawless accuracy, only to push back, tempting me where I throbbed for relief. And then he pushed that fabric inside, just enough to make my breath catch. Just enough to make the gusset slick with liquid seed. "I'm not the only one who can't stop thinking about it, am I?"

A ragged whine crackled over my lips, but I did not blink when the question came unbidden. "Thinking about w-what?"

"How perfectly you gape for me," he said, teasing me with a tendril of energy that stole my breath and made me clench where he wasn't. "That you can pretend, even as you beg so prettily."

I swallowed. "Pretend?"

"Oh, yes," he hummed, pushing his thumb between my lips. Almost daring me to sink my teeth into the knuckle. "Mustn't shatter the illusion, hmm? That you're not soaked and slick, ready whenever I feel like bending you over my mattress. Dripping wet, aching to be bred by your enemy. It wasn't *your* ankles locked around my hips." He grinned. "That would be impossible, because I'm the big bad villain, hmm? And you, the helpless, fragile little virgin. Such an elegant dance."

He kissed me, then. Stooping to catch my breath between his lips, Asher framed my face in big, rough hands and slipped his tongue between my lips. Tasting. Drinking me in, before he tugged the towel from my fingers and slung it about his own hips. Hardly bothering to conceal the furious erection tenting the fabric as he exited the bathroom with a flourish of swirling steam.

Draping my forearm over my breasts, I blushed all the deeper, even as I scowled after him.

"Have Mila dressed and fed," he said, smirking as

he pinned me with that inky, bottomless stare. "I won't be long."

Alicia dipped her head. "Yes, sir."

"Oh, and Mila?"

My lip curled.

"Please, feel free to tidy up, if you're feeling brave. I'm only too happy to fill you up again... and again... and again..."

We listened as he rummaged in his closet. Silent as the man stepped into what I could only imagine was a fresh uniform, perhaps something more casual, now that he'd been officially relieved of his duties. Humming to himself as he strode from the bedroom.

He left me, then. Alone. With Alicia. The woman who'd betrayed me for nothing but a passing, careless thanks from her master. A fellow whore for the empire, who now held absolutely no illusion that the captain had just spent the last hour indulging himself between my thighs.

Cheeks flushed with a pulsing heat that refused to fade, seething as I recovered my wits, I sat with my forearm slung over my breasts. Dressed in nothing but pink cheeks and borrowed panties, I kept my knees pressed together in such a way that stopped the slow, steady pulse oozing from between swollen, tender lips. Soaking that silly strip of fabric with a not-so-secret flood of fluids.

Eyes fixed to a scrape on my left knee that I had no memory of, the room was lit with a gentle, prominent hue of gold glowing at my wrists and throat. Evidence that the captain was with me, even now...

… when he'd gone to entertain his bride to be.

Alicia cleared her throat. "Good to see you awake, priestess," she murmured. Quiet in the tight, humid space that reeked of what had just happened. Too intimate a place to share with a woman I hated. "At last."

My jaw flexed, but I clung to my silence. My every muscle held tight enough that I'd become brittle with the need to shatter.

"How are you feeling?" she asked, and retrieved the bundle of black silks from where the captain had left them on the vanity.

"I can dress myself," I snipped.

"Of that, I have no doubt," she returned, but flung the fabric out with a snap and draped it over my shoulders anyway. Every inch the harem leader, with her cool efficiency and seeming indifference toward nudity. Twisting and fidgeting with the silken folds, coaxing them to hang artfully off my skeletal frame, until I was cloaked in Caledonian blacks once more. Elegant. The very picture of the slave I'd become.

"It's been a trying couple of days," she said, and touched my arm. Fingers warm and light, she held that contact until I met her gaze. Dragging the moment out.

A certain type of intensity burned in that lovely shade of green, but I was left to guess at her intention. Helpless without the empath to lend me insight, for her energies were… not for me to sample.

I shrugged, because I couldn't lend my voice to the pain.

She tried again. "I'm sorry for your loss. Sasha was…" Hesitating, she shook her head and laughed. "She was a woman of many talents, and a close personal friend. I'll miss her. And her gifts."

Despite myself, I was drawn from my sulking to ask, "How did you know her?"

A quick flash of straight, pearly teeth, and Alicia stooped to retrieve a fresh towel from under the vanity. One that hadn't been used more times than I could count. A towel that smelled of fresh laundry and not stale mildew of a man left to clean up after himself. "She saved my life," she said with a tiny secret smile.

Quiet, I waited for her to continue, but when she merely began to set up a box full of paints and brushes, I said, "And?"

"Talk and work, priestess. Turn, so I can fix your hair."

I moved to snatch the towel from her hand, scrubbing at my hated silver-blonde locks to force them dry.

She slapped my hands away with a hiss. "Stop that. You'll cause breakage. I got shot in the battle for Elora," she added, and produced a brush. "Not by an elite, of course. Wouldn't have been enough left of me to bother saving, and none of the good bits," she added with a lewd wiggle of her brows, making fleeting eye contact before she frowned at my hair and began to work on the snarls. "No, it was my father who did the honors," she murmured, and a quiet mist descended over her elegant features. "When the Caledonians kicked in our front door, he said he'd rather I were dead than serving the Empire. As if it were his choice, and his alone."

I made a sympathetic sound at the back of my throat.

"Lucky for me," she continued, "the old man was a terrible shot. Only managed to leave me writhing in agony before he turned the next shot on himself. The bastard." She finished brushing, then gathered my hair in one hand, and wrapped the towel around the ends. Gently squeezing it dry. "Woke up in a field infirmary with Sasha in all her quiet glory. Poor thing covered in blood, doing her best to stop the bleeding, despite the black eye she couldn't see from."

My lip curled. "Tilcot—"

"You'd think so," she drawled, a tiny, sad smile hovering at the corner of her lips. "But it was me, actually. Apparently I came in swinging. That's what the captain tells me, anyway. And he'd know, I suppose, being the one who carried me in." She laughed, then, and it was bitter as she unwound my hair from the towel. "My father. So desperate to ensure I wouldn't fall into Caledonian hands, and he all but handed me over to them himself."

Shifting, I inspected my nails. Unsettled by the similarities from her life to mine.

"I've been with the captain ever since," she added with a sigh.

For a moment, I merely watched her as she worked. Pulling at my scalp as she began to twist my hair in a complicated braid. And then I said, "You're in love with him."

Her lips twitched. "Hold this. Don't let the ends come apart," she said, and guided my fingers to pinch the end of one braid, while she moved on to another. And then she sighed. "I was," she admitted, at last. "For a long time."

Too curious not to ask, I couldn't stop the question from slipping through my lips. "But not anymore?"

"Why?" she sang, waggling her brows. "Jealous?"

My face twisted, cheeks still pink with the stain of elite lust. "Morbidly curious," I returned, and my teeth clacked together with an ivory snap. "What changed?"

"Well," she said, and plucked the braid from my fingers, adding it to her complicated twisting. "The Caledonians have a strict social class and an obsession with the breeding of their coveted, elite bloodlines. Always eager to produce a new generation of more deadly elites, most of their marriages are arranged by the royal family. These... designer couples are expected to produce offspring inside of the first two years, or see the union dissolved so another pair might have a shot."

I gagged. "Animals, all of them."

"And bloodthirsty," she added with a merry little smirk. "The women, most of all. They only carry the power genes," she said. "There are no female elites, but that doesn't mean Caledonian women are meek. Not by any stretch of the imagination."

Every priestess who has ever been has the potential to become an empath.

At this, I went very still. Too raw to do better than that to conceal the deadly secret I held. A truth I was only beginning to understand about energy wielders. That Asher was right—we were merely two sides of the same coin.

This is a truth they can never know...

Alicia laughed. "No, I have no desire to find a knife between my ribs simply because I burned a candle for a man who could never return the senti-ment. Time is our womanly curse," she said with a gusty sigh. "And I do feel for their women. To an degree. That they must battle each other for the rights to bear the offspring of men whose eyes will never stop wandering..."

"Huh," I hummed, and was made to see Carina in a new light. A desperate, pathetic sort of glow, yes. But one that lent her actions a little more reason. "Well," I said, and folded my hands in my lap. Over the apex of my thighs, where I was still wet and shamed with seed that could not root. "Not a danger for me, then."

Alicia went white. From one breath to the next, her brow glistening with a sheen of shock when her lips parted, her jaws hanging slack. "M-Mila," she gasped. "I'm so, *so* sorry. What an asshole thing to say, I cannot believe—"

I waved her off and found something of interest on the far wall. "Barren priestesses owned by an empire obsessed with breeding people for power can only be a good thing, I think."

Color rushed back into her cheeks. "I didn't... I wasn't the one who told him," she whispered, and it was her turn to find something interesting to stare at. "That... you were... untouched."

Jaw clenched, I sneered where she couldn't see, but couldn't muster the venom to snap at her. Couldn't be bothered to tell her it was me who'd told him because it didn't matter. But I wasn't moved to ease her guilt.

After all, keeping one, insignificant secret couldn't possibly make up for what she'd done. That my wrists bled gold because she'd fetched the chains for Asher without being asked to do it.

"I just..." She shook her head. "Just wanted you to know." With a dainty sniffle, she dabbed at a misty, artful droplet then clapped her hands. "Anyway. *Sasha.* I owed her a debt," she said, organizing makeup brushes from largest to smallest. "For years. She'd have disagreed with me, of course. But it's a debt I was never able to repay. Not while she was alive, at least." Alicia met my eye, then went very still. "I'll miss her every day, for the rest of my life."

Nodding, just the once, I glanced away at the sound of shouting coming from the floor below. Distracted from this moment that held too much unspoken weight.

An argument was breaking out between players whose energies I could not sample, I was left to listen and guess. Hoping it wasn't Lieutenant General Hastings returned to clap suppressor cuff on me and leave me dead in all but name.

"I left a box," Alicia said, drawing me back. Abrupt, pushy in a way I didn't completely understand. And her eyes, sparkling and green, were filled with anxiety when she too glanced toward the door and the argument unfolding on the floor below. "The last time I was here. Have you seen it?"

I frowned. "I haven't seen anything but the backs of my eyelids in what I'm told is more than a week."

"It was smaller than this one," she pressed, tapping her makeup kit with the point of her index nail. "Black. About this big. Tarnished buckles."

Bewildered, I flicked my fingers toward the bathroom door, and said, "Then go look for it in Asher's mess. I won't stop you."

"It was precious," she said, as if I hadn't spoken. Making no move to do as I said, and look for herself. "A final gift, from the Head Priestess."

Distant cursing proceeded the heavy thunder of feet racing up the stairs.

"I think," she said in a rushed whisper as our alone time came to an end, "when you're feeling up to it"—a quick, smile laden with meaning I didn't understand—"when you've got a few private moments *to yourself,* you might look under the captain's desk. That's where I would start."

12

The bedroom door bounced off the wall, announcing Asher's return with a violent flourish. "*Vile whore*," he snarled an instant before he rounded the corner to the bathroom. "Come," he snapped, and clicked his fingers in my general direction. A dark, angry cloud of temper crackling all around him as he exited the bathroom mere seconds after he'd entered it.

But my chains did not burn with a compulsion I couldn't refuse.

The compulsion ignited in my blood.

"But, my lord," Alicia began, scurrying after him. "Mila hasn't had time to eat anything—"

"Yes," he snapped. "I assumed as much. I'll feed her myself," he added, and sent his hand through his hair, then issued a bitter bark of laughter. "My apologies, Alicia. I've just been reminded of my duties to the Rawlings name. And the throne. And a half million other obligations I've been ignoring while I've been *vacationing* over the last week. It would seem my afternoon has already been booked." His lip curled. "Mila and I are off to endure a picnic with my lovely fucking bride to be."

Alicia's brows jumped, almost meeting her hairline. "A picnic," she said, halting and dubious. "That'll be... nice, sir."

He pinned her with a black glare that did little to conceal his opinions on the subject. "Then *you* go, and I'll stay here and finally close my fucking eyes."

"I haven't had time to do her makeup," Alicia returned, unaffected by the venom *or* the threat of spending time with Carina. "If you were looking for a reason to stall."

"I'm hungry," I said, and pulled myself up. Swaying where I stood, enticed by the idea of a picnic, despite the threat of the company. "You'll have to paint my face later. If there's food, I'm going."

For a moment, neither Alicia nor Asher said a word. Both merely turned to stare at me in open-mouthed shock.

And then, head thrown back to issue a startled bark of laughter, Asher grinned, his mood shifting in an instant. "Oh, believe me," he drawled, "I'm happy to paint your face whenever you want, pet. Just say the word."

Tittering behind her hand, Alicia's eyes glittered but she did me the courtesy of keeping whatever comments she might make a mystery.

Confused, I sent a bewildered glance between the pair, then said, "I don't understand."

"No," the captain hummed, "I know you don't, my little innocent. That's what makes it particularly... *precious.*"

Taking several mincing steps toward the exit, I shrugged. "Fine. Whatever. As long as there's food, paint away."

"An offer I won't soon forget," he cooed, watching me cling to the vanity as I moved. Only extending his hand when I was close enough to reach it.

It was a gesture I accepted without hesitating—and the reward was a rush of elite energy he sent coursing through my fingertips. Filling me with vigor, he lent me strength enough to stand without sweating, then pulled me close, pressed his lips against my ear, and whispered, "A taste. Just to hold you over."

Without meaning to, I groaned. Spine going loose, I became all too aware of the throbbing need in tender flesh as it was awakened at his call. By the licking flames of his heat as it blazed through my blood.

Luxuriating in the way my every forgotten millimeter throbbed, I was almost able to ignore the hint of *wrong* laced in his generosity. Almost didn't notice the whisper of rot twisting through the ecstasy, despite the way my fingers had curled into claws where they were buried in his shirt. Or that I gobbled up every drop he was willing to share and tried to reach for more—before I ran into his wall and was denied with a cold slap.

"Greedy girl," he purred, slipping one hand between us to adjust himself where his cock had grown stiff. His jaw tight as he watched me down the length of his nose. And then, "Let's get you fed, shall we? And then we'll see about painting your face."

Nodding without really listening, dizzy with even so conservative a sip, I rolled my neck. Stretching muscles long out of use, I agreed to whatever he wanted, as long as the reward was more of that potent elite energy.

Touch light on my nape, Asher's fingers curled around the back of my neck. Almost touching at the base of my throat as he steered me from the bath-room. Tossing a careless, "Thank you," over his shoulder without bothering to look back.

We paused at the top of the stairs. Poised, as if on the edge.

"Ready for this?" he asked in a low hum, because we were both feeling it.

I glanced up, and found him watching. "Does it matter?"

He snorted. "Not really, no."

"Then lead on, oh great and powerful master," I said, inclining my head.

Grinning, he pulled me in tight. Towering above me, just for a moment. Just long enough to drown me in heat and inky, swirling pools of liquid desire. "I should warn you," he murmured, and stepped back without acting on what I could plainly see lurking in his dark, Caledonian heart. Fingers tight as he tackled the stairs. "Marco isn't exactly your biggest fan."

I hummed, but that was all the wit I could muster

before we claimed the bottom step and entered the kitchen.

"At last!" Carina simpered. "I thought I was going to have to send your boy up the stairs to collect you!"

From a gloomy corner, Marco huffed. Not bothering to protest Carina's implications, his unblinking sneer was for me, and me alone. Long fingers spinning his weapon over and over and over in his lap as he watched me through a slitted glare.

One glance was all it took. One fleeting instant of eye contact with the soldier, and I remembered.

Everything.

Knew just what it was to slip into his bones as if here were an ill-fitting cloak and not a man. That I'd taken something that wasn't mine and made it into a weapon. Corrupting him as I'd filled him with my unquenchable lust for vengeance, only to set him loose on another he'd likely called friend.

An elite had died beneath a storm of his fists.

I could still feel the splatter of gore clinging to his cheeks.

Carina shifted a basket to her opposite arm in such a way that made a generous bulge of cleavage spill over the front of her dress—both nipples threatening to pop free of that distressed fabric. And with a sniff, she looked the captain up and down, tossed a sheet of silky, black hair over her shoulder, then said, "Asher, darling, I thought I asked you to change?"

"You did," he agreed, tone pleasant, despite the obvious crackle of confrontational tension in the short sentence.

She sighed. "No matter. You're free! It's a beautiful day," she purred, approaching with a seductive roll of her hips. "All you need is a gentle feminine touch, and you'll be back to your usual charming self in no time. Move, slave," she barked, and bumped me out of the way, so she might take my place at the captain's side.

I staggered, careening into the kitchen island, my hip cracking off the countertop before Asher caught my wrist in strong fingers. Steadying me.

Marco watched down the length of his nose, but made no move to intervene. Seemed almost... disappointed that I hadn't fallen hard enough to split my skull wide open and stain the tiles with spilled brains.

Even without my gifts, I knew what loathing looked like.

"Goodness, she's frail," Carina said, cutting the captain off before his curled lip and thunderous glare could manifest into a seething temper. "*This* is the golden priestess who killed a general?" She laughed, pressing her breasts against Asher's chest. "Oops. Pardon me"—she tittered—"*allegedly*." Bold, ignorant of the tempest building in her betrothed, she caught my wrist and inspected the subtle glow with an intent frown. Fingering the skin gleaming with the evidence of the captain's unique power. "That's new," she murmured. "Beautiful, the way you control her, Asher. Impressive, as always. I've never seen anything like it, among any of the others. But then, you've always been exceptional, haven't you?"

"Shall we be going?" the captain asked, jaw tight. Muscle dancing, and if I listened hard enough, I thought I could hear the sound of enamel being ground into a fine, furious powder.

"Yes!" she cried, and abandoned her grip on my skin to slip one hand around his waist. "Oh, I'm so looking forward to some private time," she whispered, and stood on tiptoe to catch his earlobe between her teeth. "Just think of the power our sons will wield," she cooed, reaching one daring hand between the captain's legs to fondle his balls. "Conceived while their sire was bound to *the* golden priestess? I already have several marriage offers."

A tinkling laugh grated at the back of my skull, and I almost asked if I was required to be present for their creation, or if I could volunteer for the Lieutenant General's suppressor cuffs after all. But the lure of a meal was enough to silence me, even when Carina said, "They'll be the most coveted elites in the emperor's arsenal! And we could start today—"

"Marco," the captain barked, nostrils pinched white. "Bring the coach around."

13

Tension.

It filled the dense air in the coach, packing it into the cramped space until there was little to do but sit in it. To bask in the total discomfort of Asher's heinous mood, and Carina's heroic efforts to ignore it.

And darkest of all, Marco's seething silence that had replaced his jovial, never-ending good spirits.

"You know," Carina purred, letting one shoe slip off her foot so she could trace the captain's inseam with her perfect, manicured toes. "There's no reason we can't get a head start on our duty to the crown today. Viridian's girl did her magic," she added, and licked red painted lips. "Apparently I've"—she tittered and leaned in, voice dropping to a low, sultry whisper—"gone into heat."

"Sounds uncomfortable," the captain replied, tone flat and cold as he stared out the window, and made no effort to rebuff or engage.

"Here. Slave," she barked, and flung her wrist in my direction without peeling her eyes from the captain's profile. "Do your whore magics. Tell your master what you sense."

I blinked. Remembering what it was to taste the woman before me, however briefly. To know her energies, her desires and pain... everything. All of it mine, at the slightest whim. A danger she apparently had no memory of, or she wouldn't be so giving. So... trusting.

My mouth watered and I swallowed, *hard.*

From my peripheral, I saw Asher move. Felt that inky glare where it burned the side of my face. His attention prickling the edge of my awareness, bypassing my wrists and throat, his awareness was in my blood. A threat poised on the edge of action. Silently daring me to take Carina's hand. To test his temper and restraint.

Daring me to see what might happen if I just... did as she asked. Took her fingers in mine... just to see if my leash had any slack. To test if he really could keep me from indulging my darkest impulses. If his control was absolute or an illusion.

Wetting my lips, I reached—

Asher snatched my wrist before I could make contact. "Mila's gifts are not available for use."

"Nonsense, Asher," Carina purred, and leaned in further still. "Don't be such a prude. The girl wants to learn, doesn't she?"

I watched her posture and preen. Aware of her every tiny movement, I was still. Lured by the shift of insidious hunger as it was awakened. Hardly breathing.

She relented with a sigh, but pressed in closer still. "I've never understood the point of owning a pleasure slave," Carina said, flippant and coy. Oblivious to the silent battle being waged right in front of her, she looked me up and down, lip curled, then shrugged. "But I suppose I can be taught. So keep her in your bed," she murmured, and elegant bejeweled fingers found Asher's knee. Trailing up. "Let her watch. Let her practice her technique on me as she cleans up your mess."

Fingers dimpling my forearm, Asher's grip grew tight enough to bruise as he watched her without so much as a blink.

Creeping fingers found their mark, and sinking pearly white teeth into the lovely bow of her bottom lip, Carina stroked the front of the captain's trousers. "I think," she said, and her wrist rolled in such a way that drew my eye down at last, "with enough... *convincing*... I could come to enjoy seeing your golden priestess between my knees as you ride her barren cunt. Shame," she added with a click of her tongue. Her wrist rolling and flexing, working in his lap as an all-too-familiar nausea bubbled at the back of my throat.

"And what's that?" the captain asked, forcing the words between his teeth as a terrible storm built where she could not see it.

"That you can't breed her, of course!" A tinkling laugh peppered the dense air with holes—holes that promised to vent the captain's temper at last. "It would've been nice to have a powerful blood-bound servant for our sons. And to think of the profits we might have made on leasing the rest out." She tisked again. "I'm sure it won't be long before they're able to reverse that nasty little side effect, and until then..."

Fingers still keeping me shackled to his side, the captain leaned in. "Carina—"

Marco threw the coach into park, and the jarring shift almost unseated all three of us. "We're here," Marco barked.

Adjusting her hair, Carina pouted. "Why not have your boy take her for a few hours?" she cooed, and worked her fingers toward Asher's belt. "We'll have plenty of time to break her in after we're married—"

"No!" Marco said at the same Asher snarled, "I said '*no*', you vile cunt," and seized her wrist in that bruising grip at last, stopping her advance without flinging her away. Shouldering me aside, he put himself between us.

"Oh," she gasped, and I watched her pupils dilate as she licked her lips. "*Oh*. I do love a man with a firm hand."

He pulled her in close. Lips hovering scant inches away from hers. "You've out-played me, Carina," he murmured, and slipped one hand behind her neck. Fingers tangling in her luscious, artful curls of glossy dark silk, he wrenched her head back and forced a primal gasp from between her lips, only to press closer still. Whispering, "A commendable manipulation," against the tender pale skin of her throat. "And after we're married, I will do my duty," he added. "I will drop a few wretched bastards in your haunted cunt. I'll smile and wave for the emperor, but make no mistake," he cooed back at her, tone deadly cold. "Mila is *mine*. Her bed is the one I will seek, if only so I might forget the horrors I've been forced to endure in yours."

At long last, Carina's mask fell away to reveal what really lurked beneath all that flowing, ethereal beauty.

She smiled.

And it sent barren winter winds howling through my heart.

"I wouldn't have it any other way, my darling Asher. In the meantime," she rasped, "you've a rather tarnished reputation to uphold. One I am *trying* to repair to the best of my considerable abilities. So lose yourself in the little whore's bed. Love the girl, if you're weak enough that you truly cannot help yourself," she said with a sniff of pure disdain. "As long as it's in the privacy of locked doors and drawn curtains, I simply do not care if you beg her to whip your ass bloody while *she* rides *your* ass, just so you can sob yourself sick in her tender embrace. But in public, she walks in *our* shadow."

Nostrils pinched white, Asher's eyes flicked between Carina's.

Back and forth, ticking a rapid beat through eyes growing more slitted with each passing moment.

And for several long seconds, I thought I could

sense something deadly fighting to erupt from a cage far more elaborate than the one he'd trapped me in.

Something that matched.

Where the empath was starving for energy, *this* beast was bursting at the seams.

The other side of the coin...

But after a beat, the captain's chin dipped in a single, tight nod. "Fine."

"Good boy," she purred, and her palm landed a gentle pat, pat, pat on his left cheek. "Now," she clapped her hands, and with that, any whisper of animosity fell away as if it had never been. "Lunch. I've brought a vintage I'm certain you're going to love, but it needs time to breathe."

He watched her gather her picnic basket, but I watched *him*. Trying to see what he strained to keep contained. To catch another glimpse of the thing fighting to rip through him so it could *burn*.

"We'll be along in a moment," he said, and lay a restraining hand on my knee.

When she and Marco had both gone, I counted to twenty before I said, "Why? *Why* do you tolerate that woman?" I laughed, low and bitter. "Please don't mistake my curiosity for any sort of concern for *you*, but this is a puzzle I just can't seem to solve. Asher"— I shoved his hand off my knee and turned to face him —"Why? You've more than enough power to make her a puppet, and none but me seem to realize it. Why do you allow yourself to be controlled? What leverage could she possibly have on you that trumps the sort of power I know you're hiding?"

His head thumped back, and for a moment, he merely watched me from beneath a fan of dark lashes. And then he chuckled. "And why not? Carina is a beautiful woman. Connected. Her lineage peppered with famous elites with nothing but the potential for more in the next generation. The Savoy's are old money, where the Rawlings' are not." He lifted one shoulder, but did not break eye contact. As if trying to say something without actually speaking the words. "Why *wouldn't* I consider the proposal?"

I returned his unblinking stare, my thoughts sluggish and cloudy as I tried to hear what wasn't said.

"I need an heir," he murmured. "And this is a match that'll satisfy the crown. But believe me," he whispered, and caught my chin between forefinger and thumb, "if I could figure out a way to keep you fat with my children, I'd scarcely give you the time to recover before fucking you pregnant again. And again."

My cheeks flushed hot, but I frowned. Refusing to let him distract me with a lewd impossibility. "That doesn't make sense," I murmured, and it was my turn to search his eyes for answers that wouldn't come.

"It's probably a blessing," he said, and sent the pad of his thumb over my bottom lip, smearing it. Tugging it down until my canines kissed the heavy air.

A question surged in my blood. One I couldn't voice without venting the horror that might come with an answer.

He heard me anyway. "The empire would take an

interest in children of mixed blood," he murmured. Carefully, as if leery of being overheard.

I shuddered, disgust rolling through my spine. "Then I would like to formally thank you for castrating yourself," I drawled. "Glad I wasn't the one who had to do it."

"Cute."

I flashed him a toothy grin, then circled back and said the first thing that came to mind. The only thing I could name as common denominator for all the times I'd seen Asher forced to do something unpleasant by his superiors. "It's me, isn't it?" I whispered, trying to reach through his wall of gleaming, stolen energy to taste his reaction. "That old money. Her connections. She's going to do something vile to me if you refuse."

A slow, deadly smirk thinned his lips. "Power is not always the trump card you think it is. This is Caledonia, pet. Things can always get worse."

"Don't be cryptic," I hissed. "If you want me to help, or at least not work against your every move, speak plainly, or ceed to the Lieutenant General and remove me from the equation entirely."

His pause was brief. "Is that what you want?"

An ugly bark of laughter burst from between my lips, and tears came unbidden. Scalding my waterline, without daring to fall. "It doesn't matter what I want," I hissed. "*I* don't matter. You've made that plain enough."

Brow creased, he frowned at me. Ebon glare swirling with an intensity I couldn't name, measuring his reaction as he tasted mine. Utilizing every unfair advantage at his disposal. And then, a nod. Not agreeing, not denying. "Not here," he said at last. "Not now. Act the broken creature she wants to see, and I'll reward you with more than just spine-melting orgasms."

I jerked my chin from his fingers and swatted his wrist. "Pig," I snapped, but turned my face into the shadows to hide the stab of anguish he could surely feel.

14

I squinted against bright sunlight. Shivering in the cool breeze as Asher stepped down from the coach and extended his hand. As if I hadn't lived as a wild thing in the forest for five years. Alone. Enduring the very worst of winters and hottest of summers.

As if I were a Tritan lady being courted by a suitor...

... and not a slave on an outing with a man and his future bride.

As if I wasn't wearing his mark, his clothes, his... seed. Stained throat to pussy to ankles in all things Captain Asher Rawlings.

But I took his hand anyway, unable to resist. Drawn in by the hunger, the tantalizing whisper of energy laced in his every lingering, covetous touch.

Marco had taken us to the edge of a well manicured park. A public place overlooking a pristine marble fountain, the park was well kept and centrally located to several shops all flying Caledonian colors. Shops that may have been the heart of a thriving Eloran economy, once. But it was now the lifeblood of the Northern front of the empire's efforts to assimilate every last whisper of competition on the continent.

"Carina," Marco said, and took her basket in hand with a ridiculous flourish. Doting on her, he took the time to send me a seething glare before he shook out the blanket with a snap, saying, "Allow me," as the blanket fluttered onto the grass.

She tossed a coil of gleaming ebon hair over her shoulder and set one glittering hand on Marco's chest. "Such a gentleman," she murmured with a nod of thanks. And with a graceful curl, folded her long legs, then glanced up from beneath her lashes to posture for the captain. The gems of her rings caught the sun as she patted the blanket next to her, lips twisting around a coy, inviting smirk that reeked of wealth and privilege.

"For the groom," Marco said, and folded a second blanket into a bundle, and invited Asher to sit on it with an absurd little bow. "A nice cushy seat for his plump, royal hindquarters."

Kicking the fold job aside, the captain followed Carina down to the picnic blanket, and hissed, "Fuck off, you ingrate," under his breath.

"Manners, dear," Carina hummed, pinning him with a shrewd glare as she rummaged in her basket.

And when the captain continued to scowl, she tilted her crown of dark hair toward the public milling about in the beautiful afternoon sunlight.

Her meaning was clear.

This was theatre.

Our audience a horde of bloodthirsty Caledonians all fighting to climb the same ladder, to occupy the highest rank they could, regardless of who was left crumpled and broken in their wake.

And Asher's tarnished reputation was corroded enough to make him vulnerable. Weak in the eyes of his people.

For a few long seconds, the captain wrestled with his temper as Marco laughed and played the jester for Carina. Amusing her just long enough to irritate the captain before the soldier tossed a lewd gesture over his shoulder and went to stand by the coach, affording the couple the illusion of privacy.

With a weary sigh, Asher stretched out his legs, crossed his ankles, then turned his face into the sun. Settling back, he lounged with arms braced behind his back. Palms turned out, elbows locked, affecting the airs of someone utterly unconcerned by the dozens of eyes and the scent of blood in the water.

And then, without bothering to glance my way, he said, "Mila," in a tone that held nothing of the man I was beginning to see beneath the mask. The cruel slave master, once more—until his fingers curled around my ankle. And with his touch, a hypnotic swirl of dark flames licked through my blood.

Enticing. Soothing my ire with a liberal dose of pulsing, magnetic *want*.

I went to him with a liquid spine and half-lidded eyes growing glassy in the glare of the sun. Numb to the aching burn of an empty stomach, I nursed at the measured sips of pure, elite power. Watching him without a blink, desperate for more. Scarcely able to hear Carina, I felt nothing but the warm glow of a fire that was no longer mine.

"Asher, darling," Carina said, an artful frown pinching her dark brows as she scoured the depths of her basket. "Ah, there it is. Here, try some of this." Producing a jar, a napkin folded around a stack of flat breads, and a spreading knife, she loaded a cracker with a black gelatinous sludge and extended her offering. "It's a delicacy in Letta," she explained. "Well known for its ability to increase a man's virility."

Lip curled, Asher watched the offensive snack from slitted glare, and said, "I couldn't possibly, no."

Carina tisked and raised one artfully precise brow. "I'm not entirely sure I was asking."

"And I'm absolutely positive I don't need a foreign delicacy to increase my appetites," Asher retorted.

Red lips spread over a viper's grin and her eyes flicked to me—*a foreign delicacy*—and her sly hum was comment enough. Without a word, she placed the cracker on her tongue.

"Keep pushing, Carina," Asher warned, and my chains surged to life as he commanded me closer without a word. "Let's all find out how far my patience extends, shall we?"

Gold pulsed and swirled in my veins, visible even in the bright, morning sunlight—and from the audience of Caledonians watching with coy glances, audible gasps at the sight of my skin gleaming with raw power.

He beckoned me closer with a flick I felt tug at my every muscle. Wound much deeper than ever before, it was a command that possessed me.

Utterly.

Written in an ancient script that had been burned into my very bones, I was ensnared. Made to crawl between his thighs, hips rolling, seduction in my every insignificant twitch. Snuggling down into his lap, I watched him. Hanging on his every breath, cradled in his warmth. Nipples tight where they poked at the fabric of my borrowed dress.

Rough fingers smoothed over my hair, traced my jaw, and cupped my face. Guiding me to rest my cheek against his thigh...

... and feast.

Gulping down everything he offered, I was left to indulge as he made a spectacle of me. No thought to anything beyond the next, desperate swallow as I basked in his excess. All but purring as his fingers traced from my temple back into my hair.

Carina's face scrunched up in a mockery of appreciation. "So sweet," she chirped, and reset her crossed ankles so she could reach for a bottle of wine already opened and resting. "Can I offer you a glass?"

"We need food, Carina." The familiar catch of calloused fingers skated through my hair before his touch settled at my nape. Massaging as the burn of the chains began to fade, the knee at my back bent to offer a cradle against my spine. "You promised a picnic, and if you brought nothing but inedible glop, we're leaving."

"But we're celebrating," she said through a pout. Reaching to pour two glasses of something pink and sparkling.

Indulging her, the captain said, "Oh?" as he fed me another slow, drugging tendril of energy. Forestalling the roar of hunger clawing at my insides. It was a distraction. A drug. Potent enough that I went boneless in his lap and didn't notice when the burn of liquid gold faded and was replaced with another sort of burn altogether.

One that ached with the sweetest poison and made the gusset of my panties slick with more than just the stain of his ownership.

"Yes, you boorish man," she chided, and passed him a glass. "You've been cleared of wrong doing for the nasty business of Harper's death. And our little golden priestess"—a tinkling laugh that carried over the courtyard and drew more than one set of eyes—"she's all *anyone* can talk about."

Dazed, my eyes flicked up and found her already staring at me with a ravenous hunger. Absent any hint of petty jealousy toward the man who made no secret of his disdain for his bride, every drop of Carina's attention was instead pinned on me. Covetous.

Of my power.

Of the status owning me might bring her.

Of the power I might lend any elite sons born of their union.

"I fail to see how that warrants celebration," the captain drawled, and shifted his seat. Wineglass poised high and clear, he moved the bright fall of braided hair off my shoulders. And with his free hand, let his fingers trickle and slip down my back. His touch light, and full of drugging, potent energy that tasted of serenity. Obedience.

A sound of mock outrage slipped over her lips, but she flashed him a brilliant smile that went no further than her cheeks. "One might argue our pending nuptials are cause enough for celebration," she snipped. "But this is a particularly rare vintage. One I collected from my private cellar just for this occasion."

Enticed, Asher sniffed at the bubbly pink wine, then sipped. "Fruity."

"Yes," she purred, but her gaze remained fixed to my face. "Summer in a bottle."

I blinked. Slow. Hazy with intoxication, but that sentence shook something loose.

A memory long forgotten. One I couldn't summon at a whim, until Carina clubbed me in the temple with the reminder.

Summer in a bottle.

A slogan from my childhood.

Sluggish, I frowned. Turning away from the feast of elite flames as horror began to edge everything else out, something cold slipped down my nape and splashed into my gut. Something horrified and stubbornly patriotic.

"It's a young vintage," Carina went on, watching me over the rim of her swirling glass. Taking her time to truly enjoy my reaction as the alarm grew louder, a siren wailing at agonizing volume where no other might hear it. My cheeks flushed hot, as cold dread beaded across my brow. "Only five years old. But that's what makes it so... valuable."

I knew, then. What it was. What she would say before the words formed on luscious, painted lips.

"Tritan summer wine," she cooed. "The very last of its kind. Bottled just a few weeks before we took Tritan, I believe." Only then did she pause to sip. Letting that small taste bubble and boil on her tongue as she sucked air through her lips and savored the vintage, groaning as if lost in the throws of ecstasy as her throat worked around a slow swallow. "I couldn't think of a more symbolic moment to uncork it."

Fury pumped through my veins. Molten, golden hatred as the empath tried to surface. To buck those chains keeping me sedated, so I might embrace the black, insatiable hatred and take my time with a more common vintage—Caledonian breeding stock.

I crashed into the captain's wall, denied. A prisoner enslaved by my own power, throttled by magic I'd traded on a whim.

Left to stew, I could do little but meet her eye and let her see the face of true malice.

But it was Asher who broke the tension when he brought the glass to his lips and swallowed every drop with a lewd groan. "You should have said," he hummed, and collected the bottle to inspect the label. His other hand growing tight on my nape, fingers dancing at my pulse. A warning. "A Tritan vintage of notable rarity is all the aphrodisiac I need."

She laughed, light and tinkling. "Oh, well played!"

Asher saluted her, then said, "Food, Carina. Mila needs real food—"

"Ho there!" Marco called, interrupting as he flagged down another coach. This one with a decidedly more utilitarian edge to it than the luxury vehicle the captain owned. Military. Muted colors. Driving far too fast to be appropriate given the number of pedestrians present in the courtyard.

Without shutting off the engine, a youth stepped from the pilot's chair. A smooth-cheeked boy I had a vague recollection of having met before.

"Collins!" Marco crowed, and clapped the boy on the back. "What brings you out on such a fine day, eh?"

Puffing out his chest, the young man adjusted the collar of his uniform. All crisp edges and ironed lines. "I'm here with a message for Captain Rawlings, soldier," he said, eyes straight ahead. "Step aside."

"Well, as you might be able to see," Marco replied, "his pending lordship is otherwise occupied. If there's a message I can pass along—"

"I need to speak with Captain Rawlings!" Collins

all but howled, cheeks pink. Dappled with anxious sweat. "It's an emergency! I haven't the time to fuss with low level footmen, peasant, now do as you're told, and move aside!"

"Low level"—Marco spluttered, hand to heart, he staggered back as if dealt a deadly blow—"*peasant*?"

Tension ignited at my back. In my blood. And with hardly a moment's hesitation, the captain was up and moving, barking, "Report," at the boy as he surged forward.

Leaving me coiled inches from Carina. No visible tether to keep me in check, but the one I'd never be able to escape.

My head tilted to the side.

Carina's chin tucked back. A tiny flinch that might have gone unnoticed by one not watching the way I was watching. Seduced by the delicate thrashing of her pulse. Hungry for any fleeting scrap of information that couldn't be gleaned by gifts I'd sold to my enemy.

She remembered.

Our last encounter.

How easy it had been for me to swallow her mundane, tasteless energy.

Somewhere deep, packed away in the reptilian part of her brain, where primal fears lurked and the nameless things were banished. Recalled only in the darkest hours.

Even if she couldn't say why, her hind brain lit up with the knowledge that she sat before a predator far more deadly than she. One who didn't know the rules of the complicated political games she played, and wouldn't have followed them anyway.

I wasn't a player.

I was the renegade.

A healer corrupted by a destroyer.

"He can't control me forever," I whispered, and let her see just a hint of my teeth. "You're hardly worth the effort, but for you"—I wet my lips with a slow, ridiculous sweep of my tongue—"for you, Carina? I'll make an exception."

She scoffed, haughty and bold. But her cheeks paled. Going bloodless the longer she looked.

"Oh, he'll punish me," I added in a reedy whisper, watching her without a blink. "I'm sure it'll be awful, even if it's just for the onlookers you so love to preform for. But I wonder... do you think he'd kill his famed golden priestess?" I sucked at my teeth. Tongue clicking. "A Caledonian wife with good breeding is a far more... common commodity, after all. Easier to replace, especially when the suitors come to him with the offers and the gifts and the empty wombs thirsty for his seed."

"You little bitch."

I hummed, nodding as my lips quirked around a tiny, cruel smile. "I'm learning from an adequate teacher, I suppose. Not the best, certainly. But..." Lifting one shoulder, I shrugged. Already bored with my new toy. "There's a price for everything, Carina. Even if you can't afford it."

The crunch of boots at my back signaled the captain's return. "It's time to go, Mila," he said, a brown, manilla envelope clutched and crumpled in his fingers. A mighty scowl etched deep into the lines of his face.

Carina cleared her throat. Taking several deep breaths, she coughed again, standing in a swirl of elegance that was just slightly unbalanced. "Asher," she said, straightening her hair, "darling, what's happened?"

"Urgent business," he replied without bothering to glance her way. "An emergency at the house. Nothing that concerns you." He reached for my hand, helping me to stand, as he murmured, "Mila," beneath his breath.

For one extra long beat, I watched Carina breathe.

And then, with the confidence of one who had no reason to feel shame and cared little for the consequences of her actions, I fell back into my role as house-broken pet.

I curtsied before the woman I'd marked for death...

... and plucked the bottle of Tritan summer wine from the blanket.

She spluttered, rushing after us as Asher guided me into the coach then followed me in. "Asher!"

"You'll have to excuse us," he said, and closed the door firmly in her face. "Time sensitive matter. You understand. But thank you," he drawled, "for the lunch. Fulfilling as usual, my dear."

"But how will I get home?" she hissed, tugging at

the door handle. Discrete, so as not to draw more attention than the commotion had already warranted.

Asher tapped Marco's shoulder, and said, "I'm sure Mr. Collins would be delighted to escort you."

15

A breath hissed between Asher's teeth, but he tore his inky gaze from the passing scenery to pin me with a sardonic glare. "Getting bold again, I see."

I hummed, shifting in my seat. "How's that?"

He plucked the bottle of wine from my fingers, turning it into a shaft of sunlight to inspect the label.

"Ah." I pinched my tongue between my front teeth to squash the smirk. "Just accepting Carina's generosity. She went to all the trouble to save a bottle of summer wine, after all. Who could possibly appreciate it more than me?"

"You are without a doubt, the most relentless pain in my ass," he drawled, but handed the bottle back to me with a quiet smirk.

"And you," I returned, "expect too much, and say too little. What's the emergency?" I asked, and ran a thumb over the gold embedded in my wrist.

His response was a terse, clipped, "Alicia didn't

bother to say," as he pulled his cannon from its holster. Checking the complicated mechanisms, he paused for just a moment before pulling on the bond to charge the weapon. Setting my wrists and throat ablaze, but only for a moment.

Breath hissing through clenched teeth, I weathered the pain without complaint, then said, "Something deadly, then."

He set the barrel atop his thigh, and murmured, "Just in case," as he turned to stare out the window.

Eying the heavy brown envelop in his free hand, I tugged it from his clenched fist and flattened the crumpled paper.

Only two words, written in beautiful script on Asher's personal, watermarked stationary.

Emergency. Hurry.
~ A

"This place is exhausting," I whispered, and let my head fall back. Eyes drifting closed for a moment as the letter fluttered to the floor.

Brows raised, Asher hummed, but that was all until his residence came into view.

It was dark.

Not a light on. Silent and still.

"Stay close," he breathed against my cheek. "Stay

silent. Let me deal with whatever comes, understood?"

I nodded. Pulse in my throat. An open bottle clutched in bloodless knuckles.

"I need to hear you say it, Mila," he said. Unblinking as he pinned me with a heavy look and did not falter.

I flicked my wrist, impatient and bubbling with anxiety. "Yes, *yes*. I'll be a good girl. Obedient, until such a time that I can overpower you and take my sweet revenge."

Despite himself and the tense, mysterious situation unfolding in his residence, the captain laughed. Letting his eyes drift closed for the space of a single breath, before he said, "Marco?"

"On your right, old man," the soldier replied, fidgeting with his weapon, he stepped clear of the pilot's chair. Utterly void of his usual banter as he scowled at the house.

"Right. Move."

As one, they melted into the house. Keeping me sandwiched between them, they slipped through the front door. Weapons at the ready. Communicating through sharp hand signals and body language.

But we were not met with the horrified screams of the mortally wounded. Not greeted by the sight of untold carnage. And the air was free and clear of the greasy flavor of vaporized elites.

Instead, the rich aroma of baking assailed our nostrils. Delicious, home cooking the likes of which I hadn't smelled in... longer than I could adequately recall. "Fuck, I hope that's not the scent of charred bodies," I whispered, stomach howling my need for something other than what the captain dolled out. "Because that? *That* smells bloody divine."

"Fucksakes, Mila," the captain hissed, sending a bewildered glance back. "A little sensitivity might be in order?"

"Sorry," I returned, hunching my shoulders. "I'm hungry."

Shaking his head, the captain muttered, "Thirty seconds. Wasn't thirty seconds before she forgot the second thing I said." And then, his senses flaring out, he said, "I think"—the captain scowled—"I think Alicia is alone. There's no one else in the house."

Marco cleared his throat, jaw flexing and bunching as his gaze remained fixed straight ahead. "Is she okay?"

But to that, Asher could only frown. Uncertain, he stepped forward, nudging the kitchen door open with the muzzle of his weapon, and—

An ear piercing scream shattered the hush.

"Alicia, *what the fuck?*" Marco hollered at the same time the captain snarled, "Fuck*sakes*, woman! We might've killed you!"

Standing in a dim, windowless kitchen, the pleasure slave was covered in a fine dusting of flour. Dressed in an apron, hair tied back in a messy bun, she was cooking what looked to be a multi-course meal in a dark and powerless kitchen.

Hand pressed to her chest, Alicia gasped for

breath, and said, "Think I might have pissed myself. You scared the life outta me!"

Marco stormed into the kitchen and took the pleasure slave by both shoulders. "What were you thinking?" he snarled, giving her a shake. "Cooking in the dark after sending a message like that, eh? *The fuck is wrong with you?*"

Color flushed in her cheeks, and something about her went soft when she said, "I-I'm sorry."

"Explain," Asher barked, tucking his weapon back into its holster. His eyes stormy, but edged in the fine lines and dark circles of exhaustion.

"Thought you might appreciate an excuse to leave in a hurry," she whispered in a trembling voice. Cowering before them, her eyes rimmed white and luminous in the shadows. "I knew—*assumed*—that—that Carina—*Miss Savoy* wouldn't have brought anything for the priestess to eat, so I put together a few of my favorite things. Made cookies," she added in a tiny voice.

"Why," Marco snarled, and forced her back a step, his grip growing tight enough to dimple her skin, "is it so fucking dark in here? Why are you cooking in the dark?"

"Fuse blew," she squeaked. "I tried to turn the oven on at the same time as the—"

"Blender," Marco said, taking a shaky breath as he holstered his weapon at last. Shoving one hand into his breast pocket, he produced a packet of cigarettes and lit one with a deep, ragged inhale. "Right. I'll be back," he added. Gruff, not making eye contact as he stormed toward the door—and almost shouldered me off my feet.

"Took it upon yourself, did you?" the captain asked, taking his turn to interrogate her as he steadied me. "To decide when I was finished meeting with my intended wife?"

"My lord Rawlings," she wheezed, aghast. "I'm— I'm sorry—"

"That's a punishable offense," he drawled, moving toward her on silent feet. "Grossly over-reaching of your station."

I slipped in behind him, set the bottle of wine on the countertop, and took my place at the kitchen island. Snagging a cookie off top of the pile.

"M-My lord—"

"And your punishment," he said, placing one steadying hand on her shoulder, "is the dreary task of cheering up that grumpy prick"—he jerked his thumb in the direction Marco had gone—"before he burns up the very last twig of my patience. Oh," he added, then turned to claim the spot on my right. "And deliver a couple of plates to my room, if you could. Whatever you've whipped up smells incredible, but I've important business to attend. I seem to recall Mila asking me to paint her face..."

For a moment, her lips gaped, and not a sound escaped her. But then a brittle laugh spilled over, and she said, "My deepest apologies, sir. I'll go about my punishment with *enthusiasm* after I've put your plates together."

I stuffed another cookie between my teeth and

took another in hand, scarfing down the calories as fast as I could.

"And Alicia?" Asher said, setting his elbow to rest on the countertop. "Thanks." He cleared his throat. "Thank you. That woman is…"

Light burst into the kitchen, and with a low hum, the oven resumed its work as the power came back on.

Donning her usual, glittery personality, Alicia smiled. Head tipped back, as if she were turning her face into the warmest glow, she hummed. "I'll bring your plates up in just a moment, sir."

The captain stood, plucked a cookie from my fingers, then claimed the bottle of Tritan summer wine, and said, "Right. Come along, pet. Better be gone before Marco returns. Don't want to make Alicia's work any harder than it needs to be."

Scowling when he disappeared around the corner, I snatched two more cookies—and then a third. "These're good," I said, spattering crumbs everywhere.

"Think of them as my apology," Alicia murmured, and all hint of merriment evaporated from her face the instant the captain turned his back. "The recipe was a *gift* from the Head Priestess. Something she cherished enough to pass on, asking that I shared it with *you*, priestess, because she knew how much you'd need it. Only you."

Her words made something in my chest wriggle.

Memories howling up from the yawning dark. Sick, painful things that wanted to fester and rot.

Frozen mid-chew, I blinked at her. Too shocked to do anything more than meet those glittering green eyes as the cookies turned to ash on my tongue. Tacky and thick. Sickly sweet.

Grease of the dead that couldn't be scraped away...

"Mila!" the captain called, already halfway up the stairs. "Move that sweet ass!"

"You understand?" Alicia asked in a low rasp, stumbling forward. Moving to seize my forearm, she said, "The Head Priestess had me deliver—"

I recoiled. Flinching clear before her fingers landed on my skin. Before her touch could betray whatever secret she was trying to spill.

Because he would know.

The instant her energy brushed against my skin, Asher would be able to taste whatever treachery might lie in wait.

Without a word, I turned on my heel, cookies clenched and forgotten in my fists, feet moving. Mind racing. Eyes unfocused enough that when I stepped into the hall, it was to collide with an unforgiving wall of muscle.

Marco.

The echo of violence sang in his eyes. The memory of what I'd done. Of what I'd taken without permission. Raping him of any choice, I'd toyed with the core of who he was and set him loose, changed. An animal on a tight leash. A monster... a weapon of my own design.

And I'd enjoyed it.

To be that strong, that sure, even if it was only the

illusion. That I'd lived it through him, the victory and the hurt. Pain... lust...

I remembered.

The joy of such freedom.

The rage and fear.

I remembered everything.

"Run along, priestess," Marco murmured, his lips scarcely moving. Scowl blazing with the promise of retribution and unfinished business. Daring me to reach out and touch...

I slipped around him without wasting another instant.

Fleeing up the stairs, my skirts kicked out behind me as adrenaline flooded my system. Fueling me as I raced to escape the graveyard howling in that deadened stare.

There was blood on his hands—but mine were soaked to the elbow in the sort of gore that couldn't be scraped off.

Breath coming hard, I closed the door with a soft click, then set my shoulder blades against the cool dark wood. Staring at the floor as I let the memories play.

I'd been murderer and victim.

I'd lived inside Marco and Dez, both. At the same time.

A conqueror whose every landed blow was another closer to suicide.

A casualty drowning in an ocean of gore, I'd spilled myself with those fists. Each blow falling with the weight of punishment that would never be enough to atone for all I'd wrought.

Asher was right.

I *couldn't* be trusted.

I'd been allowed to taste true power—and now, nothing else would be enough.

If I was given even an instant of freedom... I'd do it again, no matter how sweet the ache, nor how devastating the consequences.

Because the empath was *starving*.

I glanced up, and found the captain perched on the sill of his bedroom window. Watching me, arms crossed. Hands balled into fists where they were tucked under and over. Posture closed off, he watched me through a suspicious scowl.

Between us, a mountain of clutter that hadn't been straightened out or swept away in eight days.

Eight days, where secrets had been hidden in plain sight. Left to fester. Growing gangrenous and wretched enough that I couldn't bear the thought of touching a single one, for fear of picking at a wound that might never heal.

Settling back against the sill, he hooked one ankle over the other. Brow quirked, he didn't bother to voice the question scrawled across his face. Didn't set my blood on fire with a tendril of curious magic, or make my chains sparkle in the gloom.

He merely waited for an answer to the panic he could surely feel coursing through my veins.

I swallowed, hard. Again and again. Throat dry as

I was made to give a voice to pain I wasn't ready to address, not even to myself.

"Marco," I whispered at length, because I needed to say something. Eyes brimming with unexpected tears. "You were right. He..." I shrugged. "He definitely, absolutely hates me."

Asher sighed. Unfolding from his perch, he tugged at the collar of his uniform. "There were shards of bone embedded in Marco's knuckles," he said, loosening the buttons at his throat with hooked, deft fingers. "Splinters of Dez's skull I had to dig out with a blade before I could repair the damage to his hands."

I nodded. Inspecting the carpet with eyes that could see only memories.

"When his body was found, it was clear Dez had been attacked," he said, as his fingers moved down the line of buttons to reveal dips and valleys I couldn't bring myself to glance at. "The corpse was damaged in a way not found on any of the other casualties of the riot." He paused then, slipping out of his uniform. And instead of merely shucking it into the pile of soiled laundry taking over the room, he folded it in neat lines, and said, "Marco's been assigned to the unit searching for his killer."

Acid splashed at the back of my throat. My thin, undamaged fingers curling into fists at my sides as I listened. Unable to speak.

He took a step toward me. "We served three tours with Dez," he murmured. An explanation absent excuses, it was the truth. Exactly as hideous as it was.

No more, no less. "I'm not sure how they used to do things in Tritan, but beating a man to death with your bare hands is a pretty ugly way to end a friendship."

Unleashing a shuddering breath, I tried to swallow and choked on the guilt. The fumes of righteous anger wafting off the man as he stalked closer with rolling, unhurried steps. And without lifting my burning eyes, I said, "You were both unconscious. He was going to kill us all."

I watched his shadow shrug. Watched his feet move as he closed the gap between us, planted one hand on the wall beside my head, and leaned in to whisper, "Maybe, but who started the riot?" against my ear.

"What do you want from me?" I hissed, turning to scowl through a mist of brine. Back pressed to the door, as far from his heat as I could get in a space he owned. "An apology?" A hysterical laugh bubbled up past the clotted shame. "This is war. It doesn't matter how often you force me to beg. You"—I shook my head—"*your people* are my enemies. Nothing can change that."

For a moment, as he stared into my eyes, nostrils pinched white with every shallow, furious breath he took, the captain was still. And then, moving with frigid restraint, he wrapped cruel fingers around my throat. One by one, pinky to index, his thumb notched behind the corner of my jaw, he made me look. Pinned me to the door and lined his body up against mine. "You want to go to war with me, little girl? Have I not made your position clear enough?"

But I did not blink. "I'm exactly what you made me," I rasped and my tears spilled over, prickling against his fingers as they tracked down my neck. "Just another sleeve for your cock you'll eventually grow tired of tormenting. And when you've used me up, you'll toss me into the bathhouse with all the other whores—"

His grip silenced me before I could finish. "Careful, Mila," he crooned, ebon eyes gleaming as something surfaced in the dark. Something ravenous and jealous at the mere suggestion of someone else's hands on me.

I laughed, and it was a fragile, hopeless thing. "*Why?!*" I cried, trying to peel his fingers away from my throat. "What's the point? What more could you possibly want that you haven't taken already?"

Incredulous, as if he were staring down at a very simple child, he only adjusted his grip, and said, "*All of it.*"

A sob chattered through my lips. "There's nothing left! You've already taken everything—"

Teeth bared, he thumped his fist into the doorframe. Making the wood shudder and groan in protest. His temper frayed at the edges, enough that he slipped, losing control. Just for an instant. Just long enough to let me really feel it, the depth of his feeling toward me.

Bottomless contempt for my wretched sorrow, that I would dare to feel sorry for myself in the face of all he'd revealed. Infuriated by my inability to control myself *or* the empath, he was disgusted by my impulsive, reckless nature that was the opposite of his steely discipline.

It was *hatred*.

For all that I was.

It washed through me in a rush. Swept away from one blink to the next, as if it had never escaped from his legendary control.

But it left me ravaged and scraped raw in seconds.

Bleeding alone in the dark from a thousand tiny wounds.

Chest collapsing, I curled around a breath that wouldn't come. Collarbones jutting as my ribs hollowed out and I tried to weather the agony of his loathing.

And then a soft knock pattered on the other side of the door. "Plates are ready," Alicia murmured.

Lingering, the captain watched me down the length of his nose for the space of three breaths, before he snorted. Shaking his head, he pushed off the door frame, turned, and strode away, tossing a careless, "Come," over his shoulder.

I stepped clear of the door without a word. Watching the muscles of his back bunching and flexing as he moved.

Alicia breezed past me carrying two heaping plates piled high with food and made no mention of my blotchy, reddened cheeks. My puffy eyes. "Let's get you fed, priestess," she murmured, and, setting her bounty down atop the captain's desk, she added,

"Let me know if you want seconds. But you might have to shout." She grinned at the captain. "I'm off to do my punishment, sir."

"Good night, Alicia," he drawled without bothering to look.

Sparkling green eyes found mine without an instant of hesitation.

And then she tripped.

Artfully.

Without blinking.

Kicking something hard beneath a stack of dirty laundry. Something that was stuffed deeper under the desk as she stumbled past. "Clumsy," she murmured, and shot me a glance positively dripping in meaning I hadn't quite grasped until the moment she clubbed me in the temple with it.

... I've had something delivered to the captain's rooms...

My eyes went wide as they were snared by the past. Unseeing, blind to everything except the horrors of that doomed demonstration.

Sasha.

Her lips crinkled around a sad smile, she'd given me no time to understand before her veins lit from within.

... it isn't the answer for the rest...

The deafening clap of her trap snapping shut popped against my eardrums. Blue flames and blazing gold, I could all but feel that agony all over again. As if I were the one burning.

... I think you'll know what to do with it...

A tiny puff of air escaped my lips. A gasp hidden inside a breath that hung on an icy cloud before my face. Frost that tasted of the Void and so much pain. Where Sasha had gone, and I couldn't follow.

I understood.

At last.

Sasha's last act.

A gift.

Licking lips gone dry, I met Alicia's vibrant gaze and let my chin dip in a single, tight nod.

Relief flicked across Alicia's face, and with a false airiness, she turned back to the captain and said, "Beau will be in to tidy while you're at the funeral, sir?"

The captain nodded, making a sound at the back of his throat as he inspected the plates piled high with food.

"Tomorrow, then," Alicia said, breezing past me with a weighted glance. "All of this will be sorted out by tomorrow."

Acid burned the back of my throat. Teeth clenched, jaw flexing, I watched her go—left to wrestle the ghosts she'd brought back to life.

Only one thought echoing louder than all the rest.

This was just the opening bid in yet another sick, Caledonian game.

A game with a secret with a time limit.

But this time, the first move was *mine.*

16

We ate.

In silence, except for the inelegant sounds I made as I stuffed myself to bursting at last. I knew he was watching my every move, alert to something amiss, for he was with me. Always. That he sensed every potential deception as it grew in my heart. Ready to stop any action before it might ripen.

I stuffed any scrap of emotion down deep, and focused on nothing but how much I could fit into my mouth. That I was ravenous, desperate to consume something that wasn't charity from Asher. His energy, his... body.

When at last I could take a breath that was free of the constant ache of hunger, Asher cleared his throat.

"What will happen to Sasha's body?" I blurted. Far from subtle, a distraction that ached almost as badly as the truth I didn't want to admit.

That I was a monster with no control...

... except for the leash I'd handed to my enemy.

He sighed. "She'll be buried with Harper. Rather..." He grimaced. "As there wasn't much of anything left of him, she'll be buried in his place."

I scoffed. "The Head Priestess is *not* buried. A proper Tritan burial—"

"She was a slave, Mila," he murmured, fingers tracing the rim of a glass. "And she killed a general."

"It's an insult," I whispered. "Desecration."

He lifted one dark brow, and said, "Didn't take you to be a particularly devout supporter of the Tritan faith, given that you rejected their teachings and shunned the call of sisterhood."

It was a barb that landed true—more than he might ever know.

Anguish made me twist away from the hurt. The guilt, for it didn't matter how many slaves I'd freed, that I'd spent years trying to atone for abandoning my people during the war. It wasn't enough.

He frowned. Perplexed by the strength of my reaction. "Mila—"

"I have to pee," I blurted, bolting before he could dare to offer comfort or force me to explain.

And he let me go, because he was already with me. Monitoring me from within, poisoning me to suit his tastes, so he might feast on my energy and glut himself on my excess.

I shut the bathroom door and let go a shaky breath as the lock clicked into place, sitting in a moment of rare privacy. Perched on the toilet in a room where Asher had fucked me completely breathless, only hours before. I couldn't bring myself to glance at the shower stall. Couldn't muster the courage to turn that tap and indulge myself beneath the heated spray, even to wash away his seed. Not in there. Where he'd laid me out and set my every nerve on fire. Filling my mind with pornographic filth as he whispered depravity against my lips, my ears—then filled my pussy with the salty burn that stained so much deeper than everything else.

It was right *there* that I'd gone and done the one thing I'd tried so hard to resist.

Where I'd let him flip that coin at last and fucking *begged* for it through tears and desperate, clutching fingers.

And I knew, then. That he'd been right from the moment he'd set the terms of our game.

I was unequal to the challenge that was Captain Asher Rawlings.

Utterly.

And now he held all the power. Every last drop.

With a single, laced touch, I became a whore dying of thirst. Desperate for just another sip of whatever he would let me taste.

I'd begged.

Crawled.

Milked him dry with my ankles locked around his hips, my pussy taking great, gulping swallows of Caledonian sperm. I *needed* all he could give, and only grew greedy for more.

I was addicted.

Just as he'd promised.

Distracted by the way his eyes grew bottomless with want, for no matter the hurt or the shame or the pitiful self-loathing, I couldn't stop thinking about it.

But the clock was already ticking down.

It was only a matter of time before he claimed Sasha's gift for himself—I had to act. Whatever it took.

Jaws clenched hard enough to make my enamel squeak, I pulled a slow, steady breath in, then stood. Finished my business, I turned to the sink and was startled by the creature trapped in the mirror.

My knuckles went whiter than the porcelain I seized to stop myself from screeching.

A girl. One I didn't recognize, at first, because she was hollow. Skin papery and dry. Eyes sunken above cheekbones that had grown too sharp, when they'd once been plump and round.

But as I stared into that washed out gaze, I saw the truth I'd been trying so hard to deny.

Because she wasn't a girl at all.

I was looking into the eyes of a whore. Created by suffering, I was exactly what they'd made me.

Ugly.

Desperate.

A survivor.

I nodded.

Swallowing the bile and the rot, I nodded again and turned on the tap. Filling myself with petty defiance, I washed up at the sink.

Really washed.

A whore's bath in frigid water.

Scouring myself clean, I dabbed between my legs with cupped palms and poking fingers. Washing away any hint of what he'd left behind, until my flesh was slippery and fresh. Tender, *cold*, but no longer filthy.

Satisfied, I dropped Asher's musty, used towel on the puddle I'd made, then kicked it into the shower stall without a glance and turned the door knob.

He was there—*right there*.

I staggered back, catching myself an instant before I screeched, I wrapped my fingers around my throat, and hissed, "*Fuck!* You lurk."

Looming, somehow both relaxed and coiled, he filled the exit. Fingers hooked at the top of the door-frame, elbows bracketing his face, he was stretched out in such a way that made my throat flex as I fought not to look.

He grinned. Wicked, evil amusement crackling through the bond. "Something on your mind?" he drawled.

My cheeks burned, but I tried to sidestep him, and said, "No."

He didn't bother to match me, just refused to move. "No? Funny, I could have *sworn* I heard the call of a greedy little pussy begging for relief."

Placing both hands on his taut abdomen, I tried to shove him out of my way.

His chuckle vibrated against my hands. Muscles rippling under my palms. "I think," he hummed, watching me down the length of his nose, "we should play a game, you and I."

"I've had quite enough of your games, I think." Dropping low, I lunged for the gap between his hip and the door frame.

An unyielding grip caught me about the middle, and he spun with me. Hauling me back against a wall of muscle, he enveloped me in his scent. Squeezing too tight and not hard enough. "Don't be so hasty," he murmured against my ear, as one hand ghosted up from my navel. Catching at the billowing yards of fabric twined about my torso, he paused to cup a handful of fat and flesh—to roll first one, and then the other nipple between his forefinger and thumb—until he caught my throat in his palm. Forcing my head back, *back* against his shoulder. "I'll even give you favorable terms."

It was a trap.

I knew it, even without tasting the devious mood he was in.

But I couldn't help the question from slipping out. "What do you mean?"

A smile twitched where it was pressed into my hair. "All you have to do," he whispered, "is keep me out. Stop me from learning your secret—"

"I don't have a secret."

He laughed, but didn't bother to argue what we both knew was a lie. "Keep me out," he said again, "and you can take what you want, little empath. Feast to your heart's content. I won't stop you."

For a moment, we were held in tableau. Both of us staring at his bed without acknowledging the sinister promise lurking in dark, rumpled sheets.

What had been my nest for eight days, now loomed with the threat of what else might be done there.

The promise.

Bent over the mattress... clutching at blankets that couldn't offer so much as a scrap of protection against the man who wanted me spread at his every whim. A man who'd made me gape for him. Who'd touched and filled and coveted every secret corner I'd never wanted to share.

And I knew.

This was a game I would lose, for he was already inside.

I couldn't stand against a hurricane without Sasha's wall. I was helpless against the sort of power he wielded with painful ease, the exacting nature of his deadly control. If he really wanted to, he'd simply crack me open and spill my hidden truths himself.

But then... a tiny smirk crinkled the edge of my lips. Unseen, but not escaping notice—not from him.

He saw everything, *felt* everything.

And so, everything he would have.

My smile grew devious, despite the way my heart thrashed at the back of my throat, for it was there, in my inherent weakness that I had a tiny measure of strength.

I had nothing left. Nothing but my secrets.

One that had been entrusted to me on a dying breath.

One I shared with a traitor that was merely the opening bid in yet another game.

And one that I knew but hadn't been told.

Asher's.

The beast I could not name. One I'd only caught a few desperate, fleeting glimpses of when I hadn't meant to look. Dressed in chains far older than the ones he'd looped around the empath, he'd imprisoned it in the deepest part of his black soul.

Asher wanted me to play. To fight and resist, because he lived for the hunt... the chase. To conquer that which refused to submit, even when the advantage was his. Even when he could command my body with a stray thought, *he didn't.* Time and again, he set my wrists and throat ablaze with the *threat* of forcing obedience, but only rarely did he follow through.

Only to show me that he *could.*

Only if I refused to play.

Because he loved the fight, my leviathan.

Because we matched, somewhere deep down in the dark where the empath lurked. Dressed all in chains. Starving and wretched...

... but not alone.

Asher was hiding a secret as deadly as my own and the dots had all finally aligned.

Nature's answer to the empath. Balance of the unseen forces.

Just the other side of the coin, and so, *so much* potential left untapped.

And now it was *my* turn for artful half-truths.

He felt my interest and groaned. Lips crushing the back corner of my jaw, he sent a tendril of dark elite magic zipping through my skin. Pure energy that penetrated far too deep. Too fast for me to even attempt to brace against it or dare to pull strength from it.

Hot and hard against my back, he nudged me forward. A single step toward the bed.

And then, against my throat, "What game are you and Alicia playing?"

"Jealous?"

He laughed, beard stubble rasping against my pulse, he dressed me in gooseflesh then sent a flood. Drowning me in an ocean of power I couldn't so much as sip. "Tempted," he murmured, and placed his teeth. A gentle nip at my earlobe that drew a gasp from my lips. "Intrigued." Rumbling at my back, one forearm snaked under my arm, braced between my breasts, so his hand might encircle the base of my throat. Cradling. "And yes," he admitted, squeezing at my airway for an instant before long fingers moved up, to tease at my lips, "*jealous*. Deeply."

He dipped inside, then. Prodding my tongue, before his fingers delved deeper. Stroking. Making me taste. Drawing up a flood of saliva.

It was a lewd action meant to humiliate, even as that wave of elite energy grew heavy, saturated with a sense of obedience. Compliance that bade me answer when he asked, "What are you hiding, pet?"

Drool pooling at the taste of the man, I closed my lips around that invasive digit, and swallowed before I gagged. Sucking. It was a brainless action, one I felt a fleeting instant of regret for doing, but it was smothered beneath his groan.

Lockstep, he drove me forward another pace.

Inching closer to that heap of rumpled sheets. "Tell me."

I hissed, squirming against his heat. Clinging to his forearm, I let his fingers go without drawing blood, and said, "Can't. It's a secret," though a coy, devious little smirk.

His laugh was low and seductive, and it was a sound that curled around my throat, sent tendrils of wicked amusement singing in my blood. "Come now, pet," he cooed against my ear. "You can trust me."

"But you'll be mad," I sang, teeth gleaming through a smile that bloomed to reveal something... hungry.

"Mmmhmm," he hummed, and took another step. "And I know just how I'm going to work out my temper. Care to take a guess?"

Without answering that rhetorical question, I let him sweep through my system without a hint of war in my blood...

... and set a trap of my own.

One he couldn't help but be drawn to, for it was the exact opposite as the one he'd made for me.

A distraction made of truth—just not the one he was after.

"I know," I murmured, drugged by his influence. Intoxicated by the dark magics coursing through my veins. Reaching for it because I couldn't help myself. Couldn't possibly resist the one thing I wanted above all else. "I know your secret. What you're hiding from the empire."

He hummed and drove me forward. One pace

closer to a punishing reward. Silently commanding my secrets to spill, rough hands slipped down. Weighing my breasts, teasing peaks that begged for cruel torment.

"I know," I said again, and let my neck roll where it was cradled at his shoulder. "Know how you do it... know what you are."

"Is that so?" he murmured, lips strumming along my neck. Up, until he placed a single, delicate kiss atop my pulse where it thrashed beneath my jaw.

"I know what you're hiding"—I laughed around a hiccup—"from-from the empire. How you've managed to hold the empath back for so long. Like it was easy."

"Mmm," he groaned, and his hand fell to my hip. Kneading, fingertips finding bone where before there had been an insulating layer of fat. "Tell me," he whispered. "Say it."

"You've done it before."

A sharp nip of pain pricked at my throat. Teeth followed by wet, soothing heat of his tongue where he washed away the ache. And then, another step forward and only one more left to go before my knees would bump that mattress.

"I know," I said, "know th-that you hate me." I squeezed my eyes shut so I couldn't see that last doomed step. "*Passionately*, because you are me. Just the other side of the same coin. The order to my chaos. And the empath?" I whispered, dragging a breath through lungs that had grown frigid and stiff.

"It's only a baby monster next to the one you wrestle with every day."

He shifted, laying a trail of burning kisses along my nape, letting my words hang in the gloom. Growing heavier with every passing second, until he caught my opposite ear between his teeth, and pulled a rattling breath through his lips.

"Berserker," he said, naming it at last. Barely more than a heated whisper, it was a sound that somehow felt... wrong and seductive all at once. Three hissing syllables murmured against my ear that drew a shiver up from the base of my spine. Like naming it had brought it forth.

My breath caught, eyes snapping open as I felt him move at my back.

He spun me. A single, sharp movement that threw my balance off as my hands flew out. Catching at his uniform. Clinging to a mountain in the eye of a storm.

My enemy.

For a moment, he merely watched me. Grip so tight on the bond, I could feel nothing but the emotions flicking and dancing through my own chest as I fell forward. Swallowed by the swirling pools of inky pitch.

And then a grin. "And the warrior priestess finds her teeth once more. Figured that out all by yourself, hmm?"

I swallowed. Blinking up at him as his breath warmed my cheeks. "You showed it to me," I murmured. "When Sasha died. You used it... the..."

"Say it."

"Berserker." My throat worked. Suddenly parched. "You used it to force—to stop the riot. To stop... *me.*"

Something indescribable flicked through him, then. An emotion strong enough to wriggle free of his control, spilling over the wall erected between us, it howled through my blood. Razing my fragile resistance, he reduced me to cinders, then snuffed out the smoke in a single breath that robbed me of good sense and left me panting through parted lips as I stared up at him, bewildered.

Utterly.

And then he drove me back that last step. My hamstrings whispered against silken sheets.

"You feel it?" he hissed, and seized my braids in an unforgiving grip that twisted at my nape. Pulling my head back, exposing my throat. "This thing you call hate?"

I couldn't feel anything *but.*

The rage that burned brighter than a thousand dying elites with as many faces. Each facet a different shade of emotion I didn't know and couldn't pronounce. Crackling dark magic pulsed and lashed, and he let me look. Held me enthralled to the beast howling for my submission so it could feast and drink and gorge until I begged for that sweet torment. Until I knew nothing else.

The berserker.

The match to my empath, it sent a tsunami to wash away everything I'd ever been. Letting me feast, as long as it was from *him*. Turning my vision black, lit by shades of violet that painted the captain as he really was.

A conquering force bred and built for war.

"On your knees," he hissed, the words slipping through clenched teeth. "Taste what you do to me. What you plainly see, but cannot name."

I folded before him, knees striking the carpet with a dull, graceless thump.

"You caught a glimpse of true power and you think you know?" He laughed, low and cruel. "You understand *nothing*," he snarled, and pried my lips apart with the pad of his thumb. Adding weight to my jaw until my lips gaped as I panted against his wrist. "You play games with forces you cannot control. But" —with his free hand, he flicked the latch of his belt and did not blink—"you will learn. *I* will teach you."

Freeing his cock, he took himself in hand. At the base where his sack sat high and tight. Swollen and heavy with seed he meant to spill.

Balls flexing, he traced the length of swollen flesh with a clenched fist, and sent a bead of furious, gleaming want gushing from his slit.

I whimpered.

A tiny squeak that slipped from my lips on a hitching breath.

"*Fuck*," he snarled, and wrenched my head back. Further. Leaving me panting in his shadow. "Wider," he ordered, and held still before me when he might've plunged inside. Pausing to look. To admire my bewildered defeat as I knelt before him.

I didn't ask permission.

Didn't pause to think.

It was far, *far* too late for that.

Tongue darting out, I claimed that salty droplet. Moaning as my tongue swept the notch hidden beneath a ridge of angry flesh. Tasting, I pulled him between the points of my modified canines and was rewarded with a rumbling growl that sent waves of greed coursing through my skin.

More.

"That's it," he spat, and let me work. For the first time, despite the howling storm whirling inside him, he watched without taking. His hands tight without pushing, as if the restraint existed purely in flexing, bunching muscle. As if there were some greater victory in watching me move without the lash of burning gold.

I thanked him with a swallow when his tip found the back of my throat.

A breath stuttered between his lips, jaw chattering as he tried to gasp around a strangled, "*Fuuuck.*"

Brittle confidence surged in my heart, and I shifted closer. Making space between his feet, my knees spread where they were braced on prickling carpet—*wider*—I let his length slip from my lips. Scraping his shaft where it was wedged between my canines.

At this, he cursed in a tongue I'd never heard before. Some foreign language or Caledonian profanity that had never assaulted my ears. Guttural, breathless and desperate, and yet, his meaning was clear, even before he whispered, "I'm not going to last."

I knew it. In the gush of brine that painted my tongue and the swirling energy that danced around us in an inferno of dark flames.

And then, hips tilting in some desperate bid to ease the neglected ache weeping between my thighs, I reached for that heavy, swollen purse. Massaging his balls, I took him deeper and felt his his every muscle go tight.

Trembling fingers caught my throat, slipping where I was wet with drool, he tipped my chin back, and forced a raspy, "Look at me," through his teeth.

Lips stretched around his base, almost white and bloodless where he was thickest, I glanced up. Blinking as I was ensnared by sable depths. Helpless before him, and yet... it was *my* teeth, wicked and long and sharp, that held him on the edge.

And it was too much.

He shuddered. Feet shuffling before a guttural snarl shattered the illusion of composure. He fucked into my mouth once, twice, careful and without tether, before he wrapped one hand around his root and pulled out in a rush. Working his length in a fist gleaming with spittle, the sounds of debauchery sang out from a grip that quickly became a blur.

"Don't move," he growled, free hand anchored at my nape. Fingers tangled around braids that had come loose, he held me still, panting through his teeth, and lost control.

Just for a moment.

Just long enough to drown me beneath an ocean of pure feeling. I gasped—and stretched my ribs with a breath utterly saturated with Asher.

Up from the base of my spine, I felt him. Even before the first rope of gushing cream splashed against my cheek. Before he erupted with a hiss, I was lost.

Frozen in place, I came.

Hard.

Clenching around nothing, in time with every lashing rope of seed. I felt the impact of every searing jet not where I ached to be stretched, but laid down in sloppy ropes that burned my cheeks. My lips and nose.

"Asher—" I sobbed, over and under-stimulated.

Staggering closer, his grip in my hair turned my neck as he laid down rope after rope of come. Over the bridge of my nose, coating my lips in a thick glaze before he set his tip against my lips and ordered me to, "Taste it."

I took.

Drinking, *deeply*, I sucked him down and feasted on the beast without restraint. Still gazing into that bottomless, inky glare, I was lost in the flames. Nursing the last drops from a cock still stiff and thick and angry.

And then he grinned.

It was a quick flash of teeth, a breathy exhale through his nose. "Painted your face," he murmured, and sent his thumb tracking through the mess.

Smearing it, he gathered that spilled cream and broke the seal I had around his girth as he pushed that digit into my mouth. Feeding me every last drop.

For a moment, his words were merely that. Sounds I didn't understand until the fog lifted and he retreated behind his wall once more.

"Well." I twisted away so he couldn't see my lewd smirk, cheeks hot, still quivering with the aftershocks. "I think I prefer Alicia's paints." I licked at swollen lips tacky with his taste, wrinkled my nose, and said, "Not so bitter. And the result is much prettier."

At this, he snorted. Tongue clicking as he turned my chin first to the left, and then the right. Obsidian glare flicking over my features, he inspected his work with a critical eye. Admiring cheeks stained with the remnants of his come. Cheeks flushed a deep, shameful shade of pink, warm with a heat that refused to fade. And my hair —pulled loose. Disheveled by his hand. "No," he said at length, and helped me up. "Not from where I stand."

I went.

Legs rubbery, I let him lift me without a flicker of protest. Didn't react when he pulled at the knot tied at my nape, hardly daring to breathe when the silk fell in a ripple of liquid fabric.

He laid me out in his sheets.

Naked.

Sopping wet, my nipples rosy beads of pebbled need. The room spinning above and around me as he tugged the blankets up and let me cocoon. Back into my nest of gloomy comfort that reeked of him.

He was gone and back before the room stopped spinning. A damp, warm cloth set against my cheeks, he washed away the stains with a gentle hand, then stripped.

I watched him without a blink. Tracking his every movement, devouring every exposed inch of bronzed skin and rippling muscle. My eyes pausing on his prick. Still standing stiff, still aching with the need to slake his lust.

He made space for himself in my nest. Nudging until I rolled and gave up my back, neck twisting, so I might watch when he set one hand on my hip. Long fingers peeling me apart where I was sodden and slick, he sent his cock through my folds from behind. The glide unhindered except for a delicious friction that made me gush.

"Insatiable little virgin," he drawled, arms winding tight about my ribs, he squeezed and slipped inside on a long, slow thrust. Filling me on a guttural groan, he bottomed out. Striking something deep inside that made me shudder before my spine went liquid. "Sleep," he whispered, and made a pillow of his bicep beneath my ear.

For several long seconds, I couldn't draw breath. Shocked silent, the protest that was poised on my lips was one I couldn't utter.

Not without admitting I ached for him to move.

Not without begging him to fuck me hard from the back. To ride me until I was sobbing and begging him to come, just so I could feel that delicious kick of his cock gushing when he couldn't take it anymore.

I let one knee fall forward, thighs crossing, I squeezed him from root to throbbing tip. Trying to entice.

He groaned, sluicing through the mess, but aside from burrowing deep as he could, that was all before he succumbed to his own command.

Exhaustion pounded through the bond. Drugging and heavy, it warred with the fire still raging in the cradle between my hips.

I fell asleep to the sound of his blood rushing through his veins. An ocean roaring beneath my ear. My every appetite satisfied. Stretched, stuffed full. Debased and swaddled inside and out by a man I hated. *Passionately.*

My enemy.

Sleepy eyes glanced toward his desk, where a secret gift would have to wait just a little longer...

The morning brought bleary-eyed confusion. Dark before the dawn, in the small hours where I could still believe my own lies, my hips worked to silence the screaming ache for relief.

I moaned as I felt him grow stiff inside me. Filling me in twitching inches, slick with gushing cream that begged for the rough friction of an easy, welcome glide.

He pressed a cocky, sleepy smile to my shoulder. Nibbling at the spot beneath my ear as he rolled inside. Once, straining at my end just to feel me shudder around him. "I thought I would miss the fight," he murmured, voice hoarse with sleep. Seizing a handful of fat, he kneaded my breast. Pinched my nipple until I mewled and clenched. "But to have you like this? Easy. Soaking wet. Desperate and insatiable." His free hand slipped over my hip to cup my mound and roll my clit between his fingers. "Begging to ride my dick like you're going to drown without it?" He made a sound that was caught somewhere between lust and greed.

I rolled my neck, trying to move against him where I was pinned and skewered.

"You're wrong," he growled. "I'll never grow tired of this"—he drove deeper inside—"and I'll never let you go."

Squinting, I twisted to pin him with a bewildered glance. Shaking my head. "Please—"

He kissed me, then. Going still. Lingering, he pressed the heel of his palm against my clit, making me throb and clench, but that was all. "As much as I'm looking forward to hearing you beg for my come," he said, and withdrew, "it'll have to wait. We've got business to attend. Cousins to bury."

The funeral.

I'd forgotten.

Allowing myself to be seduced by his influence, only too happy to ignore the mysterious burden that was Sasha's gift.

Dread fluttered through my chest.

"Leave me here," I whispered, hanging on the edge of opportunity or disaster, for all I really needed was a few precious moments of solitude. "Don't make me do this," I pressed. "It's not safe." And then, sitting up when he rolled to the edge of the bed, clutching dark sheets to my collarbones, I added, "This is a mistake," as I watched him go. "A deadly one."

The captain nodded. Agreeing, heartily. "The potential for disaster has not escaped me, Mila.

Unfortunately, your presence at Harper's funeral is not an option. They need to see you." Muscles bunching and flexing when he pulled crisp, formal blacks from his closet and stepped into his pants with a little hop. "My golden priestess. Tamed. Contrite." He took a step that cast a shadow over my face as he adjusted his cufflinks, buttoned neck to navel. *"Controlled."*

A bubble of panic burst in my chest at the thought of all those people gathered together in grief.

Already, I could taste it.

Knew their energy would hang on the breeze, heavy enough that I might lick the air and lose myself from one breath to the next. A conduit to their suffering, and through me... destruction.

I wanted it, just as badly as I wanted to hide in the dark until the sun burned out, and I told him so. "But I can't control—"

"I *can*," he murmured, and knelt on the bed. Catching my chin with the back of his knuckles, he gobbled up every spare inch of my attention, and said, "Remember?" before he took my cold, clammy fingers in those that were rough and warm. Thumb tracing my wrist, where the line between gold and flesh was blurred with a subtle gleam of power. Hinting at all that went unsaid, that he alone held the empath in thrall. He alone was equal to the task that had almost killed me. "I'll know. Before you do."

I swallowed.

Because I didn't have a choice.

Not in this.

But then... neither did he.

The arrangements had been made. There was a spectacle to be made of grief, just another scene in the grand theatre that was Caledonian politics.

The next hours saw me fed, dressed, and painted.

Perched on the captain's desk, I sat trembling in the morning sunlight. My feet tucked beneath my skirts as Alicia fussed with my makeup. Before me, the remains of yet another lavish meal that had been served before dawn.

Dressed in swathes of crisp black silks rimmed in gold, the captain watched me with long legs sprawled out before him. Hooked at the ankles, his fingers pressed to his lips. Observing me, inside and out. Silent and still, except for the occasional clipped adjustments he ordered Alicia to make.

"Stand up," he said, head tilting to the side. Eyes narrowed, he picked at the cuticle of his thumb as Alicia adjusted my skirts until they hung in an artful, obscene swirl.

It was the most revealing of any dress I'd yet been made to wear. Twisted into elegant ropes, the wrap flirted with indecency in all it did not conceal. Bared all the way to the top of my pubic bone, criss-crossed to hide my nipples, my entire torso was exposed, and yet, arguably it was also the first time my movement hadn't been restricted by the accursed dress.

All of it to the captain's precise specifications. An hour of predawn meddling and preening before an eye far more critical than mine.

An act.

An elaborate distraction of the flesh, my presence was a display so he might show off his golden priestess and the power that flooded my veins with unconscious ease.

Power that no longer burned.

Power I craved enough to sit still and obedient as he fed me slow, drugging tendrils of elite magic. Sedating me with a steady drip of what I wished to guzzle until I burst.

All of it an effort to hide in plain sight, so they might be distracted by the glitter, and not see how frayed the edges had grown.

A brisk knock rapped at the bedroom door, and without entering, Marco said, "We're ready."

The captain stood. Taking slow, prowling steps until he was close enough to touch, he sent rough fingers trailing down. Bumping and catching as they traced from my shoulder cap to my palm, he collected my fingers, and said, "Ready?"

My breath caught, but I didn't bother to answer.

Because it didn't matter that I *wasn't* ready.

I didn't matter at all.

"Shall I"—Alicia cleared her throat—"tidy up while you're gone, sir?"

To this, the captain snorted. "That's not your job, Alicia."

The pleasure slave offered a coy smirk. "Yes, but with Beau overseeing things in the bathhouse, and my only real chores being to make the priestess presentable, which isn't hard"—she winked at me—

"and to deal with Marco, which is quick and painless—"

A strangled yelp came from the other side of the bedroom door. "Oy!"

"—and even a little boring, if I'm honest. I find myself with hours, and hours, and *hours* of free time," she drawled, inspecting her nails as the sounds of a man strangling on outrage continued to pepper her airy words.

Head thrown back, the captain uttered a bark of startled laughter. "My apologies, Alicia! I hadn't realized I'd given you such a dull and tedious chore as that!"

"It's been a trying few days," she replied with a playful sniff.

"Well, if you find yourself with *hours* of free time," Asher said, one hand on my nape as he steered me toward the exit, "unencumbered by the tediousness of house breaking an untried pup—"

"Fuck me dead!" Marco hollered. "The injustice! The slander!" He swung the door open, leaned around us to pin Alicia with a heated stare, and paused long enough to make her cheeks flush beneath her smirk, then said, "I'll see *you* later," in a low murmur. Lingering with eyes narrowed, his body language was a promise that might have sent a chill through my blood, if I'd never met a better predator.

Unruffled, Alicia blew the soldier a kiss, peels of dainty laughter chasing us from the room.

We left Alicia standing by the captain's desk. Smirking, she wiggled her fingers at Marco before she stooped to gather some laundry. Sparkling green eyes fixed to me, I watched when she tucked a featureless black case deeper under the desk.

Sasha's gift.

From one desperate whore to another, Alicia's meaning was clear.

Time was running out.

I nodded. Throat tight at the thought of what I would have to do to earn enough trust to be left to my own devices long enough to open that damned box.

The cost would be whatever dregs of dignity I still possessed.

Grumbling under his breath, Marco escorted us from the captain's rooms. Down the stairs, through the kitchen, and out into the crisp, morning sunlight. Without a word, he opened the coach's door and stepped back as I claimed my seat.

Avoiding eye contact, avoiding touch without openly glaring.

"You're in a better mood," the captain drawled as he took the spot beside me.

"*Was,*" Marco returned, and shut us inside before he slid into the pilot's chair.

The captain sighed. Silent when we began to move, he shook his head and turned to stare out the window at the passing houses. Second in a line growing long enough to lose count, it seemed all of the Northern front would attend this event.

All of them gathered in one place.

A veritable buffet of energy unguarded. Ripe...

That bubble of panic fluttered and trembled once more.

My breath stuttered once before it stilled, frozen in my chest. Threatening to burst at the slightest whisper of opposition.

Dark eyes flicked to my face. Chips of obsidian obscured by shadows that gleamed from hooded lids. And then, "It's only a few hours."

I shot him a look, because we both knew what might happen in a few *minutes* if I were off my leash.

He grimaced through a smirk. "It's not ideal," he admitted. "The Lieutenant General won't be the only one watching, and we cannot afford another... spectacle."

An indelicate snort puffed through my nose at the understatement of a lifetime. And I shuddered, swallowing back the bile at mere thought of piercing, stormy eyes and dreams of compliant, living corpses.

Lieutenant General Hastings.

Forehead dewy with anxious sweat, I turned to scowl at the passing houses. At the translucent reflection of a girl I no longer recognized, if I'd ever known her at all. A girl courted by death, who wouldn't act, even if she could.

"I'm serious, Mila." Fingers biting, the captain claimed my wrist and made me look. "Don't give Hastings another reason. Don't make eye contact," he murmured, and pinned me with the full weight of that inky, unblinking stare. "Give him exactly what he wants to see. No more. No less."

Broken. Obedient.

The very picture of a Caledonian slave.

I swallowed, throat clogged and growing thick with the weight of such an ask. And then, inspecting the lewd hem of my silken scraps, I nodded. Just once. Just enough to acknowledge the part I'd play in this artful, obscene dance, without having to voice what felt like betrayal.

"One day at a time, pet," he added, and sent his thumb over the gold gleaming at my wrist. Sending a ribbon of power through my skin, letting me sip— and through that tiny taste, I caught the unmistakable flavor of anxiety and knew I wasn't the only one dreading the funeral.

"Oh, *good!*" Marco snapped from the front seat. "We're making deals with the Lady of Death and Corruption now, are we? Brilliant choice, mate. Seriously"—his knuckles went white and the leather of the steering wheel groaned in protest of clenched fists—"your best plan yet. Tell me, and this is an unrelated question, but has your brain begun to rot in your advanced years, or—"

"You about finished?" the captain snapped, and the window into his mood clapped shut between us before any hint of that blackness might spread and infect.

"Oh," Marco hummed, "I've got a *lot* more to say. You're just too cunt-drunk to hear it."

"And what, exactly, would you have me fuckin' do about it? I can't—"

"Sounds like Hastings is making an offer you shouldn't refuse," Marco returned, and dark brown eyes flicked up to scowl at me in the mirror. "Instead, you're making deals to keep her just the way she is. As if there's nothing wrong with that little terrorist. As if she didn't slip inside me like an ill-fitting coat barbed in razorblades—"

"Right, and which one of your brilliant plans did you want me to go with?" Asher snapped, and his grip on my wrist grew tight enough to bruise as he scowled at the back of Marco's head. "The one that absolutely gets me killed, or that'll probably get us all killed?"

Marco slammed both palms on the steering wheel hard enough to make the whole cabin tremble. "You're not the one who has to deal with it!"

Asher laughed, low and full of spite, brittle where it tested the seams barely holding together. "Is that what you think I've been doing for the last nine days? *Not* dealing with it?"

"She didn't crawl inside *your* mind," Marco hissed. "She didn't use *you* like a whore and leave you soaked to the eyebrows in the blood and brains of a man you fought three campaigns beside. And the next time it happens," he said, and met my eyes with those that were full of hatred and accusation, "it won't be you who has to choose which monster might be worse." He threw the vehicle into park with a jerk that almost sent me sprawling to the floor. "So, yeah," he sneered, "if you're asking me which of my brilliant plans I'd rather go with, it's the one that doesn't end with me being forced to put *you* down, you complete fuckin' knob."

I blinked. Shocked as a memory surfaced. Marco standing on the podium, cloaked in dust and ash as a riot surged out of control. A thousand different moving targets, but his weapon—spitting green flames and deadly, grim determination—*had been fixed directly to the captain's heart.*

A breath leaked from my lungs, and with it, clarity.

I wasn't the only one who knew Asher's secret. That a berserker lurked beneath that thin veneer of Caledonian civility.

Because it was a beast Marco had been ordered to kill on sight.

18

The Tilcot manse.

Sweeping and regal, it had once been an opulent estate of Elora's wealthiest patrons. But now? Every inch had been transformed by swathes of black fabric rimmed in gold. Stamped with the Tilcot coat of arms where it was draped over the three story building, Caledonia's colors fluttered in the breeze. A somber monument to its late occupant.

Wrapped in fine dark silks, Carina materialized at the captain's elbow as if he hadn't abandoned her in the park at the earliest convenience without a backward glance. A somber smile fixed firmly in place. It was a perfected expression just wide enough to be seen without appearing garish.

Mournful enough to be mixed with a few sniffling sighs.

Without missing a beat, she looped her arm through the captain's and fell into step. Unruffled by yesterday's insults, she chose to soak herself in the attention, the adoration and condolences afforded to his intended bride. Artful tears sparkled at her waterline, though her kerchief remained suspiciously dry, despite her dainty hiccups and trembling fingers.

The long driveway was lined with a hundred soldiers dressed in their formal attire, and I watched from beneath lowered lashes as we walked at the head of the funeral procession. Five short paces behind the late general's wife and newborn son. A woman whose name I couldn't recall, whose face was shrouded in a black veil as she wept noisily before the throngs of onlookers. The infant clutched to her breast was swaddled in black, gossamer silks, fast asleep. Oblivious to his mother's display of grief.

Blissfully unaware of the monsters all around him.

I followed. Eyes downcast. Skin gleaming with power I couldn't taste, itching with the weight of hundreds of eyes as I trailed along in the captain's shadow. On display for the first time in eight days, I maintained my end of the bargain and gave them my best impression of a broken thing.

Contrite.

Obedient.

Absent any whisper of spirit that might need to be crushed beneath a storm of black, Caledonian boots.

The funeral procession entered a courtyard lined with row upon row of pristine white chairs untouched by the ugliness of war. Out of place, it was a grotesque show of wealth that left rot bubbling in my stomach.

There was a pause before the ceremony began. A few moments of mingling amongst the grievers that reeked of political flirting. Of games and careful maneuvering that brought a fetching glow to Carina's cheeks as she accepted condolences on Asher's behalf and played her part to a degree that left me shaken. In awe of a woman who held no power, except for what she might manufacture from her own vicious cunning.

She was more than the treacherous organ between her legs.

She was... *better* at this than me.

By a margin so utterly out of my reach, I'd assumed her to be just another whore owned by the empire, and failed to see her for the player she really was.

"Tragic," she said, quiet and demure. "And to blame his dear cousin, just because Asher's priestess is one of rare power?" She sniffed, leaning into the captain, one elegant hand spread over his heart, toying with the buttons. "It was *awful*," she whispered, injecting a little tremor into her lilting voice. "Even the suggestion that my beloved couldn't control the girl? Absurd slander." She laughed, high and tinkling. At home in her element as she worked to repair the captain's reputation. Painting him as untouchable.

The captain left her to it. Jaw tight as Carina

moved through the well-wishers at a pace that made my head spin.

But when a wraith appeared at Asher's elbow, he softened immediately. Turning to embrace the Tilcot widow with a gentle murmured, "*Tyra*. How are you?"

"Asher," she choked, and that was all before she was sobbing into his shoulder.

"How is he?" the captain asked, retreating so he might lay a hand on the infant's ruddy brow, where he was swaddled in dark silks.

"Fatherless," Tyra hissed, knuckles white. Her red-rimmed scowl darting from face to face to face—anywhere but the bundle slung over her arm. "But he thrives," he muttered, distracted. "Quiet. Sleeps most of the time. The wet nurse tells me he's eating well enough."

At this, the captain made a happy sound at the back of his throat.

Tyra's chin snapped back, her attention sharp for just an instant when she barked, "I cannot *believe* they wouldn't let you out to see him! Fucking barbaric. Believe me, Killion Hastings will think twice before he dares to bring charges against a member of *my* family ever again."

"Yes," the captain drawled. "It's been a trying few days, hasn't it?" One hand on her mid back, he guided her from the throng and left Carina to her political games. "What's the boy's name?"

The widow's smile was watery, though she didn't turn that smile down. Couldn't so much as glance at her son. "Samuel Harper Tilcot. My mother picked it.

Convinced me he should have his own name. So he wouldn't be made to walk in the shadow of his father." She pressed one delicate, trembling hand to her lips, swallowed her grief, then added, "So he could be his own man."

"Wise woman," the captain murmured, and claimed their seats in the front row. Letting Tyra sit with a grimace, her weight balanced on her right buttock, the infant shifted to her left—closest to me.

Curious, I peered into his macabre swaddle. The tiny, mushy face didn't look as corrupt as the father, despite the clear resemblance to the man. And I reached for my power, meaning to test the boy's energy. To see if he'd inherited his father's status as an elite, or if he'd favor his mother's mundane energies.

"What are you staring at, slave?"

It was an ugly snarl. One that sent me stumbling back with a shocked gasp, my hamstrings striking one of the pristine chairs with a clatter that drew more than one curious set of eyes my way.

The captain reached for me, an instant too late.

Big hands cinched tight about my ribs.

Hands that did not belong to the captain.

The touch was unfamiliar and repulsive all at once, and when I flinched toward the captain, that grip only grew tighter. Forcing me to stay in place as warm digits slipped beneath the edges of my dress, teasing the hem of the fabric. Where I was naked and exposed.

I went still, nauseated when I dragged my eyes off

the ground and found the captain staring at me with an equal measure of frozen horror.

It was a man.

One I recognized by touch alone, a man whose energy was familiar enough that I knew just how deadly the trap without needing to see his face.

Nevertheless, a warning exploded in my blood, freezing me in place as my wrists and throat burned with the captain's power.

But more than that, it was the look on the Asher's face. The stony fear he allowed to spill over his wall, seething through my veins.

And then, from behind, a low, soothing hum I knew to dread. "Rawlings." It was a greeting as much as it was a summons. A quiet murmur that didn't suit the presence of the man whose heat enveloped me from tailbone to nape.

"Lieutenant General Hastings," Asher returned, inclining his head without daring to take a step.

"Excuse us a moment, dear," the Lieutenant General said, and jerked his chin toward a quiet corner of the courtyard that was quickly becoming anything but.

The Tilcot widow sneered, struggling to stand as she hissed, "Killion Hastings, *this is a funeral.* Where is your decency? How dare you—"

"Peace, Lady Tilcot," the Lieutenant General murmured, but his fingers only grew tighter on my skin. Biting where my ribs tucked in and floated above my hip bones. "I'll return Captain Rawlings to you in just a moment," he murmured. "You have my word and deepest apologies, Tyra, but this is official business. We won't be but a moment, I'm sure. Rawlings," he said, tone clipped and frosty. Offering no room for arguments or compromise. "Come along."

Planting a kiss on Tyra's cheek, the captain patted the infant's head, then turned to follow. Leaving me trapped in the clutches of a man who wanted me ruined.

Nausea splashed at the back of my throat as I tried to leash my reaction—but even that was lost to me.

A wash of tingling numb spilled from the crown of my scalp, all the way down, past where the Lieutenant General's nails bit at my skin, to pool in knees that were turning liquid with each horrified, involuntary step I was made to take.

The captain.

He pulled on that poisoned barb lodged behind my ribs, draining me through the bond. Taking every drop, except that which was required to keep my feet moving, he left me floating and dizzy. Too drained to muster a reaction worth noting—even to a man like Hastings.

And not a moment too soon, for on my next breath, I felt it.

Like disembodied eyes rolling through my muscles and nerves. Severed, but all-seeing, Lieutenant General Hastings stole through my skin, his magic penetrating deep. Forcing me to still, I was made to endure every horrible second of his interest as he swept through my blood. His inspection the clumsy prodding of a full-blooded elite attempting to use the gifts of a priestess. No finesse, and even less skill.

But inspect me, he did.

When he found nothing but the echo of the captain's energy, he retreated in a rush of callous disinterest that left me reeling once more. Releasing me, he tugged a handkerchief out of his breast pocket and wiped his hands clean, then said, "A fine day to bid a great man farewell."

The captain hummed and lay a possessive hand on my nape. Tugging me tight to his side, before letting me draw in a single ragged breath.

And with it, the return of warmth.

The burn of molten gold familiar in its agony.

Asher forced my hands to remain limp at my sides. Loose, when I wanted to curl hooked fingers into claws and sink them deep into the belly of the man who asked, "And how is the girl today?" as if he hadn't just licked the inside of my skeleton and sneered at the flavor.

The captain glanced down at me, his expression speculative, as if he'd forgotten just what lurked in his shadow. As if he didn't know exactly how delicate an act it was to force me to do nothing. To *be* nothing. "It's hard to say," he said after a moment. "Most of what she says is garbled nonsense"—he chuckled, long fingers almost touching at the hollow of my throat—"but *I've* slept, and I think that's more important."

"Ah," the Lieutenant General hummed, and

clasped his hands behind his back as he guided us around the front of the audience. Past the casket, and off to the side of the courtyard, where he claimed a sliver of privacy in the shadow of a mighty pillar draped in Caledonian black and gold. "Well rested, and back in control. Good. *Good.*"

A grin flicked across the captain's face, but before he could reply, I caught movement that ensnared my entire being with a visible snap.

Pale, silver-blonde hair shifting in the breeze.

Rail thin, long slender arms that hung loose from shoulders with sagging joints.

And her eyes.

Sunk deep, rimmed in dark, purple shadows.

Pupils blown wide enough that what might have once been a vibrant, icy blue, was now merely a tight ring of color that stared and stared and stared, but saw nothing at all.

Utterly vacant in a way that made my stomach lurch as acid splashed against the back of my throat as an image flashed between my temples.

Staring forward without blinking. An ominous wall of unflinching power that stood sentinel around the Head Priestess. Obedient slack-jawed slaves doomed to die in crackling blue priestess magic... men reduced to dust that might never be scraped off...

I almost wretched.

Couldn't stop myself from taking a panicked half-step back as I stared at my reflection. *My future.* A girl who'd been a priestess, but was now little more than a well of power running dry. Used up, until all that remained was a desiccated husk that blinked and obeyed.

Lieutenant General Hastings' priestess.

A living corpse programmed to follow at a distance. To obey.

Her throat ringed by a burnished, ugly gold. Impure... and yet...

She was the very picture of Caledonian perfection.

"I brought a gift for you, Rawlings," the Lieutenant General said, and produced a black velvet bag that clinked when it changed hands. "As promised."

The captain loosened the ties and peeked inside. "And the crown gave permission?" he asked, tone light, despite the tingle of warning that sparkled at my wrists and throat.

With a shrug, the Lieutenant General said, "Given the special circumstances, I'm confident you'll get approval."

"Thank you, sir. But"—the captain tucked the bag into his jacket pocket—"if it's all the same to you, I'd like to wait until it's in writing. I've already pushed my luck more than I should have with Mila."

For a moment it seemed that Lieutenant General Hastings might insist, for it was obvious enough that he wished to clap the contents of that bag around my wrists himself. That he'd ushered us off into the shadows for but one reason—to watch the blue flames in my heart flicker and die.

Irritation rippled across his features, flicking through that narrowed, stormy glare. But then, with a tight smirk, he said, "Suit yourself. And again," he added, clapping the captain on the shoulder, "my condolences for your loss."

"Thank you, sir."

"Oh, and after the service," he added, "I'd like to schedule a meeting."

The captain cleared his throat. "Certainly, sir. May I ask what it's regarding?"

To this, a sly grin spread over the Lieutenant General's lips, and he said simply, "Your future."

He turned to leave, then, and with him, the ghost followed a score of paces in his wake. Her body moved before her head felt the silent command, before her eyes caught up to the action. Giving the illusion of a puppet jerking to the orders of unseen hands. A phantom tethered to Lieutenant General Hastings, bound in iron and gold, forbidden from slipping into the Void until there was nothing at all that might be of use to the empire.

When the shaking started, it came from deep inside. Down deep where the well of power had gone cold, frosted over with a fine layer of dust. Where a monster lurked. Howling at her bonds. Clawing and raging and trapped with no outlet, but that which was made of her own power.

Through blood and bone.

A breath rattled through my teeth, chattering.

The captain surged into me, wrapped both hands about my shoulders, and pressed me back. Back, until my spine bumped the pillar and my world was filled with *him*.

He stooped. Lips set to my ear, he murmured, "Just breathe. Breathe with me, Mila. That's it," he droned. Inhaling with me. *For* me. "Slowly, now. In and out."

Teeth clattering, I shook my head. But I couldn't find a single word for what I'd just seen. Couldn't describe so exquisite a horror as *that*.

I could only obey.

Long fingers moved to cradle my throat, his thumb pressing at my pulse. A tiny, invisible gesture laced with a heady sip of elite strength that fed the fire that wasn't allowed to burn. "This is Caledonia," he said when I took another breath, unprompted. His touch was gentle—his words a hideous excuse. And his eyes? They'd gone liquid with something that almost tasted like pity. "It can *always* get worse."

I swallowed back the lump of nausea on a nod.

Focused on drawing one breath in, just so I could force the other out.

"One day at a time, pet," he said, voice low as he murmured his new mantra. The words hot on my cheeks as he let me drink from that bottomless cup and lent me a soldier's endurance. "And we're almost through today."

I almost laughed.

The grass was still wet with dew—the morning sun not yet hot enough to burn it away.

But when the storm had passed, my nerves well tempered by waves of lapping calm, he set one hand to my lower back and drove me back to his place in the front row. Stepping around a line of formless, well-dressed blurs—only to find Carina already seated in his place. Her lips pressed to the Tilcot widow's temple as she whispered against tear-stained, blotchy skin.

Red-rimmed eyes darted to my face—a face that twisted into something hideous at the mere sight of me, and for the first time, I was grateful to Carina for injecting herself into the captain's life. That she'd taken it upon herself to absorb the grief of a woman who loathed me on sight.

Before the widow could voice that hideous expression, the captain's fingers caught me beneath the chin. And in a voice that brooked no argument, he said, "Kneel," and pulled the very breath from my lungs. My knees went boneless, and with lingering contact, he took all that he'd given. Filling my chest with a liberal dusting of frost that left me sagging before him.

Before *them*.

The audience watching with a thousand, thousand eyes.

And then, with the tip of his gleaming formal boot, he dragged a pillow out from beneath his seat and arranged it on his right.

So I might slip into his shadow, as far from the widow Tilcot as I could be.

Without a word of protest, I knelt on my designated cushion. Sweating liberally in the cool morning breeze.

Hands balled into bloodless fists, I refused to see anything but the tattered edges where flesh met gold.

Refused to see the baskets of tropical flowers hanging from white pillars. Blinded myself to the enormous casket stamped with the Tilcot coat of arms, where it was partially concealed by a neatly folded Caledonian flag. Trying not to drown in the light breeze that was saturated with the scent of grief and mixed perfumes.

And I shut myself off from the wraiths of my homeland. The bowed, silver-blonde heads that speckled the front three rows of the audience as they began to settle on cushions all around us.

I focused instead on the way my ribs stretched the silky strips of fabric as I dragged in one breath after another, ignoring the sweat that trickled between my eyes, dripping down, where it traced the bridge of my nose.

And so it came as a shock when soft fingers landed on my wrist, a gentle touch followed by an breathy, "Greetings, sister."

A priestess.

A *living* priestess with icy blue eyes, watching me from beneath a fan of pale silver lashes. With rosy cheeks, and a gleaming white smile hidden beneath a sheer veil. One of rare potential, whose light, airy presence was a lure that caught the attention of an untrained monster starving in the dark.

I jerked away with a low hiss, leaning into the captain's thigh.

Terrified of the sudden ache swirling at the back of my throat. Where I was parched. Desperate for just a little sip...

19

"You must be Mila," she murmured, voice low enough to evade the Caledonians above us. A practiced hum spoken through lips that hardly dared to move. "I'm Carly," she said, watching me without looking. "They said you were with"—she coughed, nostrils flaring white as she swallowed and swallowed again—"they said you were with Sasha when she died."

For a moment, I could do nothing but look. My throat clogged with something bitter I couldn't name as I took in her attire. That her silks were only half as revealing as mine, her makeup subtle and not the flashy paints of a well-used whore.

But I nodded.

Just once, before I tore my eyes from her achingly familiar face and forced my scowl back to my ragged fingernails.

"Did she... did she suffer?"

The question startled me enough that I glanced at

her and found honest anguish scrawled across her elegant brow. Her eyes pinched at the edges where they were glassy with unshed tears.

I hesitated.

Sick at the mention of the most horrific thing I'd ever seen. Balking at the reminder that flashed behind my eyes, where it was seared forever into the backs of my retinas, mocking me with every blink.

A blazing deity cleansed in flames, surrounded by the flaking ash of those she'd chosen to die in her honor. Drained of their vitality, enslaved by a master who gobbled up every last drop of their magic until there was nothing left but a husk. Hollow men who couldn't stop the wind from howling through their flesh. Their veins growing blackened with blood turned to char...

They'd crumbled together, six followed by one. Priestess and elites, spines twisted by exquisite agony as they were swallowed by the Void. Screaming. Choking on blistering, burning pain...

I'd felt every horrible moment.

I *still* felt it.

Knew exactly how hard *that* noble death had been.

Jaw flexing, I ground my molars until they squealed. Trying to throttle the revulsion that warred with the want. The desperate hatred of all that had come next.

Because it had been tainted by a thing I couldn't help but want to taste again. A thing that promised to bask in the glow of death wrought by my own doing.

Bloodlust.

I was ruined.

Drawn to pain and suffering, lusting for freedom, if only to wreak havoc. Just so I might drink down the fumes of suffering caused by my own hand, until I was cloaked in swathes of unlimited power.

Nausea made me shiver.

Loathing what I was, rejecting it, I clenched my fists and jaw. Again and again and again.

But the empath forced my head to turn toward this woman reeking of soft, priestess magic for nothing more than the promise that I might know it again.

Just one sip.

Just once more...

Above me, a leviathan stirred. Winding coils of pure wrath about my throat. Forbidding my impulse—feeding my desire with the billowing fumes of elite energy more potent than any other.

Because I was allowed to drink—as long as it was from *him*.

I swallowed, and it was thick.

Did she suffer?

Unsure if Carly had come seeking honesty or platitudes, I chose the latter.

And lied.

"No," I said. "It was... quick."

Carly pressed her hand to her heart. Lashes sparkling with what I might only assume was relief, she gobbled down my answer in a single, greedy swallow. And then, "She's in the casket, you know."

I jerked. Eyes flicking back to her face once more.

"It's a secret." She grinned, showing teeth. "One poorly kept. There wasn't enough of the man to lend the casket any weight, so..." Shrugging, she picked at a fleck on her thigh, then said, "Even the worst Head Priestess shouldn't be buried, much less one of *her* status."

I hummed, but that was all.

"It's a shame we weren't permitted to preform the proper burial rituals, but given the circumstances... I'm sure she understands."

From the opposite end of the courtyard, the Lieutenant General made his grand appearance, and with him, a hush fell upon the crowd of grievers. Silence punctuated by the choked sobs of the Tilcot widow, it was the sort of quiet that felt charged. Heavy.

To the Caledonians, it was merely the scent of their divine privilege. Evidence of their right to rule.

But my eye went to the wraith floating in Lieutenant General Hastings' shadow. To the nameless girl with burnished gold poisoning her blood. The girl who'd been a priestess, whose eyes were black, and whose joints sagged beneath the weight of limp, useless arms.

"It's a desecration," Carly murmured, and I flinched, willing her to be silent. Willing her voice to remain unheard in the presence of a man who wanted to clap a set of suppressors on my wrists. A man who wanted to watch me strangle on a collar worse than anything I could imagine.

I ran my fingers through grass still damp with dew, sweating freely in the chilly morning.

I just had to get through the day.

The Lieutenant General took his place at the podium, then turned to place big hands on the casket gleaming in the sunlight. Paying respects where they were due.

Because General Harper Tilcot hadn't deserved such pomp and show.

But Sasha had been a master.

Turning once more, the Lieutenant General let those stormy grey eyes pass over his audience. "We are gathered here today to bid farewell to a great man. General Harper Tilcot—"

His widow cried out, guttural sobs shaking her frame hard enough that her chair groaned in protest and Carina draped her arms around those trembling shoulders. Cooing nonsense into her ear with artfully painted lips.

"General Harper Tilcot," the Lieutenant General said again, "leaves behind a beautiful, *loving* wife, and cherished newborn son."

"It's a desecration," Carly said again, her voice low but *strong*. Heavy with meaning that made me look. "On pain of punishment, we will not allow such a violation." A weighted pause, and then, "Are you with us, sister?"

My heart squirmed where it was impaled by a poisonous barbed hook. Pinned to my ribs, bleeding through a thousand tiny cuts all at once, for I knew that look. I could smell the reek of what she offered as it oozed from her pores.

It was a trick that had bitten me too many times

to count, for my deepest scars weren't from the fire of elite weapons.

Not from the lash of cruel whips, chains, or brutal, punishing flesh.

No, those earnest, wretched lies had *always* come from the simpering promise of friendship.

Again, I pressed against the captain's thigh. Seeking comfort from the man who'd let me see what he really was.

A man who lived in the shade between truth and lies, but made no apologies for what he was and felt no shame.

My only ally.

My enemy.

He let rough fingers tangle in my hair, rewarding me with a ribbon of elite strength that made me shiver and cringe away from this priestess and her pretty lies.

And so, from between the points of my modified canines, I hissed an ugly truth, "I am not a priestess, and you are not my sister."

Something painful flashed across her brows, there and gone before I might give it a name. But she schooled her features, nodded, and offered a tiny, sad smirk, before she said, "Something I hope will change with time."

Before I could respond, she set her hands on her thighs. Palms up, the gold at her wrists caught the morning sunlight and threw glitter into my eyes. Blinding me for the instant it took for Carly to start humming.

So quiet at first that I wasn't sure of the source. Couldn't separate it out from the confident droning voice of the Lieutenant General as he spun beautiful lies about a man who'd been a monster.

But then another voice picked up the hum.

And another.

And another.

One after the next, each of the priestesses in the audience sang the same quiet song of mourning. Each of them assuming the exact same position where they knelt on silken cushions at their master's feet. Palms up. Heads bowed.

The Caledonians began to shift. Uncomfortable in their seats as they tried to locate the source and didn't think to look down. Discounting the slaves they thought already too beaten to consider even the smallest act of rebellion.

A delicate heat surged through the air, and acting on some unfelt trigger, the priestesses' song escalated as it evolved.

Entrancing all who might hear it, designed to wash away anger and fear. To leave nothing but a sweet sorrow felt through the ages. Loss. Grief. An ode to suffering, and a loving farewell.

The priestesses sang in a language understood somewhere primal. Remembered in the blood, where ancient ancestors had gathered around a fire and celebrated their dead.

I was enthralled.

Drawn to the shimmer of raw power wetting the wind, I watched through wide eyes, unable to blink.

Hypnotized by a flavor more beautiful than the pure, unfiltered chaos of the riot. It was the very wind itself. Delicate and trying to be precise.

Reaching for the sort of focus they couldn't quite grasp.

Awed, I bore witness as the storm swept over me —*around* me. Leaving me untouched in the centre of a cyclone. Alone in the heart a blizzard, surrounded by priestesses who knelt with spines unbent. Their silent protest a sweet song that shivered through my skin with fingers that burned with the beautiful ache for sisterhood.

Beseeching.

To join them and belong.

I pulled a breath between the points of my teeth...

... and inhaled the intoxicating aroma of unity.

The warm embrace of friendship. Of everything I'd rejected as abhorrent, because I'd never known anything but pain.

It was right there.

And it reeked of longing.

"*Mila.*" Heavy, biting fingers landed on my nape. A warning as familiar as my name on his lips, laced with addiction and the promise of satiety that would never be realized.

But their magic touched me too. It sparkled in my every breath, clinging to my skin in a fine, sparkling mist that caught me in a sweet embrace.

Gooseflesh cascaded down my nape as war raged in my blood.

On my left, a juggernaut so jealous of my attention, he could never share it. Not even with me.

On my right, a sister I didn't want, but desperately needed. A woman who had nothing, except what precious little had been left to her—and she shared it with selfless abandon.

But she had *friends*. Women who sang with one voice and shared the fumes of their gifts in a beautiful dirge of love and loss.

As if it were drawn to me, my bottomless hunger, layer upon layer of priestess magic dappled my skin. A warm spring rain that dredged up a shiver from the base of my spine and saw gooseflesh cascade down my nape. Touching everywhere I was exposed, every whorish inch gleaming with all that remained to my people.

Dangerous and tempting and beautiful, all at once.

Enough that Asher's fingers grew tighter at the base of my skull, and with a quiet hiss, he surged through my blood. Militant. Efficient, he pulled at me until my lungs grew cold and tight once more. Snatching the priestess' power for himself before I could do more than catch their scent.

A tiny sound of protest left my lips, and I watched as the nebulous cloud of priestess magic turned toward me. Pulled in by the gravity of the monsters hiding in my blood, it passed through me...

... and went directly to *him*.

A plea left my lips, soundless, but desperate

nevertheless. One he felt, because he was already inside.

He only pulled harder.

Horrified, I watched. Helpless as the priestesses stumbled. Their voices growing ragged and thin as they strained to accomplish some undefined goal, but their magic went to serve yet another Caledonian master.

Asher.

I turned to look, and found eyes painted black. Jaw clenched, sweat beading on his brow as he worked. And his skin—it looked too tight. Stretched around too much as he drank, and drank *deeply*.

I knew then, what he was doing.

What he was.

Priestess and elite, both.

That he was both sides of the coin at once.

Question and answer.

Berserker and empath.

Complete.

Because of me.

Because I had given him everything I had, and let him feed me drugging, perfect lies designed to keep me sedated. Manageable. Numb to the hurt. My fire snuffed all the way out, just so I didn't have to manage the suffering.

A breath caught at the back of my throat.

Something brittle shattered.

And through the cracks, the empath howled. Strangled by a thing that matched, a better monster whose teeth and claws were sunk deep inside as it feasted on priestess magic.

Magic that had to pass through me, *first*.

It was right there. Already warm and tingling on my palate, far from pure, tainted by the elites who'd enslaved them, but it was power all the same.

A cinder.

It reached down through the dusting of frost, down through the guilt and the horror and the secrets, all the way through the grime and self-loathing that had coated me since the day Sasha had died...

... only to crash against Asher's wall.

I recoiled from the pain, curling in, to defend against a thing that had no physical form and needed no permission to slip through my pitiful defenses.

Something sparked.

Something I thought had already gone stiff and cold and bloated with rot.

I gasped. Staring up at what little remained of the miasma swirling in the air. The tendrils of pure priestess energy reaching out, on pain of punishment.

And I knew.

It wasn't enough.

They weren't enough.

Even unified in sisterhood, they couldn't muster the raw power needed to concentrate their magic.

Because Sasha was dead.

And it was my fault.

My skin tingled. Itching and too tight as I

watched those ghostly tendrils reach, even as they were drawn in, to me, pulled away from their goal.

"Mila, *don't,*" Asher hissed, and I felt him begin to drag me under. Drugging me placid as he looped bands of burning gold about my throat.

It was too late.

He was too late.

They needed a conduit.

And I would give.

Neck rolling, I let it wash over me. Palms fisted in my lap.

Asher cursed.

My right hand darted out, seizing Carly's wrist in a grip that was sure to bruise. And through that contact, I didn't merely welcome the storm—I *became* it.

Connected, a part of a whole, I understood. For one brief, glorious instant, I knew what I was meant to do.

Through me, they would have justice.

Feasting, I dragged every drop of priestess magic through Carly's skin and gave it focus, for it was my turn to wield a weapon—and I chose a thing that matched.

Berserker.

Asher snarled, but it was swallowed by a note of triumph. The priestesses voices rose in pitch, until their song grew sonorous and escalated beyond any reasonable hope that it might continue to go ignored.

The Lieutenant General stuttered to a halt, and in

his silence, the priestesses sang. A quiet, breathtaking refusal to see their beloved Sasha buried...

... when she was meant to burn.

When the eyes of the Caledonians turned at last to their slaves in horrified awe, my eyes fluttered closed. Blind to the display of shimmering magics they couldn't see, my head fell back as a breath filled my chest and stretched my ribs.

I didn't need to break Asher's wall to touch the core of his power—the berserker was already loose. Already inside me. All I had to do was lose the war being fought behind my ribs and let him have exactly what he wanted.

The empath.

All of it.

Too much.

Too fast.

I groaned when the tide flipped, and all that tantalizing priestess magic surged into him. When he was made to choke down every last drop, until his unshakeable control began to splinter. Growing frayed at the edges. Stuffed full, his seams bulging under the strain.

Another wave pulsed through me. Power Asher couldn't swallow fast enough to stop what was coming.

Because I handed over the empath, just as I'd promised.

But for one, glorious moment, the berserker was *mine.*

As if thrown, a spear of pure energy launched

through me—too fast for any to see—and found its mark.

Face ashen with impotent fury, as if he knew what might happen, the Lieutenant General stepped back, away from the podium. Back from the heat building beneath swathes of Caledonian blacks, he took his undead priestess by her nape and hauled her tight to his side.

And not a moment too soon.

Another surge of power rippled through the air, and the priestess' dirge hit a climax that echoed through my marrow, before it fell silent with an almost deafening boom. And with it, every last drop of priestess magic fell upon the casket. Seeping through the cracks. Coating the flag and the flowers in a fine, glimmering dust.

A dust that began to smoke.

At first, a few wisps of curling white that might've been incense—until the flowers began to crisp.

Entranced, I watched. Witness and stranger, both, held in silent thrall for the space of three breaths that seemed to drag on for decades.

And then, with a crack that blew my hair back, blistering heat erupted through the wood.

The same shade of Sasha's eyes.

Icy, crackling blue flames.

A Tritan burial fit for a Head Priestess.

Fire so hot, it consumed the casket in a matter of seconds and sent the first three rows of the audience staggering back with cries of pain and confusion. Leaving nothing but row upon row of silver-blonde heads bowed in loving respect as they endured the heat and bid her farewell.

But I was robbed of my moment to grieve with them.

My gaze torn from the quiet beauty of her inferno. My senses were totally ensnared by what I had unleashed.

Head turning in slow, halting ticks, jaw hanging slack, I blinked and looked directly into a blazing sun.

My enemy.

20

Time stuttered to a full stop. Frozen from one blink to the next, and all it took was a single glance.

Just one instant, and I was utterly, *helplessly* enthralled by obsidian eyes reflecting blue. By the titan blazing before me, cloaked in billowing flames of pure, raw power that didn't lash out at the silence, or fill each passing moment with directionless flailing where the empath was meant to thrive.

Asher.

But not as he'd been.

Standing rigid on my left, swirling flames of gold engulfed him but did not burn. He was power in the flesh, a leviathan unmatched by anything that had ever come before.

And every last drop of his attention was fixed to *me.*

He stooped.

His smile was predatory.

His fingers cool when they curled around my throat and his thumb notched in the point beneath my jaw. Forcing my head to tilt until my breath wheezed through my kinked throat and he dragged me to my feet. And then, in a low, cultured hiss meant for my ears alone, he said, "You're going to pay for that."

I could only stare.

My fingers still clenched about Carly's dainty wrist, made to watch when he seized my connection to the priestesses and snared their attention.

He let them see.

What he was.

What *I* had made him.

That in my lonely grief, I had freely given to their captors what I had denied my own people.

The last weapon we had left—and I had used it to make something new of a Caledonian elite.

Not an empath.

Or a berserker.

He was balance.

Because of me.

Their collective alarm whined at the back of my skull as he stood and let us all look. Exposed at long last, and yet, he remained absent any tender scrap of remorse, for this was a private show. Time was bending around his heat, distorted and warped by the perception of the collective as we watched in horrified awe.

A blink for everyone else, whose eyes were captivated by the funeral pyre.

An eternity for those doomed to sense energy they had once been born to use.

Point made—that I had never been with them—he severed my connection to the priestesses with an effortless flick. Reducing me to little more than an untrustworthy whore who gaped at his command.

A pet on a leash.

But even a dog born in captivity could bite the hand that feeds—

"No," he said, and it rumbled through my bones. Banishing the thought before it began to so much as whisper of rebellion, he tugged on the threads of power he'd layered into my muscles. Called on the commands he'd written inside my marrow, and drew me back with a feast unmatched by any other.

Spine going loose, I melted in his hands. Contained in an ocean of flames. Courted, seduced, and betrothed to the liquid inferno only he might offer me.

In an instant, I was lost. Happy to drift and never be found.

From a far off, watery distance, a commotion pattered against my ears.

And, as if watching from outside of myself, I saw the Lieutenant General take the stage. Firearm glowing hot in a clenched fist. His was a power that was pale and dim to my eyes that had seen the breath of something all-but divine.

"I want every man who owns a priestess in the dining room, *right now*," he snarled, white-lipped with fury. And then, pausing to let his eyes land on each and every one of the women gazing cooly back at him, he forced, "And bring them with you, gentlemen," through clenched teeth.

The captain held me back as the courtyard emptied of the funeral goers. His grip was loose on my nape, because the leash he held was anchored so much deeper than mere flesh.

A tide of power buoyed me closer, and I moved on boneless legs. Drunk, luxuriating in the sensation of rough hands keeping me steady.

"Asher!"

My head swiveled. Drawn to the alarm in that voice, for it rang louder than the crowd, louder than the roar of power washing me clean of any pesky, stray thoughts. A memory fluttered through the fog —of a riot full of armed soldiers who fired at civilians.

But only one weapon had been aimed true.

Marco.

He shouldered through the layers of my mind, bursting through the misty haze to appear before us. White-knuckled alarm and blazing, hissing cannon aimed true. "Asher—"

The captain lifted his hand, calm in the face of his would-be assassin.

In response, the soldier glanced once at me, met the captain's eyes, and quirked his brow. A question unspoken, but heavy with the shades of murder.

"I expect this meeting is going to be something of a *monster*," the captain murmured, not blinking as he held Marco's gaze. "We're going to be late, but"—he shrugged—"I've already dealt with the biggest problem. Not your plan or mine, but you were right. She couldn't be trusted."

Dark glare flicking back to my face, Marco sniffed. Fidgeting with his weapon for a moment before he said, "You're certain it's handled?"

"For now," the captain returned, and an arrogant little smirk twitched at the corner of his lips. "I'll tell you about it when we're done here. Don't wait up."

I shook my head, reaching to trace that tiny smile with the tips of my fingers. "Something new—"

The captain caught my wrist and stole my voice without bothering to glance in my direction. "Please escort Tyra and her son to their rooms," he said. "We'll be fine."

"I'll help you get them settled," Carina volunteered. In the crook of her elbow, she cradled the infant—his tiny head tucked tight beneath her chin —and with her free hand, she struggled with Tyra's dead weight.

The widow was slumped over in her chair, unconscious.

And then there was movement. The sensation of time thawing around me as I gazed up at the hard edges of the captain's profile with dewy, soft eyes. My feet and lungs all moving at his command, I was left serene. Unconcerned by the deep ocean of rage I could feel boiling beneath a calm surface. Fury that was restrained by necessity, merely waiting for the moment that it might be unleashed.

On me.

I was dimly aware that we were packed into an intimate room. Ringed by an audience of nervous elites, the priestesses were all corralled in the centre. And me, with no memory of walking.

No memory of anything at all except the halo of power I saw with every blink.

The doors banged shut.

"So," the Lieutenant General said, voice deadly calm as stormy grey eyes flicked from face to face, searching—until they landed on me. "Which one of you started it, hmm?"

For a moment, silence dominated that tightly packed room.

Silence where a leviathan crouched over its kill, ready to defend what it had claimed. No matter the cost.

Unaware, the Lieutenant General took a step, watching me without so much as a blink, when he should have been watching Asher.

Movement caught my eye. A twitch in the shadows, where a ghost with wide, blank eyes and sagging joints was imprisoned. The only priestess *not* caught in the web of sisterhood.

"I'll ask just once more," the Lieutenant General said, his every syllable measured and crisp. "Which one of you started it?"

My eyes drifted back to those that were stormy with accusation.

Asher's fingers bit at my nape as he pulled me closer still. Vicious jealously winding tighter about my shoulders.

A light, cool touch landed on my wrist, and I looked at the woman who stepped into the Lieutenant General's path.

Carly.

Her chin lifted. Defiant and steely, she nudged me back, and said, "I did."

But my eyes landed on something grotesque.

Black, cracked skin. Blisters seeping red and glistening where they ringed her dainty wrist.

Burns.

Seared in an unmistakable shape.

My palm tingled.

Horror prickled through the icy, soothing numb as my gaze traced the path of each digit where I had held her in a clenched fist—*where I had branded her with my touch.*

She tucked her hands inside the folds of her skirt and faced the Lieutenant General head on. "It was me."

The Lieutenant General's glare tightened as it shifted to her face. "Is that so?"

Colonel Viridian pushed through the women to stand at her side, spluttering. "What is the meaning of this—"

"It's simple, sir," she murmured. "I overheard mention that the Head Priestess was to be buried in General Tilcot's place, and did my sworn duty as her successor. I alone knew the incantations for the funeral pyre. It was me," she said again.

But another priestess stepped forward, and shouted, "She's lying! I was there too," she hissed, all stiff lines and righteous fury. "I overheard the same conversation, but *I* was to be the next Head Priestess."

"No, it was me!" said a third.

"Liars, all of them! I started the fire!"

A ripple of nervous energy shivered through the elites.

But a glassy smile spread across my lips.

Eyes narrowed, the Lieutenant General was silent as his gaze scanned the women standing defiant before him. Calculating as each and every one of them stepped up to claim responsibility for the fire.

All but me, and the ghost floating in the Lieutenant General's shadow.

"So," he said when they finished. "It's to be a group punishment, then."

"Anything public will make martyrs of them," said a man with sallow cheeks who claimed his priestess and tucked her neatly behind his bulky frame.

A giant man stepped forward, and laid a gentle touch on the shoulders of an unusually tall priestess. "And every time my Bella is sick or injured," he rumbled, "I'm affected on the field."

"I'll pay reparations for Keelie's part in this debacle," yet another elite offered. "But I won't see her harmed in any way. And not for a crime with no clear culprit and no victim."

A breath caught in my throat, and for just a moment, my smile grew watery.

"No victim?"

Still smiling, I turned toward the new voice.

It was a woman, dressed in a widow's blacks. "No victim?" she said again, but this time, it was a low hiss laced with outrage.

"Mrs. Tilcot," the Lieutenant General said, "please. This is a private meeting, so if you'll—"

"And this is *my house*, Killion!" she shrieked. "You cannot tell me what to do in my own house."

"Tyra," he said, but it was in the low soothing tones reserved for children and cornered animals. "You need to calm—"

"Don't you dare tell me to calm down, Killion Hastings." Stalking forward, she sliced through the elites to stand amongst priestesses. "Not in this house. Not today. No," she hissed. "*No.*"

"Tyra," he said, and spread his hands. "You've had an exceptionally trying day. And you know I'm happy to help in any way I can, but—"

"Sasha killed him," Tyra said, chin tucking in, spittle strung between top and bottom lip. Her eyes rolling white. "You know she did. And"—she laughed, high, and leaning toward shrill—"after everything he did for the little whore, now Harper's son will grow up fatherless. *I demand justice!*"

Quirking one steely brow, the Lieutenant General hummed. "Do you now?"

For a moment, it seemed Tyra had run low on fumes. That she was wilting before her audience of powerful men protecting their most prized possessions. I could see it in the way her wild, dark eyes swept the women. Flicking from face to face to face without ever really seeing anything at all.

Until her crazed glare landed on me.

And flicked down to my lips.

Lips that were still absent-mindedly curled around a misty smile I'd forgotten to bottle.

Incandescent fury ignited in the widow's eyes. "You asked what you could do to make it better," she said, and stood tall. Spine going straight and elegant. Proud. "That's it," she said, lifting one trembling arm to point—at *me*. "I want blood."

21

A chilling silence filled the dining room. Quiet that lasted for three heartbeats and a thousand years.

And then Lieutenant General Killion Hastings began to laugh.

Head thrown back, he stepped into the circle of elites, scattering priestesses as he cut a path to stand before the Tilcot widow with long, confident strides. Cruel, unforgiving when he took her cheeks in cupped hands—a new mother still ragged from childbirth—and offered nothing in the way of empathy for her pain. Her loss.

"That you think I would tolerate losing a single priestess is absurd, Lady Tilcot," he murmured, deadly soft. Thumbs stroking the ridge of her cheekbones. "But to insist I should voluntarily offer up their lives in some kind of... romantic publicity stunt? That tells me you're delusional."

She spluttered. "Killion—how can you say that?!"

she cried, clutching at his formal jacket with desperate, hooked fingers. "By decree of Caledonian law, murder is an offense punishable by death—"

"Shh, shhh, shhhh." Thumbs stroking, he hushed her gently. "To say the late general's slave was even capable of murder is merely a working theory, as of yet unproven by anything other than wishful thinking and womanly hysteria."

"Womanly hyst—*Killion!* How dare you suggest—"

"Even *if* they possessed offensive capabilities," he said, and pressed her back, clear of the tight cluster of priestesses. "Even if there was undeniable proof before an auditorium of blood-soaked witnesses that a priestess had committed murder with her bare hands, I still wouldn't entertain your silly commands." Without breaking eye contact, he clicked his fingers and summoned a soldier. "Please escort the Lady Tilcot to her rooms and see that she is made to rest."

Wary, braced for violence, the soldier put hands on her shoulders and tried to turn her toward the exit.

Fingers curled into claws, she lashed out at the soldier and snarled, "This isn't over, Killion!" as she was dragged from the room. "This isn't over!"

But the Lieutenant General flicked her threats aside, and said, "I'll make arrangements to meet with you in private. That will be all, Lady Tilcot."

When the dining room had cleared of her crazed shrieking, the Lieutenant General clasped his hands at his lower back. Head tipped toward the ceiling as he took a moment to centre himself.

And then, "It would seem that things in the North have been allowed to devolve under the late General Tilcot's reign. Slaves running about unchecked, and worse"—he laughed—"the elite soldiers of the Caledonian empire, seemingly reduced to doting nursemaids who balk at the notion of just punishment."

The man who offered reparations cleared his throat. "With all due respect, sir, I don't think—"

"No," the Lieutenant General spat. "Apparently you *don't* think, Patelle. This is a sentencing, not an open forum. I've already made my decision. And after seeing the way you lot coddle these slaves, I can see it's intervention sorely needed."

The tension in the air grew brittle enough to snap. I could almost see it floating there, crinkling on each held breath.

But I was apart. Drifting as the captain's hands held my body pinned in place, while my mind was somewhere else entirely. Observing from a lonely island in the middle of an ocean of scarcely contained power, while a leviathan circled my tiny refuge. Swimming at such an impossible speed that the wake of his every lap was nearly enough to drown me in crashing waves of liquid fire.

Locked away in the privacy of our linked minds, he watched me with the unflinching focus of an apex predator. Daring me to move, as if I could manage to simply draw a breath without his allowing it.

A discrete cough made me jerk, startled.

I blinked and found the Lieutenant General standing before me. Hands still clasped behind his back. A sickly, pleased smile oozing across his lips when I focused on his face in slow, halting ticks.

"Apparently," he began anew, "you've forgotten a very simple fact. These slaves are assets owned by the empire. An asset you are permitted to use in your service to the crown." Elegant, cool fingers curled beneath my chin, and he guided my head back, so he might look deeply into my eyes and see the nothingness inside. "But they belong to the Emperor *first*, and we cannot abide rebellion of this nature without dealing swift, irrevocable justice for the disobedience and insult to the crown."

From the corner of my eye, I saw the ghost move. Drifting closer, she approached her master as if summoned. The dirty gold at her throat and wrists gleaming as the Lieutenant General drew on her power and slipped into my skin. Meaning to taste. To touch what did not belong to him.

But I was secreted away, utterly beyond his reach.

He couldn't penetrate the leviathan's thick skin, or slip through his greedy coils to see what lay beneath, and the Lieutenant General wasn't nearly refined enough to sense the deception woven into me on a foundational level.

He smiled all the same, pleased by my apparent placid obedience. "Commendable," he murmured, giving the captain a tight nod of approval before he turned to the other elites once more. "These slaves shall be fitted with suppressor cuffs. The question of their obedience entirely removed from the equation."

For a moment, not a sound escaped either priestess or elite.

Until pandemonium filled the gap.

The elites spoke all at once, their voices clambering to be heard. One escalating over the next, until the yelling began to swell.

"You can't do that!" Patelle snarled above the rest, his Caledonian complexion going ashy. His fists tight balls clenched at his sides.

"And why not?" the Lieutenant General drawled, turning to face the other man head-on. His head tilted slightly to the side. "I think you'll find it's a fine compromise." He swung one hand toward the nameless priestess who wore his mark, lips quirked and full of smug arrogance as everyone looked at the pitiful creature who made his cheeks glow with pride. "Free access to their many charms, and above all, unflinching loyalty to the empire."

Even on my island, I felt the revulsion. The horror.

I looked to the ghost. To the hollow spots at her shoulders, where the joints sagged from disuse. Her glassy, empty gaze framed by sheets of thin, silver hair.

The priestesses are all gone. Taken. Enslaved. So much potential left untapped, each one holds a secret the empire can never possess...

My breath hitched in my throat. A whisper of cold

fire plucked at the back of my mind, begging for violence and untold carnage—

The captain spun me to face him. One fist bunched in the fine hairs at my nape, while the other found an anchor on my breastbone. Fingers spread, he forced heat through my skin. Drowning me in choking fumes of unsullied might.

Unable to resist, I went limp against him. Gazing into a black sun, my bones went rubbery and loose. Melting around his rigid frame and cutting, harsh angles.

Insulating me in heavy blankets of frost, he pulled on every unseen weapon. Tugged at every thread he'd woven so much deeper than bone as he dressed me in layer upon layer of cool, drugging calm.

Every advantage unquestionably *his*. My throat and wrists ablaze with forced obedience, he robbed me of any hint of rebellion. Snuffed out the fight with a snarl of command and followed through on every promise of retaliation.

It wasn't a cage meant to hold me forever.

But it was enough.

A distraction that swallowed time and distorted my perception of reality, for my next blink brought me to a dining room all but emptied of outraged elites and horrified priestesses. The temptation to seek vengeance removed while I'd been consumed by a greater threat, and only the vaguest memory of a clipped, "That will be all, gentlemen. Dismissed."

Aside from the Lieutenant General and his ghost, only Asher and I remained.

"Have a seat," the Lieutenant General said, motioning toward several clustered chairs at the end of a large banquette table. Claiming the head of the table for himself, he spread a crisp manilla folder out before him and began to read.

His every muscle tight, braced for battle, the captain took the offered seat and left me standing in his peripheral. Slightly to the left, and back, but locked in within easy reach, where he could see my every breath. Fingers steepled, chin resting on his thumbs, he cleared his throat and said, "May I ask what this is about?"

Instead of answering, the Lieutenant General licked his thumb and flipped a page. Stormy eyes flicking over the text, he hummed then turned another.

"Quite the impressive resume," he said at length. Still reading, his brows jumped as he nodded. Lips quirked. "Several tours in the West—which is nothing to sneer at. Commendations from ranking officers. Impeccable record out-pacing even bonded elites tasked with similar exercises, but—" He glanced up, eyes flicking over to me. Framed by a frown, before his gaze returned to the captain's file. "But the instant you claimed this girl, it all stops when it should have launched you into a new category altogether. Suspended from duty for *'extraordinary risk to empire property, and inability to use his power without also killing the girl.'* Can you explain this?"

The captain cleared his throat, leaning forward in his chair. "I can, sir," he said, split between holding me in thrall, and dealing with his commanding officer—the only outward sign a damp brow and flushed cheeks. "As I said earlier, Mila was never trained as a priestess. Never taught to throttle her gifts, and remained totally ignorant of her potential until I put my mark on her throat. And then her flaws became mine."

Frowning, the Lieutenant General hummed. Calculating, he tapped the index finger of his left hand, before he said, "Go on."

"Before Tritan fell," the captain said, "it's my understanding that Mila's father disobeyed Tritan law to keep her identity a secret. Refusing to send her to the temple for training. After the fall..." Snorting, the captain huffed out a breath. "She spent every waking moment of her time working toward a single goal."

"To cause as much strife for the empire as she could. Yes," the Lieutenant General hummed, "we heard tales of the Wood's Menace, even in the capital."

The captain nodded. "I'm sure you did. She was quite the accomplished little terrorist, given what she truly was. But Mila's power, the empath, it's... unstable by nature. And I inherited that flaw." He snorted, shoving one hand through thick, dark hair. "A punishment for my greed, I suppose. That after everything I sacrificed in the West... *I* was the danger on the field. Unstable, unusable power more likely to kill my own defective priestess, than killing rebel scum. That's why she'd been seeing Sasha. To undo decades of bad habits and install some version of discipline she *should* have learned in the temple, under Sasha's tutelage."

Stormy eyes fixed to the captain's face, the Lieutenant General was perfectly still when he said, "And was it successful?"

The captain didn't hesitate. "No. Not remotely. She only saw Sasha twice. There wasn't enough time."

For a moment, the Lieutenant General said nothing. Did nothing but watch. Calculating. Eyes ticking back and forth. And then, "That's... unfortunate."

"It might've been, yes," the captain drawled, and sat back. Beckoning for me, without bothering to glance my way.

And I went.

With boneless limbs, I melted into his lap. Curled up with my cheek pressed to his heart. Blinking dewy, glassy eyes at the man who burned with dark flames and let me sip at his fumes.

The Lieutenant General's eyes narrowed. "Explain."

"Mila is well in hand, sir, and I've got you to thank for that."

"Is that so?"

"I'll admit," the captain said, smug as he turned to stare into my eyes, "it took some doing. She held out far longer than I expected might be possible, but then, she did spend five years alone. Surviving the elements and evading the empire entirely on her own merit."

"An impressive feat, certainly," the Lieutenant General said. "But how did I help?"

The captain tapped his fingers on the smooth, wooden tabletop with a dull thunk. Once, twice, before he cupped my cheek. "You were unsettled that I'd worked so hard to contain her after the riot," the captain said, and his thumb tested my lower lip and found it pliable. "Enough to offer suppressors to ease my burden. And it was then that I realized my mistake. She's not a liability," he said, and slipped his thumb between my lips. Letting me taste. "She's a blank slate. With no Tritan education, and less control over her power, it was nothing to turn that power against her. A simple flip of a coin, and now she obeys my every command."

Frowning, the Lieutenant General leaned closer. "How can you be certain?"

"Mila," the captain murmured, and caught me under the chin with one curled knuckle. "Who owns the empath?"

A flood of lust soaked through my blood. And I heard the echo of my voice saying, "You do, Asher," as if lost in a memory.

The captain's grin made my own cheeks ache.

"Remarkable. Do you think this methodology might be replicated?" the Lieutenant General asked. "It could be significantly cheaper than using the suppressor cuffs, *and* have less impact on the issue of their fertility."

"I don't see why not," the captain hedged, running his fingers through the complicated twists spilling down my back.

"*And* you can use your weapon? Without killing the girl?"

Lifting one shoulder, the captain shrugged. "I'm happy to demonstrate when the cease-fire in honor of Harper's death has been lifted."

"Well," the Lieutenant General hummed, leaning back. Folding his hands, he watched the captain through narrowed eyes. Jaw bunching at the corners, until he said, "This is welcome news, indeed. As you're probably aware, we've had a recent... shall we say... *vacancy* in the ranks that can't go on much longer."

Eyes gleaming, the captain sat forward. "What are you saying, sir?"

"How does *Major* Asher Rawlings sound to you, son?"

"It sounds like a fine bottle of expensive scotch," Asher replied, and stood. Shaking the Lieutenant General's hand with enthusiasm. "Thank you, sir."

"Fantastic. Then it's settled." The Lieutenant General clapped his hands, stood, and tucked his paperwork beneath his arm. "We'll get you and the girl back to the capital to make things official."

For a moment, I felt ice shiver through him and into me. Something that tasted of alarm. "The capital, sir?"

"Certainly." Sniffing, the Lieutenant General adjusted the cufflinks at his wrists, one after the other, before he lay a heavy hand on the ghost's nape. "Fighting rebels is a waste of your talents, son. Can't teach the young, unbound elites your methods if you're killed in action by a lucky shot."

Clearing his throat, the captain pushed me off his lap and stood. "It'll be a relief to be back in civilization," he said, careful and full of tact, despite the bubble of panic fluttering at the back of his throat. "But my bride-to-be is here, and I know she's got plans—"

The Lieutenant General shrugged. Careless when he turned and his ghost went with him. "Change them. I've ordered a shipment of suppressor cuffs for the priestesses of the Northern front, and I expect you to be packed and ready when the convoy makes a return trip." He paused, then. Clapping one hand on Asher's shoulder, he smiled, and said, "Congratulations, Major. You're going home."

22

*H*ome.

The word echoed around my skull. Bouncing between my ears in a distorted concert of all the many things that made my heart twist with the ache of longing.

A vicious, guttural curse hissed through his teeth as he shoved one hand through his hair, and with the other, he collared me with long, calloused fingers. Blanketing me in layer upon layer of insulating power that forced me back. Down. Where he'd left me marooned on a spit of land in a vast, forgotten ocean. Where it was dark and there was nothing at all.

Nothing except for *him*, and what he was beneath a man's skin.

The leviathan rose up before me. Seething with the sort of fury contained by a grip that was brittle and doomed to crumble—a flavor I knew well, for it reeked of vengeance.

Held in check by the scant need for privacy, so he could vent his fury without the risk of being discovered.

As if from far, *far* away, I heard his gruff command to, "Walk," when it was snarled against my cheek. Felt my feet move and knew the light was shifting around me as I was made to walk without seeing.

He commanded my body with insulting ease. Held me rapt and entranced by the storm when it began to break against me and left me unable to blink. Unable to so much as glance away from the pure, raw beauty of the man whose fingers were tight on my nape, but whose touch went so much deeper than flesh.

But I remembered.

Bits and fragments all smashed together in the jumbled mess that was the smoking wreckage of my mind, but enough to stare into the unblinking glare of an unimaginable power and know I was apart. That I would weather the punishment I'd earned, and come through it battered, but alive. Mostly whole.

Because beneath the frost, there was a tiny blip of heat untouched by the glacier that had crushed everything else.

A cinder that meant to endure.

And it had begun to smoke.

Too late, and not nearly enough, but it was all I had.

Pulling the threads of my attention in, bit by

broken bit, I gathered the dregs of my mind and turned my back on the storm.

There was... peace. A certain type of silence found only in the whirling heart of a tempest.

At my feet, a tender glow.

A fosterling of dainty, fragile energy that had escaped notice.

All it took was a glance.

Just a single instant of attention, and a spark ignited in the smoke.

The sweet ache of fire spread through my muscles, begging for *more* as it moved to consume all that I was. All I might have been, until I'd sold it for nothing. Rejecting what I was to spare myself the pain.

But this time, I embraced it.

The hurt.

The guilt.

The endless, wretched self-loathing, and all I'd given up to avoid admitting one undeniable truth.

That I was not enough.

I had failed.

A willing vessel, I let it spread through my blood, feeding the empath's fire with pain until my ribs stretched on a breath. One born of my own volition that leaked between my lips before I dragged another breath in and dared to face the storm once more.

Wicked amusement grinned back at me, for he was with me even now. In this one, small rebellion. Two pathetic little breaths. A few blinks to prove sentience. And one soggy refuge already saturated by the stink of my enemy.

Everywhere.

He was everywhere.

So deep inside, he could count my every heart-beat. Knew the exact flavor of my mood before I knew it myself.

But in that perfect, exacting control... a flaw.

For he was *right there*.

Close enough to touch.

A towering giant, sharing my prison.

Not quite Asher... this was a beast that matched. One that had been imprisoned in the depths of his black soul.

The berserker.

Watching me with the sort of greedy jealousy I had only caught a glimpse of. Covetous, but restrained. Waiting...

... for me.

A tiny, coy smirk spread over my lips as I stood before him. Exposed. Vulnerable and weak. Defeated, and yet... unbroken.

Awake at long last.

Warmth spread, heating me from within.

I drifted closer to the beast, fingers tingling. Reaching toward the blistering cold swirling around us both. Drawing us closer, until there was nothing between us but miles of loathing and lust, and so very much I couldn't begin to name.

And then I knew.

This, too, was my fault.

I had driven him to do this. To follow through with the threat of forcing my obedience, because he'd been cornered between discovery and condemning me. His secrets all-but exposed, he'd been forced to cannibalize the very thing that had kept us separate. The source of his legendary control was the price for just one more day.

His wall.

It was gone.

A prison built to hold us both, now unable to contain either.

Still, he hadn't rushed to rebuilt it, but waited. Watching as I gathered myself. Poised on the very edge of action.

After all... he lived for the hunt. Loved the fight. The reward of conquering a thing that could never truly submit, not for long.

All I had to do was resist.

I closed the distance between us and touched the beast.

Power surged through my skin, igniting my senses as I burst through the fog. Surging up from the depths on a tide of power I could touch but not taste. Buoyed by a better monster, who paced at my back and followed me up.

Free.

Gasping, I came awake with a snap. Staggering, sweat blooming across every generous inch of exposed skin, I was only barely able to catch myself before I crashed into the kitchen counter as the world around me shifted on its axis.

Time thawed.

My senses returned to me in a callous slap that left me reeling and nauseous. Trembling as I tried to swallow everything that had happened while I had been *contained*.

I was standing in his kitchen, already back in the house he occupied with no memory of how we'd come to be there.

Hunched over the island countertop, clutching at the edge with white knuckles.

Dressed in silk, my every lurid inch exposing me for the whore I'd become. Bewildered by the gaps in my memory.

Heat lined up at my back. Heavy. A weight I recognized in my skin. One that didn't make me flinch—I curled.

Male. The flavor of possessive arrogance, and something... primal. Something not quite right.

Rough fingers took liberties. Callous, catching at my scraps, he traced the flare of my hip, fingers bumping up, over my ribs. Teasing between my breasts where beaded tips strained against black silk. Up, to circle my throat in a grip that flirted with murder and trembled with scarcely contained need.

The need for retribution, payment for allowing the priestesses to touch what belonged to him. Punishment for my endless disobedience.

And for clenching, slick heat to yield to all that was thick and rigid. Swollen, fit to burst.

A tiny puff of air was the only question I could muster.

But he understood the barest whisper of confusion that surfaced in my befuddled head.

Instead of answering, he pressed a grin into my hair. Took a breath that rattled against my skin and sent a ribbon of gooseflesh tumbling down my back. And with it...

Fear.

It pushed all else out and filled the void with barbed, rusty terror.

Because I knew.

It *wasn't* the man draped over my back.

It was the monster.

And then, lips caressing my ear, he peeled back the last of the layers and let me take a stuttering breath not throttled by the choking fumes of his power.

Because he wanted me to feel it when he whispered a single, cursed syllable against my skin.

"Run."

23

Savage, liquid heat pulsed through me, and with a desperate squeal, I dropped to my haunches and rolled to the left. Scrambling to stand before cruel fingers might find purchase in my hair, I spun around the corner of the island. Panting.

He was gone.

Twisting, heart thrumming at the back of my throat, I braced for violence. Eyes flicking at a manic pace as I scanned the gloomy, windowless kitchen and found nothing but a weighted dark.

A dark that grinned.

Ice washed down my nape, and, sliding one foot to my left, I inched back. Away from shadows bundled too tight. Shadows that shifted to reveal the flash of teeth inside a predator's hungry smirk.

Berserker.

He was loose.

Untethered… fixated on *me*.

And Marco was nowhere to be found.

Run.

I bolted.

Thighs whispering, silk snapping out behind me, I sprinted away. Blind with panic, I bounced off the far wall before I found myself staring down the length of a hall. Muscles weak from my days as his pet, bedridden, adrenaline alone lent me the strength to fly. And for three whole breaths, there was nothing but the sound of my heart thrashing in my blood. My lungs rattling as they stretched and strained for enough to sustain my wild flight.

Instinct drove me up.

I took to the stairs without a thought more complex than gaining the high ground. Seizing the bannister in a sweaty palm, I let my momentum swing me in a tight circle so I might surge up. Around. Righting myself with a whine of helpless panic.

But instead of taking the steps three at a time…

… I tripped.

No longer the Wood's Menace, who slid through the tree tops with death-defying ease, I was bested by a set of rickety old stairs. Betrayed by the mark of my station when my whore's gown was caught on the railing, sending me crashing into the steps with a strangled yelp and bruised, throbbing shins. Skinned palms.

He was on me before a ragged sob spilled over my

lips. Rumbling deep in his chest, heavy as he took a breath and set his teeth against my shoulder. Playing at the tendon with a bite that promised pain, but instead, plucked at a chord that sent an electric wave zipping through my blood.

I hauled my limbs beneath me, bracing on hands and knees as I tried to buck his weight when it fell across my back. Snarling, I reached for leverage with trembling, hooked fingers. Tried to claw my way free of him, even as a wry chuckle puffed against my nape.

Too late, I realized what I'd offered a man reduced to his most basic instinct.

A female on all fours.

Hips tilted up and back, as if ready to take my punishment as a whore ought.

Fucked raw from the back.

Bred. By a monster who matched.

Wicked amusement heated my spine, and without missing a beat, he planted one palm between my shoulder blades. Taking advantage, he drove me down. Down into the rise of the steps. Making space between my knees, he fit his body against mine and let me feel the pulse of his arousal when it kicked against my core.

Exhaling a shuddering breath, I whined. Baring pointed teeth where he couldn't see the confusion warring with the want.

The rasp of hot, rough hands found an anchor at my hips. Skin grating on skin, he slipped inside where my dress sagged open. Fingers dipping around the jagged edge of my hipbones, to tease at the crest of my mound as he leaned back. And with the other hand, he seized a handful of fat and muscle. Kneading, he let his thumb trace the curve of my ass in a languorous stroke. Bottom to top, tugging at what was secreted away behind a pathetic scrap of fabric, he made a fist of that handful and squeezed. Notched against me. Savoring, even as he shivered against me.

There was no mocking, taunting banter. No seductive lure wound through my nerves to feed me elite energy laced with lust.

He didn't bother to flaunt his power or force me to acknowledge how my body was reacting to him.

To this.

And I couldn't bring myself to speak the lie.

Not now, when I clenched at the low, possessive snarl that rasped against my shoulder. Not when I gushed in answer to wandering fingers and straining male flesh.

I was what he'd made me. A whore who'd failed time and again. My every passionate declaration had gone unfulfilled, replaced with such sweet poison. He'd seen me changed to suit his lewd desires. Left me helplessly addicted, just so he might feast on my energy when it was aged to his exacting needs.

A willing sacrifice, I'd already begged for more. Already cried out his name and let him brand every last piece of me with his signature. His mark. His seed. I'd sobbed in delirious relief when he stretched all that was swollen and needy, and turned to him for comfort, time and again.

It was nothing to do it just once more.

Because my body remembered what it was to burn beneath bruising, clutching fingers.

Gasping, my back grew tight as I arched. Pressing back, trying to entice, I set my cheek to cool wood and lifted my right knee one step higher. Leaving the other perched on the lower edge, muscles twisting as I freely offered what was already his.

He moved.

An inky shadow, he wrenched my silks aside, tore free of his zipper, and spread me with a sweep of his thumb. Pumping once, twice, his fist worked against my thigh before he sent that blunt tip through sticky, desperate folds with a possessive hiss.

I gasped, exhaling a ragged groan. Eyes squeezed tight, knuckles bloodless as I clenched hooked fingers and flexed my left calf. Raising up, just a little more.

He obliged me.

Reduced to wild, rutting instinct, he bullied through tight, swollen flesh and seated himself in a single, punishing thrust. Stretching my pussy wide open, only to pause. Straining against my end.

Where I was dead. Entombed in liquid Caledonian gold.

Rumbling against my ear, breath hot, he slipped his free hand around my hip. Stole beneath the folds of silk to cup my mound. Two fingers swirled at the base of my clit, drawing up a hitching sob from the bottom of my lungs.

"*Please—*" I gasped, hips tilting to take all he

might offer without spilling a drop, if only he'd douse the flames he'd set in my blood.

But he drew back. Left me throbbing as his digits painted a slick trail between the jagged bones of my hips.

There was a moment suspended between breaths. A brief instant of confusion, before it all came crashing down.

Power.

It surged through his touch. His every point of contact, from his palm to the tip of his cock, sent power zinging through my veins.

His command, it pooled low, behind my pelvis.

Swirling and building, it battered at the very last place I'd never thought to guard, because it was a place both coveted and *wasted* by the Empire of Caledonia. Rendered barren and infertile by their hasty greed.

"A-Asher, what—"

I felt him smile, then. Wicked when he withdrew just enough to stroke back inside. Filling me with a possessive thrust that sat heavy against my end, bumping something that saw my eyes roll back on a haggard gasp. Testing, searching for something outside my scope he fed me power and drove me to madness.

I sobbed.

Twisting where I was speared, I hiccuped and tried to move. Begging with the slide of slick flesh, I bucked beneath him. Sending one hand down, my fingers bumped over his, where he palmed the stretch of skin below my bellybutton but went no further. Down to the spot that throbbed and ached for his touch. Slippery with cream, I caught that neglected bundle of nerves between my first two fingers and spun a circle at the base.

Hesitant, shying away from the intensity of the sensation. Shamed by the need I couldn't possibly resist.

My pussy fluttered. Growing tighter with each maddening, clumsy circle.

He growled.

Not quite a man.

Not quite my enemy.

But I turned to him for relief all the same.

He dumped power into my womb, fucking me in tiny, punishing thrusts that sent ripples through muscle and fat. Skin clapping against skin, his grip tight on one cheek of my ass, he grunted as he peeled me open. Making me gape as he rode me hard and ruthless, even as I began to swell with the power pooling between my hips.

Ripe.

Fit to burst.

Pleasure crashed into my brain. Contorting my spine, robbing me of breath, I came hard enough to force him still. Milking his length in pulsing waves that begged for the punishing lash of seed that couldn't root.

He denied me.

Content to let me writhe, breath hot at my nape, his attention was instead ensnared by his work. By whatever nebulous goal a berserker might have with my barren, frigid womb—

My breath caught.

Ice washed through my shivering muscles an instant before a glimmer of understanding lit a horrible candle in my brain. Feeding my orgasm with dawning horror, even as I shuddered and shook where I was impaled by the instrument of my doom.

Amusement licked through my blood, and he answered my unspoken question in a voice I'd never heard before. "*You are mine,*" he crooned, and began to ride me anew. Each deliberate thrust cramming another wave of energy through the gates of my sterile cunt. "Mine to use..." He curled around my back, covering me from thigh to nape, and set his lips to my ear. Nipping at my lobe, he sprinkled a pinch of pain into the riot of blinding pleasure. "Mine to soil..." Power dripped down my thighs, mixing with my come as he sluiced through the mess, and said, "Mine to *breed*..."

"You can't!" I cried, and let my right knee drop down to meet the other. Reaching for leverage on the steps—succeeding only in finding myself more deeply pinned to the wood. "The empire would take an interest—"

Silencing my protest, he wrapped the fingers of his free hand around my throat, and with the other, drove power through my skin. A tidal wave of pure, brute strength. Every spare drop, funneled to the spot frozen in a golden cast.

I tried to buck my way free. "*Asher—*"

But he was deaf to my terrorized pleas.

Razing what little remained of my pathetic will, he sent a command howling through my blood. Crackling dark magic that demanded I submit to this.

My breeding.

Possessing me inside and out, he rode me with a savage intensity the man could never endure.

But the beast?

He was awake... free of his chains, and utterly fixated on *me*.

A weapon capable of unimaginable destruction, or impossible change. He was balance. Empath and berserker both. A warrior priest born to go to war with the laws of nature. To make something new... or force life into a desolate tomb.

With sheer force of will, he meant to override the effects of my chains.

Restore my fertility.

Fuck me pregnant.

Each thrust was a punishment that pushed the very air from my lungs, even as he crammed me full of dark, insidious flames. So much, so fast, so... *full.*

Even as his cock grew thick enough to ruin, he forged on. Panting. The sounds of wet, raw fucking rained down on my dewy back as I took it all.

I was nothing but a vessel. Empty, until he decided to fill it.

A tiny squeak spilled over my lips as the pressure began to push beyond what my body could endure, and still, he continued. Snarling, the fabric of his uniform adding obscene texture as he wrenched my head back and rutted with wild abandon.

"*Come*," he snarled, and hauled me up, flush to his chest as he pummeled at my womb with the last of his strength.

I went.

Falling, going completely rigid, I convulsed in his arms and milked his cock for every last drop, my breath frozen until one hand found a swollen breast —forefinger and thumb twisting to offer a cruel pinch of sweet torment—while the other landed over mine at last. Cupping my fingers with his, he strummed my clit with sure, slippery eddies that made me choke.

An explosion burst the dam.

He roared. Seating himself deep as he might go, he filled me in a way that robbed me of breath and blanketed my vision in a shower of sparkling black stars.

And inside my head, an image painted in colors I couldn't name. The slit of his cock fitted to a tiny crack at the gates to my womb, he pumped his seed inside. Laying claim where no other could possibly go, where I couldn't spill a drop.

I sobbed.

Just once.

Over-stimulated, coming at his command with a pussy full of come and potent dark magic, my eyes rolled back as he continued to work. Going limp, I let his power drag me under. Robbed of breath and every last ounce of sense, I tumbled into the blissful dark.

Where my unspoken questions might never be answered...

... and a berserker couldn't rewrite the laws of nature...

24

I blinked.

Cheek mashed against slick, damp wood, breath ragged and shallow. Ears ringing with the howling of my blood as it surged through my veins. Running thick enough with insidious magic that I could hear the echos of the endless war raging between both sides of the coin.

A battle almost won.

One I couldn't endure again, not without a weapon to give me an edge against the most powerful man on this side of the veil.

But there was a moment of calm. An instant of peace where I was left stained and forgotten. No more consequential than the spoils of war. Defeated, already tasted... but not quite devoured.

And so I watched, trembling beneath him as the searing crackle of his energy turned in once more.

Any notion of rebuilding the wall between us long

abandoned, I felt it when a more worthy opponent surfaced. That the man strained to reclaim his iron-fisted control over the beast. That even now—as he panted against my ear, still locked as deep inside me as he could get—he fought the urge to begin anew. To rut at my back until the possessive flames finally guttered out, or he died trying to crack through the golden cast guarding my womb, so his child might—

A tiny, hiccuping sob spilled over my lips.

And in a rush, I understood his purpose in a way not obvious in the heat of the moment, for my head was a wasteland of chaotic, jumbled thoughts not my own. All except one.

Escape.

Fingers curled into claws, I moved to seize that narrow window while his attention was turned in, *away*. Dragging myself out from under him, I claimed one step.

Mindlessly possessive, he snarled and drove back inside. Hips bucking against my ass, teeth fluttering at my shoulder.

Frozen, breath caught, I waited for the next fragile moment. A splintered instant that offered me the chance to slide off his cock. Uncoupled in a gush of cream that flooded my thighs in a lewd river of liquid shame, I fought not to moan at every second of friction. Hyper sensitive, swollen to bursting with the berserker's magic, slicked by a torrent of his sperm, I nearly pushed back. Nearly impaled myself once more, before I caught that impulse between my molars and crushed it with a whine of cracking enamel.

A rattling breath ghosted against the cheek of my ass, snagging on the fabric of my rumpled silks as I left him to his inner war. The stubble of his beard rasping at skin made tender by desperate, clutching fingers as I stole another step. Inching away.

Sucking my bottom lip between pointed canines, I bit down until I tasted the coppery tang of blood. Latching onto the nip of pain, trying to find my center, I claimed another step.

And then another.

And twelve more after that.

Forging ahead on hands and knees, I climbed. Each millimeter I could put between us was precious. Each moment of dragging silks, bruised knees, stinging palms, and ragged breath not fogged by his influence was another all to myself.

Sweating freely, I claimed the landing with a little flutter of victory as I pulled myself up. Swaying as I stood, I glanced back. Down...

... and nearly feel into icy chips of glittering obsidian.

He was watching.

They were watching.

Frozen in place as he fought to master himself, right hand planted in the middle of one step. The other clinging to the railing spindles, he was hunched as if still covering my back, his brow damp and glistening. Lips parted, cheeks flushed, his formal blacks were rumpled and disheveled.

My throat flexed, and as if unable to stop myself, my eyes ticked down. To where his shirt was untucked. Down to the spot where his pants sagged around an open fly. Where he hung heavy. Angry and unspent. *Exposed.* A rope of pearly glaze strung between his swollen tip and the step he'd fucked me into.

I staggered back from the edge.

But my wrists and throat did not burn with the searing lash of forced obedience that would put an end to my flight before it had even begun.

He didn't so much as levy a single tingling, golden threat in my direction.

He smiled.

Because he *wanted* me to fight. To run, just so he might chase. So he could conquer what should have been impossible to invade, and continue to feast on the spoils of war. Drunk on the fumes of uncontested victory.

Fingers spread wide, I clutched at the bannister, legs all-but boneless until I tore my eyes from that narrowed, slitted glare. Slipping into the shadows, I fled. Bitingly aware that the hunt had merely begun anew, and the time for apathetic indifference was over.

The next move was *mine.*

The half-dozen steps to his bedroom were a marathon in restraint.

A careful opening bid in a game I was going to lose.

I knew it.

Didn't bother to question the outcome any more vigorously than I tried to stop the flow of time.

But in that acceptance, there was a tiny measure of power. In the knowing that I might trade with the only coinage I had left, that I would lose with intention but *also* reclaim something of myself.

I spilled inside the room that had been my tomb and shut the door with a haggard breath. Grateful for a moment to think.

It didn't last.

I gasped—the bedroom was transformed.

Gone were the stacks of dirty dishes, the piles of laundry and empty bottles of wine. The windows had been thrown open, carrying off the scent of stale fucking with a gentle afternoon breeze. His bed had been redressed in handsome, dark sheets that beckoned me to sink into that welcoming embrace and forget my frivolous, doomed flight. And there, centered on his desk, the opened bottle of Tritan summer wine, a platter of fresh fruit, and baked goods were waiting to sate my endless hunger.

"Fuck," I whispered, because Alicia was equal parts miracle worker and traitor.

A traitor who hadn't deserved a second chance, but in my bottomless apathy, I'd given her exactly that. Trusted her to keep a deadly secret on the off chance that she wouldn't sell out a people not her own for a pat on the head.

Gait unsteady, panic bubbling at my throat, I cursed myself for every moment squandered on selfish, decadent indulgence. That I had dared to allow myself the luxury of grief, drugging myself with elite fumes just because I couldn't bring myself to look at my gruesome inheritance.

But it was right where Alicia had left it—tucked neatly beneath the captain's desk. Out of sight, but not quite hidden.

Sasha's parting gift.

Either a solution to all my many unanswered questions, or merely the opening bid in yet another Caledonian game.

A sound from beyond that closed door made me lurch into action.

Unhurried, measured steps creaking up the stairs. Each footfall heavy with confidence as he closed the distance between us. Enjoying the moments between, he strummed the bond anchored in my heart just to stoke the whirling panic sloshing in my gut.

Just to let me know... *he was coming.*

Moving before he'd been able to master himself, the man and the monster now shared a single goal. Hunting together, as one, to reclaim but one prize.

Me.

Asher wanted my power, my body, and my obedience.

But the berserker wanted my blood... my future.

Together, they would take *everything.*

Panic clawed at my throat, a strangled squeal ripping free of chapped lips as I lurched forward.

There wasn't enough time!

I needed more. A distraction that would allow me to open that damned box.

Whatever it took.

Shaking with the force of my heart hammering at the backside of my ribs, I stooped to seize the battered, simple case, darted into his bathroom, and dumped it in the shower stall before I let the panic bubble over.

Because he could feel it, knew the exact flavor of my every emotion, but he couldn't know my thoughts.

So I submitted to the flood. Let him feel my terror, the last noxious fumes of hope as they guttered out beneath the deluge. The tender wisps of feminine interest that fluttered to life as he drew near.

Everything I was, exposed to his inspection.

I showed him that the haze of placid indifference had been replaced. Washed away by something far more deadly.

Acceptance.

Because we matched.

Because it wasn't *just* Caledonian seed wetting my thighs.

It was the hunt. The chase. Knowing that no matter how hard I fought, nor how fast I ran, he would catch me.

That I *wanted* to be caught.

Yearned for the fist in my hair, the fingers tight around my throat. The punishing grip of desperate hands and the burning splash his seed—it was a drug.

Mine.

For he would let the empath feast, as long as it was from him.

One side of the coin would take everything not offered.

The other would spend until there was nothing but dust and smoke.

But together, they were balance.

Feast and famine...

.. and I was starving.

I bolted away from the bathroom, away from the last place I wanted him to look.

A booming crash made me yelp, whirling toward the sound.

The door bounced off the wall, kicked open, left sagging from twisted hinges. And there, framed in shadows and splintered wood, *Asher*.

Disheveled. Rugged. His black gaze cut to the bathroom, first. Suspicion etched in his every line, he narrowed his eyes. Trying to find something out of place. Astute, cunning as always, the man saw right through me as if he could smell the deception.

I staggered back, heart full of terrorized panic as I inched away. And when my hands found the sill, I glanced over my shoulder. Down at the street below, as if contemplating jumping from a second story window just to escape his wrath.

It was enough to break his focus—he pinned me with a slitted glare.

I recoiled from that storm of seething rage. Inched closer to the edge.

Teeth flashing, fists clenched, he surged forward

half a step. "*Don't,*" he spat, but still, my chains did not burn.

I glanced at the bed. The crisp, clean sheets that had been a refuge and a prison.

Head tilted to the side, he took another rolling step then paused.

My grip squeaked on the sill, and I let my knees go soft. Braced to jump.

He moved between blinks.

Faster than I thought possible, he closed the gap. One hand landed on my hip, but the other found an anchor at the base of my throat. Face to face, he towered above me. Trembling with a fury reserved for me alone, he pressed forward. Making me bend backward as he tipped us both over the edge and impaled me with twin chips of icy obsidian.

Fingers curled, I lifted my hand. Hesitant, I let my fingers land on his chest. Let my digits spread as I marveled at the heat billowing off a landscape of ridges and valleys that was at once so utterly foreign, and yet... familiar.

Beneath my palm, his heart hammered a wild pace and I felt him recoil an instant before he seized my wrist in a grip meant for splintering bone.

Guarding his vitals, coiled and ready to defend against attack.

Because he remembered.

That I had tried to kill him like this, once.

That I'd been closest to victory when I'd embraced what he'd made me.

A seasoned whore.

One who'd tasted the salty brine of his seed and begged for more. Pussy singing for his touch, for the punishing ache of his cock as he whispered obscenities against my ear and bred desperate obedience into slick heat.

I'd gaped for him.

Crawled.

Begged.

Needed.

"Please," I whispered, and wet my bottom lip with a flick of my tongue. Spine arching over the windowsill, I went loose and docile against him. Giving him my weight, trusting him not to break my wrist, I lifted my feet and hooked them around the backs of his thighs. My silks gaping in a lewd spread, I tipped my hips back and offered myself as that last, desperate distraction.

Nostrils pinched white, he took a choppy breath. Shuddering as wet heat kissed where he was rigid and thick.

"I"—I swallowed, throat dry and reedy, and tried again—"I need..."

His head tilted a few degrees. Enough that the deep inky, black of pupils blown wide caught a curious glimmer of light.

"Please," I whispered. "It hurts to want you like this. To *need*—I've never... I don't..." I shook my head. Blinked. And with an effort that left me scraped raw, I uncorked the dam. "I need to feel you," I panted, and let my tongue sweep over the points of my teeth. "Touching me. F-fucking me. Again and again and again, because..." I abandoned my grip on the sill and reached for his fly with the trembling fingers of the hand not caught in a merciless grip. Catching him where his zipper sagged, already sticky with a glossy white sheen. "Because I can't help it, damn you," I gasped, core clenching when I took him in hand. Letting velvet and steel slip through my fist, I stroked him from tip to base and back. "Can't stop thinking about it. What you do to me. The way you taste..."

His lips parted on a ragged, low growl. But he didn't blink. Didn't move as I worked my palm over his length.

"I know you can feel it," I murmured, and let my thumb sweep over his slit, through a bead of furious, slippery want. "How badly I need you to do it again. *Already*. That I haven't stopped dripping for you—" I pumped once, twice more, and then sent his tip through sodden heat. Slicking him with the honest truth of my words as they dripped from honeyed lips. "Because I can't help myself, and no matter how much you hate me, no matter how much it hurts, I still need it."

Pinning me with a slitted glare, his black gaze flicked between my eyes. Searching, rigid, resisting me even as I laid myself bare and threw myself at his mercy.

Fat, shameful tears spilled over my lashes, and I choked on a bitter laugh. "It's what you wanted, isn't it? To ruin me so deeply, so completely that I could never escape you?"

At this, his cock kicked where it was poised to

obliterate me. A spike of sick, male jealousy lanced through my blood. Possessive rage cooled only by my destruction. It was satisfaction born by my words—words he didn't so much as attempt to deny.

Because I was right.

A fragile smile cracked my lips. Laced with so much that would remain nameless, hardly more than a grim flash of teeth, but a smile nevertheless. "You win. I have nothing. I *am* nothing," I said, voice watery and quavering with each syllable that spilled over my lips. Damning me. "Just a whore. An empty vessel, begging for your"—my breath hitched—"your come. Helplessly addicted, my every cursed step haunted by the ache for you."

Slipping my free hand up, careful not to touch the spot where his heart thrashed in his chest, I tried again to pull him inside. Leveraging hooked heels, I stretched as far as he'd let me. My fingers falling to trace the bow of his bottom lip, just once. A gentle pass that let me feel his shallow breath on my knuckles. The prickle of stubble shading his chin.

"Please," I whispered, and moved to pry his fingers away from my throat. Guiding him down, over the snag and catch of black silks covering nothing of my nudity. Over the bump of jagged ribs and the soft hollow between. All the way. Past my belly button to find where I was slick and hairless, weeping for him to move. To take. "It hurts," I said again. Fragile. Raw. Grinding against the head of his cock, our fingers intertwined, and I painted delicious little circles around the base of my clit.

Inky eyes darted down. As if reluctant to be distracted, but unable to resist the sight of what he'd fought so hard to claim. Now freely offered.

Nostrils pinched white, a tiny breath puffed over his lips. A shiver rippled through unyielding muscle.

"I have nothing left," I whispered. "Nothing that's not already yours. The empath..." I whispered, and shifted to take his length in hand once more, leaving him to toy with that rigid bundle of nerves. "This p-pussy..." Stroking him, I tried to pull him inside. "All yours. And I need you," I murmured, palm slippery with his come and mine. "Fuck me, Asher," I said, pulling him closer with my heels. Straining toward the back corner of his jaw, so I might press a single word against his skin. So he would feel it, when I said, "*Hard*,"

He snapped.

Filling me in a single, vicious stroke, he obliged me at last. Releasing my captured wrist, he let me cling to him as he surged inside. Impaled, filled to my limit, his balls flexed where they were mashed against lips gone almost bloodless with the stretch.

Calves burning, I squealed and tried to move against him. "Please," I gasped, and wound my fingers in the short hair at his nape. Thighs clenching as I tried to grind against his root. "*Please—*"

His grin spread against my cheek. A prickle of smug victory as he flexed inside me, savoring the wet heat.

"Asher," I whined, begging without an ounce of shame. Trying to appeal to the man, pleading for his cock to ruin me, as only a whore might. And admitting it had become *easy* in the space between breaths. "Please fuck me. *Please.*"

With a low snarl, his hands found the backs of my thighs. Lifting me off his prick in a slick glide of willing, melting flesh, just so he could drop me, surging inside once more. In plain view of anyone on the street below, he pummeled tender flesh.

Claiming me.

Every last inch.

And then, with clenching fists he kneaded the globes of my ass and peeled me open. Making space for himself, he took my weight from the windowsill. Adding leverage to work me over his length.

Thighs and hips rolling in a taut wave, writhing in his hands, I helped him ruin me. Using him, ankles hooked at his lower back, I pressed closer and inhaled his breath.

Our chins bumped.

Panting, my eyes darted up, only to find myself ensnared by pools of inky pitch. Eyes that were level with mine—until he lifted me up. Setting my back to the wall with a thump of sweat-damp skin.

And as his hips rolled into mine, I kissed the man I hated. Lips crashing into his, reveling in those that were at once soft and rimmed in prickles, I devoured him with clashing teeth. Dragging him with me into the seething dark.

Tongue plunging into my mouth—tasting me— he spun toward the bed. Taking three surging steps, before he dumped me on my back and followed me down without missing a beat.

Stuffed full, made to take all of him, I groaned. Letting the points of my teeth scrape at his lips, I feasted.

Drunk as I gulped him down and begged for more with flexing calves and tilted hips.

I wouldn't last.

Couldn't.

Hypersensitive to the point of madness, I urged him to go deeper. Harder. Kissing the man as if his lips might cure me of this poison, I welcomed my doom. Ripe and tender, aching for his touch, my breasts jiggled against the fabric of his formal blacks with each weighted impact of his heat. Rumpling pristine sheets as his cock sluiced through petals slick with treachery, I clung to him. My fingers wound tighter in his hair, desperate, my body wrapped around every part of him I could reach.

Invading with an obscene stretch, he burrowed inside. Tied to me in a way that would never be scraped clean.

"Please," I said against his lips, my every muscle growing tight. Shivering with the building weight of my climax. "Asher, please don't stop."

He shuddered.

Cock swelling, making me gape for him as dark flames crackled at my edges and something hungry licked at my pulse. Something wicked and cruel that took a greedy sip of my energy and dragged at the fabric of my tattered soul.

"I could keep you like this," he rasped, on the edge of falling, but for a moment... he resisted. Ridging the wave. "Sweet. Docile. Drunk on pleasure, your every need tended." His pace increased as he rutted between my thighs, luxuriating in the mess I'd made for him. "Mine forever."

I blinked.

Staring into an alien gaze. Pupils blown wide enough to swallow me whole. It was a bottomless hunger. Monstrous and insatiable.

One I recognized at a glance, for it had been mine, once.

Before I was nothing.

Before I was *his*.

Helpless as he edged between two paths, made a passive observer as he weighed his options—between snuffing my fire or feeding it—I went still beneath him. Lungs frosted over with a layer of dust, my breath stilled as he toyed with the threads of absolute control woven through my skin. Inky black stars sparkled at the edge of my vision. Tunneling around him, framing him in the lazy flicker of hungry, greedy flames.

And I didn't care if he made me a ghost with sagging joints and empty eyes.

I'd already accepted it. Committed everything I was to this—the opening bid in yet another game, or... my last act.

Chin tipping back, I exposed my throat to the beast.

Surrendered to the better monster, for my fight was over.

Hands falling away from the soft, sweat-damp curls at his nape, I let him take until the cauldron went cold. Quiet. Haunted by phantoms too tired and drained to fight chains that couldn't be removed.

The abyss yawned.

And in its gaping maw, a bone chilling void that welcomed the weary. The defeated. Those who were slipping beyond saving... reaching for... peace.

"*Mila.*"

It was a command spoken in a voice I couldn't ignore. Thick with alarm. Panicked hatred of that peaceful nothing where possessive, jealous rage wasn't welcome and couldn't fester.

His lips crashed into mine.

Demanding I yield to the breath he forced into frozen lungs, the man pulled me back with the hook lodged behind my ribs. Begging me to fight, he sent a cinder tumbling into the depths.

"Mila," Asher said again, pumping me full of cock. Surging inside with easy, sure strokes, both palms cupped my cheeks. Engulfing my face as he drank me down and filled me up. Inhaling my whine of agonized pleasure, he forged on. Letting it build with the sort of expertise that sent my eyes rolling back, my spine bowed as I was pummeled into silken sheets.

It was too much.

Just enough.

Perfect.

"Ash—"

He kissed me when I broke.

Tasted every moment of ecstasy as it shot through my blood and that cinder began to smoke. Resisting the urge to pump his come as deep as he could, just for the pleasure of watching me fall apart.

Chaos raged between my legs.

My every muscle seized in an orgasm that stole my breath and bent my spine. Pussy rippling as I shuddered beneath him.

His forehead dipped, bumping mine as he gazed into my eyes and saw everything, all together all at once.

"Fuck*sakes*," he rasped, growing thick. His sack drawn tight, spreading to either side of his cock as he splintered at last. Torn right down the middle when it became too much. When he'd dragged it out beyond what either of us could endure, and that first jet of come splashed against my womb. Kicking so deep inside, I came all over again.

Milking his balls dry of every precious drop.

25

I lost time as we lay there. Locked together, sharing breaths as he panted above me and wallowed in his perfect victory. Luxuriating in my defeat, his cock throbbed inside me. Pulsing when he sent the occasional lazy gush of seed into my depths.

A fine tremor shivered through overwrought muscles. His and mine. Flitting from one to the other in a seamless flow of unfiltered euphoria.

It wasn't until he shifted that I felt it.

Only when he moved to wiggle free of his rumpled shirt. When he braced on one arm, and tore at the buttons fastened at his wrist with his teeth, straining to remain buried to the hilt for just a little longer. A smile pressed to my lips, he peppered me with little kisses that tasted like more...

... until something foul slithered into my gut.

Regret.

Creeping, horrified realization of what I had done.

That from this, I might never recover.

My very last thing of value given in exchange for a prize I hadn't seen. Gambled away on the words of a woman who'd betrayed me—who'd cost me my freedom—for a chance to know the last wishes of a woman who'd died in my place.

The captain frowned, his interest piqued, and sent a barb of curiosity rippling through my system.

An unconscious search that fed him the details of my turbulent emotions, but not their source.

"Tell me," he murmured, frowning as he slid one hand up. Under my arm, scooping beneath my nape to cradle the back of my skull. Making me look, when I tried to squirm away. Tried to hide the salty burn of shame scalding my eyes.

"I—" My voice caught, hoarse with the cries he'd wrenched from my throat. "It'll be"—I swallowed—"good? Between us?"

Head tilting, he stared down at me with that bottomless gaze. Curious. A little alien. Still haunted by the beast, still slavering for the hunt.

I tried again. "You won't... won't give me to your men when you're bored?" I asked, giving voice to the vulnerable, trembling pieces he'd flipped over. The ugly things he'd forced into the light, exposed, left to wriggle and worm. "Won't let them earn a turn to treat me like a whore if—*when*—I slip?"

Something soft flitted between his brows. "No, Mila," he murmured, petting stray wisps of silver-blonde hair back from my face. "You'll beg, but only for me."

I nodded, shifting my feet where they were spread around his—and felt the seal stretching gooey petals break. A trickle of warm come gushed from my depths, an intimate lick that oozed where he had begun to soften. Where I gaped for him.

Willingly.

Heat burned in my cheeks, tears blurring my waterline as I nodded again and tried to hide my face so he couldn't watch the next words tumble forth. "Will you make me forget?" I whispered. Tiny. Fragile. "Everything I've lost, so it doesn't hurt so much to want this? To want... you."

He moved. Cupping my chin, fingers gentle on the edge of my jaw when he said, "Your fight is over, little warrior."

Tears spilled over my cheeks, then. Tracking back, to prickle at my temples. "And this is enough?" I asked. "You won't make me a ghost?" A watery hiccup clattered between my teeth. "With dead eyes and sagging joints? Like the Lieutenant General's p-priestess?"

At this, he hesitated.

Just long enough that the unmistakeable lash of pity contorted his face.

My breath caught in a trap of frigid horror. "Nooo. Asher, you—you *can't*—"

"It's over," he said again, sad, frustrated agony scrawled between his brows. "We're being sent to the capital."

I shook my head, letting the tears fall. Trying to bargain. "To train the elites in your methods. So we can s-save the priestesses from a living death like—"

He scoffed, derisive and full of soft scorn. "Have you ever been to the capital, Mila? Have you any idea what it's like for Tritan slaves there?"

My lips parted, but I couldn't force a denial through them.

It didn't matter.

"I warned you," he murmured, voice hard. A flicker of anger igniting in obsidian depths. "Time and again, over and over. I warned you not to draw attention from men like them. That there would be consequences and they would be horrible for both of us." His jaw flexed. Nostrils pinched white as he shook his head. "I did everything I could think of. Invented new methods not even imagined by your people or mine, and *still*, you fought me at every turn. No matter how futile, how endlessly fucking stupid or hopeless. And now I have no choice. No more plans or last resorts. I have to—"

"Please," I gasped, weeping quietly as my tiny world began to burn in hopeless, wretched flames. Because I knew what this was, even without my crutch—it was a farewell. "*Please* don't do this."

He touched my lips. Gentle. Almost wistful as he tugged at the bow of my lower lip, avoiding eye contact when he whispered, "I have to break you."

Keening low in my throat, I shoved at his chest.

He caught my wrist. "Mila—"

"Please," I rasped again, straining against his

weight. "Let me go." A gasp lodged in my throat, hurting where my lungs were frigid and overfull. "Just to the—*I have to pee.*"

Watching with guarded eyes, he took a sip of the panic flooding my system. Searching for deceit.

And for a moment, I thought it was well and truly over.

That he would loop bands of burning, golden compliance about my throat and douse the flames from my heart once and for all.

But he nodded.

Pulling out, he rolled to the side. A terse, "Don't be long," chased by a nod, he looked away. Occupied by arranging dark sheets stained by what we'd done, giving me the illusion of privacy so I might grieve in peace.

Legs almost boneless, I fled without glancing back. Staggering through the door to the en suite bathroom, my cheeks burning with the fall of salty anguish. With the heartbreak tearing me to pieces.

Separate but not alone, I stood in the quiet found behind a closed door. Dragging great, heaving breaths between clenched and pointed teeth. Trembling in the cold, dim light. My silks hanging from my frame at odd angles, no longer doing a thing to conceal my nudity, I was bare.

Dripping.

Frozen.

Unable to twist my neck and glance at the box I'd given everything I had left to protect. One last secret.

The only thing that stood between me and oblivion, if there was even half a hope at all.

My knees wobbled before they buckled. Kissing the tiles in a dull thump, I caught myself with sweaty palms. Gasping, tears racing down the length of my nose. Unable to give a name to the feeling pouring from the wounds shredding my chest to garish ribbons.

Trapped.

I was caught in a box with no window and no escape. Forced to trust my enemies, or lay down and accept my doom.

Knuckles going white and bloodless, I clenched my fists. Dragged a whistling breath through my nose, and crawled into the shower stall on hands and knees. Bruised, soiled, my hips swaying as I fought for each pathetic inch until I was curled in the darkest corner of the shower stall with a harmless, unremarkable box clutched to my chest.

Tarnished silver buckles gleamed in the gloom. Mocking me.

I flicked the latch with my left hand, and with the right, flipped the lid on hinges that squeaked a tiny protest.

A black velvet bag, cinched tight. Too small to be a weapon, too light to be anything I might use to free myself.

I set the box aside, fingers clumsy and shaking. Pulling on the strings as if watching from outside myself.

Four golden, mismatched rings tumbled into my palm.

A set I recognized.

Rings that were a perfect match to those that were sunk into my flesh—a complete set of unused, Tritan chains.

The very set that General Harper Tilcot had tried to use to steal me from the captain, before he'd fallen into his own trap.

Nausea splashed at the back of my throat, and I choked on acid, swallowing a scream of violent frustration and bile. That Sasha would give them to me, that she would use her last moments to have them delivered to *me* and not Carly—to not use them herself.

A huff of laughter bubbled up from the bottom of my gut. Quiet, teetering toward madness, for her plan wasn't the brilliant musings of a tragic genius.

Neither a savior swooping in at the last possible moment, nor a vehicle of untold carnage and destruction.

I've had something delivered to the captain's rooms... Something I think you'll know isn't the answer for the rest.

And I did.

Know.

Because it was the last weapon we had left.

The chance to take something corrupt and make it new. To force new life into a barren tomb and rewrite the laws of nature so they might suit the downtrodden. The enslaved.

My fingers curled around the soft gleam of gold, and I let my head thump back. Striking tile, I pulled a steadying breath between my lips...

... and nodded.

Resigned to my role in the end.

Because I was just another whore. Ridden into battle by a master who worked from beyond the Void. A vehicle of great and terrible change.

It wasn't the answer for the rest. Not a solution for the peaceful women trained to be healers. Invaluable women of the Tritan faith, and the last keepers of our wisdom.

But *I* was apart.

Not a priestess.

Nor an elite.

A new thing both dangerous... and expendable.

I think you'll know...

I nodded again.

Tears running unchecked down blotchy cheeks, I felt a cinder flicker in the smoke.

Tiny. Dainty, but burning with the hot snap of generational rage.

Escape from him, from our infernal bond, came with a price I'd never meant to pay.

But I stood. Jaw bunched tight. Knuckles white, four golden, mismatched circlets clenched tight in my fist. Heart burning with grim determination.

The only way out, was in. *Deeper*. To seize control of a lonely island guarded by a better predator where the empath had been marooned.

Because to set her free, Mila had to die.

∼

Oooooph. Brutal cliff, but I hope you're not too spicy with me. If you are, come holler at me in The Daniverse over on Facebook, where you can also win free things, get sneak peaks, and find the very rare pics of my face skin. Which I post sometimes. Usually zoomed in way too close and accompanied by a weird story about my daily, fantastical life as a Chaos Demon and all the fuckery that goes with it. Also, love or hate it, leave ya girl a review. Go. Do it now. Actually, you'd better leave a funny one, like, "Porn hub has nothing on this series." Or, "I slid off my chair while reading this book. IYKYK. Five Evil Nips, highly recommend."
Just because I think it's funny, and I am not good enough at my job to stress over what my sales page looks like, but reading funny reviews brings my day joy.

If you like the cut of my meat sails, join my Newsletter for the occasional dark comedy nugget like, "Zombie porn and German Parents," or "Eye Contact, Kiosk, and Vengeance." Oh, and books, sometimes.

It has been a truly insane 15 months on my end, and I would like to apologize for the huge delay in publishing. I left myself tonnes of space between the publishing of Frost to Dust, and what I THOUGHT would be the release of this book, you know... just in case something came up. Because I was about to give birth to my daughter, and thought, it'll be fine! I'm only editing an already written series.

Well, flick my nips, baybeee. Something came up. My daughter, Danger Danvers, is a class six hurricane. Walking at 10 months, running at 12. The only hours I can actually work are between 3am and 8am, where I can get a most of a whole work day in before any chubby baby arms are sinking into my tepid, wretched coffee and slapping down on my keyboard because the mere sight of my laptop is an affront to her entire lineage and how *dare* I do something that isn't paying her every spare ounce of my attention.
Poor me.
My adorable, sweet, brilliant little girl wants to hang out with me constantly, right? What a horrible life event.

Kidding, obviously. I'm obsessed with her. It's creepy. I honestly just stare at her and smile. And when she's sleeping, I watch videos of what she looked like last week, because I miss her, even when I'm thrilled that she's sleeping for a few hours and I'm getting a few precious minutes to pretend I inhabit the flesh of an adult female. But something had to give, and it took me a really long time to realize that, why, yes! I CAN function on 5 hours of sleep and write in the small hours when no one is pulling down my shirt and shouting, "YAH YAH YAH YAH YAH YAH YAH!!!".

So anyway. Book was late, I'm sorry and also not.

Also, this series was never a trilogy. I don't know how that rumor got started, but don't flame me in the reviews because you were hoping for an ending in this book. There is still 3 whole-ass books worth of content to publish, as the OG readers will remember.

Smoke to Cinder: The Last Tritan, Book IV is coming soon.
But just a warning, going forward, I am doing things differently. I will never again set up a preorder without the manuscript being completely finished and ready to go. I can't handle the stress, and I don't write well under that brand of pressure. It's just not for me. That said, I'm absolutely hyped for this year.

Magic happens in the small hours, and evil has my nips so, so hard...
~Myra

FREE BOOK! Download Swallowed by Darkness now!

"Thrilling, addictive, a bit horrible, but oh so entertaining and funny—truly unique—I loved it!" ~Goodreads reviewer

RAVENOUS INNOCENCE, TRITAN EVOLUTION, BOOK I

Want more Tritan? More Mila and Asher while you wait for Smoke to Cinder? Good news! There's an alternate Tritan universe called *Tritan Evolution*. Which is NOT this series. Not the exact same world, though they have many overlapping themes, events, and characters. I cut my author teeth in a weird corner of the internet for free porn stories, where The Last Tritan (the one you just read) was originally published. Tritan Evolution, however, is the result of me breaking free of that original pen name, to publish my works on mainstream vendors. They're very different stories that can be read separately, despite sharing similar elements.

Download Ravenous Innocence, Tritan Evolution, Book I now!

I wasn't supposed to be here.

Wasn't allowed to walk amongst my fellow citizens, enjoying the beautiful, sunny day. I'd been forbidden to stroll through the over-crowded market, unattended and unprotected. To do as I wished without the express permission of my father —and the accompanying escort—was to invite dire, world-altering consequences.

It wasn't safe.

I smiled, soaking up the sun and watched a jewelry merchant hawk his wares. Watched as he snared the attention of a tall, willowy woman, seizing her elbow before she could pass his display. Tugging, he pulled her into the shade beneath his tent and the flapping azure awning, thumb stroking the pale skin of her upper arm. Directing her gaze to follow a trinket with his free hand, he bedazzled her with glittering stones and polished silver that danced in the shadowed half-light.

I pressed my palm to the pendant perched on my breastbone, torn. As of yet, I hadn't actually done anything deserving of consequences. Had, in fact, done nothing but watch, enthralled by the market's chaos. Thrilled by the colors and scents of the Tritan people, I watched from the sidelines. Pretending I was just another face in a sea of silver-blonde, Tritan heads, to whom words like 'consequences' and 'unsafe' did not apply.

But I wasn't one of them, blood or not.

My fingers tightened around my pendant, considering as the precious, ugly stone glittered in the sun, tossing distinct shades of blue, green, and purple onto the street before me. Simply being here was a risk to everything my father and I had sacrificed over the years, surrounded by the crush of unsuspecting masses, each more sightless than the last. Most unable to sense the ki burning thick and sweet in the air. That such a power could go unnoticed by so many was a blessed curse from the Goddess herself, drowning me in the temptation to reach out and touch them... to blend in. To taste the living flames of their ki and know *normal*. To *be* normal, if only for a few stolen moments.

I clenched my fist, letting the tarnished family heirloom bite the meat of my palm. At once concealing the scatter of blues, greens, and purples before they were recognized, and letting the stone drink deep of my life force. It feasted with greedy abandon, starving for ki willingly given. Storing my excess in its stony, cold heart in return for blessed, numbing calm.

A service only the Glaith could provide to one such as me.

I shuddered, drained, for now, but conflicted. There wouldn't be another chance as perfect as this, what with my father occupied by some important State Senate meeting and my target already marked. In fact, everyone who might take an interest in my actions was in that meeting. The rest, the Priestesses with their keen ki-sense, were locked away, deep in the heart of the temple.

No one would recognize me here. None could sense what I really was beneath the Glaith.

And yet, I hesitated, eyes fixed to the merchant conducting his business. Fingers tight about my pendant, keeping myself firmly in check. My father had given *everything* to keep me free. Free to live and make mistakes. It was a debt I could never even begin to repay, and yet, in this, he was *wrong*. The man was blinded by his need to protect and coddle. Couldn't see the raw potential simmering in my veins... desperate to be set loose...

I grinned.

If it were possible to harness my birthright, I alone would decide how it would be used. Not my beloved father. Not a faceless, tyrannical High Priestess, moored in tradition and secrets, who would claim me for the temple simply because of what I was.

Me.

Alone.

And if I failed? Consequences were only for those foolish or weak enough to get caught.

Finished with his sale, the merchant kissed his customer's wrist and tucked a handful of coins into his purse, setting pale eyes to scan for his next conquest before he'd finished with the last.

This was it, then. My moment. I let the pendant fall. Let it settle above my shift, separating its numbing influence from my skin and leaving myself vulnerable—for in its absence, the rest washed in.

Ki.

My accursed birthright.

Awareness burst inside my skull. The ki of every man and woman in the market—of Tritan blood or otherwise—called to me, whispering their secrets all at once. Begging me to reach out and touch, to drink until I'd filled the bottomless, ravenous void. There was no bracing for it. No way to prepare for the kiss of the Divine. And here, in an overcrowded market separate from the Glaith for the first time in four years, I swayed, staggering under the weight of their ki. Knuckles white and jaw slack, suffering an endless, blazing inferno writhing just out of reach, I struggled to master it before it swallowed me whole.

The stone in my pendant was warm now, working to consume the flames I'd fed it, to store the ki I couldn't contain alone. I could feel the heat through my shift, knew it would need time to cool before I could feed it again, lest it overheat and sear my skin. Four years, my pendant of Glaith had protected me, shielding me from any consequences my existence might provoke. Numbing.

Too long.

Knuckles white, I forced the whispers back, straining to bank the flames of their ki without reaching for the Glaith. And then, taking even, measured steps, I merged with the busy foot-traffic, letting my country-folk carry me toward the jewelry merchant. On my lips, a practiced smile. Careful to evade skin-to-skin contact with the press of the crowd, I focused on the pendant swinging between my breasts. Glaith was the only guard and escort I needed. A safety net giving me permission to meet the merchant's eye and dance with a viper.

"Goddess be with us," the merchant trilled, stepping into my path. "Such a beautiful young lady! My dear, you simply glow with *youth!* Come," he said, butter-soft fingers finding purchase on my elbow, guiding and hustling me into his shaded tent. "I have just the thing to complement those striking eyes."

I blinked, straining *not* to look at his fingers upon my skin. Swallowing a groan as his ki blazed through me, my focus narrowed to him and little else. Both a relief from the roar of the crowd and a painful, intimate burden, but I allowed him to lead me into the shadows. Listening to his ki whisper tales of false smiles and sharp instincts as that thumb traced a trusted pattern on my skin.

"It's a pleasure to make your acquaintance, miss..."

Insincerity oozed through my skin, and I knew he didn't care. Knew it was a tactic to lure me into a false trust so he could relieve me of more coin. But my first name held no power, gave him nothing that could bring my father into this or lead the merchant to realize who I was, if my efforts here went sideways. So I smiled, and said, "Mila," tapping two fingers to my temple. My tone light. Carefree.

"Mila," he breathed, returning the gesture of respect. "Beautiful name for a beautiful girl, but"—he hooked a single, slender finger beneath the pendant's chain, *tsking*—"oh, no. No no *no!* This simply won't do. I cannot bear such an outdated, battered piece distracting from your radiance, my dearest Mila."

"It—" I cleared my throat, taking a tiny conservative sip of his ki. Looking for deception, only to find genuine distaste for an outdated, battered piece worth more than everything else in his shop combined. "It was my mother's," I said, letting him taste old sorrows.

The grip on my elbow tightened, light eyes widening. "Ah. Well. The Goddess can be cruel, for all her wisdom. I'm so sorry for your loss, child. Come," he said, fluttering bejeweled fingers. "Sit. I have the perfect piece to soothe such pain. Why don't you take your dear mother's pendant off, and I'll have it cleaned? Perhaps we can replace the jewel in the center. How about a nice sapphire to match your eyes, hmm? I happen to have a selection of loose stones for just such an occasion."

Pushing my ki through the pad of his dewy thumb, I trapped his hand on my elbow and directed his attention away from my pendant. Toward the case I'd seen a week prior while perusing the markets with my father, for I'd already chosen what I'd be leaving with today. "You are too kind, sir, but I couldn't. I haven't enough coin to—"

"Nonsense," he breathed, pulling me deeper into the tent. Something akin to fatherly instinct lit up my senses when he dropped the hyper-cheerful sales pitch and said, "Everything is negotiable, darling. *Everything*. Remember that lesson, and you'll do well in life."

A tentative, fragile smile spread across my lips, no less effective for all that I'd rehearsed. "Thank you."

"I won't hear it," he said, patting the back of my hand. Each pat landed with a burst of ki behind my eyelids. Dazzling. Enthralling. "Now let's find the piece with 'Mila' written on it."

I smothered the grin begging to be set free, allowing him to guide me around the tiny shop, hand in hand. Flitting from one display to the next, the merchant remained unaware as I slid beneath his skin. Drinking just a little *deeper* to learn him from the inside out, while he filled my every cell with power and confidence.

I'd been *right*.

This was right, this Divinity thick in my blood was *mine*.

The light shifted, signaling the arrival of another patron, but I didn't spare the newcomer a glance, instead driving my merchant to stop before a display of brooches. It took little more than a tiny *push* to make it his idea to open the case.

"Oh, darling, *yes*. This is it." He lifted the brooch, letting it catch the gloomy half-light. "It's far from the most valuable piece in my collection, but it was made for you. I feel it deep in my bones."

Did he now? The Glaith hung heavy about my neck, the most innocent expression I'd rehearsed fixed to my lips. "It's beautiful," I whispered, inspecting the savage likeness of a snarling wildcat with tiny amber eyes.

"Isn't it? But I'm selfish." He winked. "I simply

cannot go another minute without seeing it against your skin, my dear."

I returned his smile, tilting my chin back as he pinned it to my shift. And yet, my fingers lingered upon his skin, maintaining the connection with that which had become mine. "Thank you," I breathed, meeting his eye. Watching his pupils dilate. "It's beautiful. It must also be... expensive?"

The merchant blinked, pulse pounding at the base of his throat, unable to tear his eyes from mine. Unwilling, for he too, could taste the Divine. Through me. "Ex-Expensive, yes. Yes. But for you," he said, licking lips gone dry, "I'm happy to see it go."

What would it hurt to take just a little... *more?* To drink just a little deeper from my merchant and celebrate this tiny victory? My fingers tightened on his wrist, mouth watering, hungering for his ki. He wouldn't notice the absence, not really. How could he miss what he couldn't sense? What he'd *never* sense, for he was not of the Blood.

"A fine choice," came a voice from behind, making me jump. "Not sure it's worth the risk, but a fine choice, nonetheless."

Heat rushed to my cheeks, fingers jerking free of the merchant on a startled gasp. Fist crackling with stolen ki, I spun to face the fool who dared disturb me.

He caught my wrist, standing too close, fingers rough and warm—but utterly devoid of ki.

I blinked.

Blinked again, turning the full strength of my

senses upon him. Nothing. Not a lick or whisper of ki. "Impossible," I breathed, meeting eyes darker than pitch, trying to wrap my head around the contradiction standing before me. Every living thing had ki to some degree, for without it we were nothing but fuel for the next generation. And yet this man, obviously so full of life, possessed nothing of the sort. Unless...

My eyes dropped to his neck, absent a chain that might have swung with a pendant like mine. Dressed in formal black and gold, dark hair cropped close and kept neat, the man had the gall to smirk at me. Clean, sharp jaw framing a handsome face, his were *not* the features I was accustomed to seeing. Too dark, build too big to be of Tritan blood. My gaze dropped further still, to the hand on my wrist—and the chunky, masculine ring sitting proud on his pinky finger.

Glaith.

I knew without seeing those distinct blue, green, and purple shadows scattering the light. Knew what the ugly stone set in a foreign family crest meant. But... "Impossible," I said again, though this time it was a dry squeak. This time, I pulled away, for he *couldn't* be what I thought he was. The Glaith was coveted by Tritan's *Priestesses* for its responsive reactions to ki. This *man* couldn't possibly know what his ring was truly worth.

It was a coincidence, nothing more.

Trying to step back, I tucked my pendant beneath my shift, reuniting the warm stone with my skin, just in case. When the Glaith touched my breastbone, it pushed everything else out, deadening my forbidden senses once more. Turning my knees to water as it swallowed the Divine.

"The brooch," he said, ignoring my attempt to free myself from his grasp, though those dark eyes tracked my every movement. Tracing the pendant beneath my shirt. "How much?"

The merchant blinked, still under my sway even without my touch on his skin or my ki thick in his veins. "F-For the lady, nothing. A gift, sir."

"Take your hand off—"

"Nonsense," the intruder returned, fingers tightening on my wrist. Near to bruising with the unspoken warning. "You have a living to make. To earn nothing from an item of such fine quality is a crime where I come from."

I bristled with the implication, spluttering, the reprimand plain enough.

"Well," the merchant breathed, each passing moment pulling him further from my influence. "If you insist—"

"I do." The intruder dropped a few foreign coins into the merchant's outstretched hand. "Besides," he continued, full lips twitching when he met my bewildered scowl once more, "it's my pleasure to part with the coin if it'll buy me a few moments of the lady's time."

I wrenched my wrist free at last, pressing a trembling hand to my throat. "Do I look like a commodity?"

He turned those obsidian eyes down at me,

invading my space with a single step. "You'll have to excuse the presumption, but I rather think you'd prefer if I *didn't* say what I think you are."

"And I think *you'll* excuse my rudeness, but I don't care what you think I am—"

"Asher. Captain Asher Rawlings of His Majesty's Imperial Army."

A Caledonian.

The heat rushed from my cheeks, taking my breath with it.

A Caledonian. Goddess, with all my power, how could I have been so bloody stupid? So blind?

I swallowed the bubble rising at the back of my throat, and said, "Right. Well, Captain Asher Rawlings of His Majesty's Imperial Army, I don't care what you think I am. Because whatever it is, I can assure you, you're wrong."

Asher hummed, low at the back of his throat. Inky eyes glittering with something I couldn't name.

And then, without speaking another word or breaking eye contact, he removed his ring.

Download Ravenous Innocence, Tritan Evolution, Book I now!

ALSO BY MYRA DANVERS

Swallowed by Darkness ~ **FREE**

- Grab your free copy of Swallowed by Darkness now!

The Last Tritan

- Flame to Frost, The Last Tritan, Book I
- Frost to Dust, The Last Tritan, Book II
- Dust to Smoke, The Last Tritan, Book III

Tritan Evolution

- Ravenous Innocence, Tritan Evolution, Book I
- Insatiable Corruption, Tritan Evolution, Book II
- Lavish Destruction, Tritan Evolution, Book III

The Feral Court

- Renegade, the Feral Court, Book I
- Giaus, The Feral Court, Book II
- Sickle, The Feral Court, Book III

Atom and Evil

MYRA DANVERS

USA Today Bestselling author, Myra Danvers, is best known for her compelling mix of unique science fiction and dark fantasy worlds that feature feisty heroines, antihero men, and of course, proper villains. Though you may not always know who is who until the final pages...